THE SALARIAN DESERT GAME

J. A. MCLACHLAN

EDGE SCIENCE FICTION AND FANTASY PUBLISHING
AN IMPRINT OF HADES PUBLICATIONS, INC.

CALGARY

The Salarian Desert Game

Edge Science Fiction and Fantasy Publishing
An Imprint of Hades Publications Inc.
P.O. Box 1714, Calgary, Alberta, T2P 2L7, Canada

Acquisitions Editor: Ella Beaumont
Interior design by Catherine Murray
Cover Design by Marija Vilotijevi

ISBN: 978-1-77053-114-7

EDGE Science Fiction and Fantasy Publishing and Hades Publications, Inc.
acknowledges the ongoing support of the Alberta Foundation for the Arts and
the Canada Council for the Arts for our publishing programme.

Library and Archives Canada Cataloguing in Publication
CIP Data on file with the National Library of Canada
(E-BOOK: e-ISBN: 978-1-77053-113-0)

FIRST EDITION
(20160628)
Printed in Canada
www.edgewebsite.com

For Lori Christy

Your tough critiques and reader insights
make my books better,
So this one's for you.

"This is the most important decision of your life:
Who will you choose for your friends?"

~ Master, speaking to the fifteens

Table of Contents

Chapter One

Fortunately, I'm alone in my student room when my comp emits a low, despairing moan.

I freeze in my chair, staring at it. It's silent now. The screen looks normal, nothing different. I'm convincing myself I imagined it when another, louder wretched groan begins.

They know about last night, I think. My hand lifts involuntarily to wave my comp off before I stop myself. The awful noise will just resume whenever I reactivate my comp, louder and even more agonized, and what if my roommate is in the room with me then? Besides, I need to access my creds, and until I deal with this, everything else on my comp is frozen.

"Okay, *Flickis,* I'm listening," I mutter in Kandaran the code words I chose to open this message board. I don't often swear, in any language, but I was ticked. I didn't want the O.U.B. installing their unbreachable firewall on my comp, so they could message me in private. I don't want any messages from the O.U.B. Not that they care what I want. I tried to disable it after they installed it, and I'm pretty good with code, but like they said, unbreachable.

The screen shatters. At least, that's the image I get. And from this broken-glass image a calm, emotionless voice states: "Report to Number One Prophet's Avenue on Seraffa, 05-14, Planet Year 108, at 1600 hours."

Today. In one hour. They have to know about last night.

Now I really want to swear.

Nevertheless, at 1600 hours exactly I'm standing outside the door of Number One Prophet's Avenue. I'm not as frightened as I was last time I was here, but I'm scared enough. No one shows up for a meeting with an Adept of the O.U.B. without their heart pounding and their palms sweating.

1

What will they do if they've found out I'm going to Salaria? That's all I could think about as I walked all the way down the Avenue. There's a Prophet's Avenue in the capital city on every world, and Number One always houses the O.U.B.'s planetary administrative offices. The rest of Prophet's Avenue is lined with residences for the Select stationed on the planet. The transit strip let me off at the end of the street. The whole way down the avenue to Number One I imagined a Select or an Adept at every window, watching me.

I haven't done anything wrong! I wanted to shout. But I doubt if anyone can walk down Prophet's Avenue without remembering every single thing they've ever done wrong, and I can remember a lot. I don't think it would have the same effect if I added, *recently!*

It's a religious order, I remind myself. The Order of Universal Benevolence. As in faith. As in religious services.

As in moral accountability.

That last one's where the trouble lies. Because I'm going to Salaria whether they want me to or not, whether they're paying my way at the University of Translators and Interpreters, and expect me to stay here and attend classes, or not.

I'm still trying desperately to remember the scene at the embassy when I told Jaro I was going to Salaria. Was there a Select within hearing distance? No matter how hard I try, I can't recall. I take a deep breath and decide to assume they don't know. Yet.

It's impossible to keep anything from the O.U.B. They train from childhood, heightening their six senses to a nearly inhuman level. The smallest twitch of a muscle in my cheek or shift of my eye will tell her I'm lying as clearly as a full confession. For as long as I'm here, I'll have to avoid the topic of travel entirely. I can't even let myself think about it. Or about Salaria, or the Salarian Nightgames, or family, specifically sisters…

The door opens. I raise my chin, stand up straight, and desperately begin reciting the declensions of regular verbs in Oodan in my mind.

2

Chapter One

A middle-aged female porter dressed not in the blue and white habit of a member of the Order of Universal Benevolence, but in a simple blue and white jumpsuit, stares out at me. I stop conjugating verbs, for now.

"Come in, child."

I hate that. I enter without answering, but I'm tempted to say, *Sure, old woman.* Since she's exaggerated my age down, why shouldn't I exaggerate hers up? But it's possible she meant her words kindly, to put me at ease, and I wouldn't be meaning mine kindly, so it wouldn't be the same. Rude is when you're nastier than they are. I try to keep things equal. Agatha would say we should try to be nicer than others are to us, not just equal. Since we were stuck together so long on Malem, I thought that was a great philosophy—for her, toward me. The other way around was a stretch on my good days.

I'm rambling. It's good practice. Rambling thoughts create fewer expressions to read. It's not as good as focusing on something else, like reciting verb declensions, but easier to maintain.

The porter leads me to a waiting room and asks if I'd like something to eat or drink. Her voice is pleasant but she doesn't smile; in fact she shows as little expression as a Select. Well, any Select but Agatha, who's my friend, even if she is a Select. Probably because she's a little incompetent in the no-emotions department.

I'm about to accept a drink, just to show I'm not nervous. Then I remember I accepted one last time and my stomach was in such knots I couldn't drink it and had to pour it into one of the plants. I sneak a glance at the nearest plant. The soil looks pretty damp already.

"No thanks," I say.

The porter nods without speaking, and leaves the room.

I wait. There is nothing even to look at in this room. I should have brought my wristcomp. If I had known I'd have to wait this long, I would have. I wish I could afford the implant, then I'd always have access to it. I could be brushing up on my Salarian. It's a tricky language and an even more prickly culture, and since I intend to leave on the first ship going there, I could use every spare minute to—

The door at the far end of the room slides open. It's almost 1700 hours, I'd like to say to the house attendant standing there to escort me, a male this time. I stifle my annoyance at the wait and follow him down the hall to a smaller room with three chairs, one of them behind a desk. A woman in the blue and white robes of a Select is sitting in the nearest chair, with her back to me. The attendant waves me to the other chair in front of the desk. It all looks plain and unimposing—until the Select turns to look at me.

Agatha! Now I know I'm in serious trouble. My face doesn't know it, though; it breaks into a grin before I can stop it. I haven't seen Agatha in months, and I thought it might be a year or more before I did. She rises at once and comes to me.

The Select don't hug. They don't touch unless there is a clear need. They are reserved and calm at all times, not unkind, but not familiar.

Agatha throws her arms around me. "I didn't hope to see you, Kia," she murmurs.

I feel myself tear up, and blink hard. I wish she was more like a normal Select, because now it's going to be really hard to say no when they ask me what I think they're going to ask me.

Agatha drops her arms and steers me toward the seat beside hers. The calm expression of a Select slides over her face just before an Adept enters through a door in the wall behind the desk.

The Adept is also wearing the blue and white robes of the Order, but all I notice are his eyes. They settle on me with an intense, unwavering attention that makes me feel completely exposed. Meeting Agatha threw me off. I'm not prepared for the Adept's gaze and I freeze, unable to move. I can't even remember which

Oodanian verb I was in the middle of conjugating when I walked in. I struggle against his cool appraisal. He doesn't look angry or cruel or judgmental. Why should he? I'm not here to be judged. Am I? Is there something I've done I don't know about?

Beside me, Agatha moves. "Should we take our seats?" She asks the Adept, all innocent-faced, as though she has not just interrupted his cool control. I look quickly down at the chair in front of me. To be, I think, and in Oodanian: ooma, ooba, oosam...

The Adept folds his hands on the desk. "Please do," he says, still looking at me. Most people don't resist the O.U.B. like I'm doing, I realize. We were a little less formal when I was on Malem with Agatha, but that was another Adept, not this one. I bite the inside of my lip. Oomar, oobar... Well, it's too late to take it back now. Oosamar...

"Have you done something you do not want us to know about?" he asks.

My sister flashes through my mind—exactly what he wants me to do: think of whatever I want to keep from him. I force myself to think of another verb, any verb. Once you get the verbs, the rest of a language is easy. It's the action that drives a thought, nouns are just added detail. Actions speak louder than words... I let my mind ramble. "No," I say. Not yet, anyway.

It's all a game. Why can't they just stop, and have a normal conversation? My cultural training kicks in, answering that question. We notice what we are taught to notice. I couldn't stop myself from noticing if someone frowned or smiled at me, and drawing conclusions about what their expression might mean. It's cultural, and automatic. It's just that the Select and Adept of the O.U.B. are trained to notice so much more, and to draw such accurate conclusions. If I had nothing to hide, I'd feel as though I was talking to the most understanding person I've ever met.

Who wants something from me. Agatha and I are not here

together by chance.

And when I find out, it will not entirely be a request. The O.U.B. are paying my way, they know my past; a past I don't want anyone else to find out. The longer we delay that talk, the more likely this Adept is to find out—from me—about my sister and Salaria. About last night.

"Why am I here?" I ask him.

"Kia Ugiagbe," he says. His voice is calm, but it resonates in the meeting room, which suddenly seems too small to contain him. "There has been a vision."

Beside me, Agatha sits in her chair still and expressionless, but I can feel a heightened alertness in her, an excitement, since I know her so well. Also because she's not always as careful at hiding her emotions as most of the O.U.B. are.

I sit very still, too, holding my face as expressionless as I can, but inside I'm groaning. Not again. I don't have time for a vision, I have to get to Salaria. No. I stop thinking of that at once.

"This is not something that can be ignored," the Adept says, more or less accurately reading my response, even though I'm deliberately not looking at him.

I try to think of a polite way to ask if it could at least be postponed. The last time they had a vision about me, it happened shortly after I was born and they didn't act on it till I was sixteen. Which I still am. Fulfilling two visions in the same year seems a bit much to ask. Couldn't they envision someone else for a change? I can't quite think of a suitably pious way to express that, either. And really, since knowing Agatha… well, I'm a little more open-minded to spiritual stuff than I was. It's just really not convenient right now. For reasons I can't let myself think about while the Adept is watching me.

"Do you not want to know who is in the vision?"

I look up, surprised. "I thought it was me."

"Why would you assume that?"

I flush. Do I really think everything revolves around me? "Because… because you brought me here… Isn't it?" I don't even try to keep the relief out of my voice.

"Not entirely. It is about the Select you went to Malem with." He looks at Agatha, who sits up even straighter in her chair, almost hopping off it, in fact.

What about A—her?" I almost say Agatha's name before I catch myself. The Select don't divulge their names outside their order. I shouldn't even know Agatha's, but she isn't very good with formalities. The Adept is looking at me, and since I looked up, I'm trapped in his gaze. Knowing Agatha's name isn't a secret any more.

"Then why am I here?" I don't know how I say it. My voice feels frozen under the Adept's stare, but I have to know what he wants of me. I'd also like to know what he wants with Agatha. I thought she was safe on Malem, in the company of another Adept who could, I hoped, keep her out of trouble.

Agatha couldn't conjugate the verb *to be* in Central Ang, the easiest language in the human universe, unless I wrote it down for her. She's probably said something terrible, without meaning to, that's why she's been taken off Malem. But what can I do about it now? I am not, absolutely not for any reason, ever going back to Malem. If they need an interpreter for her…

"We do not explain our visions," the Adept says.

Not to the subject of the vision, I remember. That would influence the person's behavior. So it is about me, too. I can tell he knows the minute I realize this. Well, let him know, and know that I know he knows. Living all that time with Agatha on Malem taught me a bit about reading miniscule expressions, too.

"You have questions I cannot answer at this time, except to say that this Select needs an interpreter. One who speaks Salarian."

"Salarian?" I can't keep the surprise from my voice, let alone my face. Why does Agatha need to speak Salarian? She's not... surely they wouldn't send her to—

"Salaria?" Agatha says, her voice sounding strange.

The Adept turns to Agatha. "Yes. You are going to Salaria. Unfortunately, it is necessary."

I don't know whether to laugh or throw up. How could they send her there? Agatha can't speak Salarian. She grew up on Seraffa, same as me, and speaks only Edoan, our official language.

"I will go where I am sent, Adept," Agatha says the words of obedience calmly. Usually even I can read her expression, when she's not deliberately hiding it, but this time I'm baffled.

"Don't send her there!" I burst out before I can stop myself. "She doesn't know Salarian! The Salarians are the most easily offended people in the human universe!" She won't stand a chance of getting home alive, I want to add, but I don't need to tell him Agatha's foreign language skills are non-existent.

"Your concern for the success of our mission on Salaria is commendable," the Adept says, as if he believes for a moment that that's what I'm worried about. But he will not—and his cool eyes let me know that I should not—suggest for a moment that a Select of the O.U.B. is not capable of accomplishing the task they give her. "And you are correct. The Select will need an interpreter. We want you to go to Salaria with her."

"I expect that was in the vision, too," I mutter, ticked at how neatly he's cornered me. "I'm not going. You can't force me."

Agatha looks at me. If the vision has us there together, and I don't go with her, it can't be fulfilled. Which means there's no reason to send Agatha.

Except that I will be on Salaria. I have to find my sister.

"We do not force anyone to do anything."

Technically correct, but not exactly accurate, I think. Before

I can repeat my refusal, he completely throws me by turning to Agatha and saying: "An important woman, a Coralese lady of the lakes, played Salarian Die at the Salarian Nightgames last night. She lost. Her family has approached us to investigate and ascertain she is being well treated."

I sit with my mouth half-open, staring at him. I remember the lady; she threw her die just before my sister's turn. "You're going to buy her back for them?" It's all I can do not to scream the words. If they're buying a lady back, they might agree to do the same for Oghogho. I remember hearing her voice in the crowd around the gaming table, swearing the oath to abide by the roll of the die. My sister's voice. Why was she even at the Salarian Nightgames? I fought my way through the people, desperate to stop her, but I was too late...

The Adept turns his intense focus on me. I catch my breath. I want to look away, but I can't, I'm trapped by his eyes. He can't read my mind, but my expression is clear enough.

"You know we do not alter the choices people freely make. And the Salarians never, under any conditions, sell back indentured servants. They must work off their debts. The lady's family has only asked that we ascertain she is being treated according to interplanetary humanitarian laws."

"But, if you can do it for her..."

Agatha touches my arm. "What is it, Kia? What's wrong?"

"If we do it for the Coralese lady," the Adept says smoothly over Agatha's question, "the Salarians will know we are concerned about all of their indentured servants. We do not need to call attention to each one of them."

"Kia, is someone you know in trouble?" Agatha persists, despite the clear redirection of her superior.

I shake my head. *Do not call attention*, the Adept said. If I want his help, he has laid out the rules. "It's just that... I was at the Salarian Nightgames last night... interpreting." I add quickly, before Agatha can imagine any other reason. "I saw them all, the ones who lost."

Agatha nods, as if she believes a sudden fit of compassion is in my nature. It makes me feel worse than I am, that she so easily believes me to be better than I am.

"Why now?" I ask the Adept. "Why weren't you concerned with their living conditions before?"

"We might ask you the same thing."

I blush again. I knew, everyone knew, what happens to those who lose at Salarian Die. I remember the people around the game table, cheering for those who chose to play, booing those who backed away. As if someone else's life was merely a game. I didn't do that, but I didn't object, either. I didn't even sign that interplanetary petition to ban the use of Salarian crystals mined by slaves, last year. My brother Etin did. He converted the *Homestar* to a more expensive drive system to avoid using their navigation crystals. That's probably why he and Oghogho are in debt. But I was busy studying languages, I didn't really care. I'm only concerned now because now it's my sister who lost at Salarian Die.

"We have always been concerned about those in need on every planet," the Adept says. "But we do not enforce our faith on others. That has been done in the past, and always failed, as you know if you have studied history. You have been raised in the Order, you know our ways. We encourage, and when the time is right, we weigh in. Gently. On Salaria, the time has become right for us to weigh in, and because the time is right, an opportunity has presented itself through Lady Celeste of planet Coralee."

"You want to increase the pressure on them to free their slaves?" I ask.

"Indentured servants. Human slavery is illegal across the human universe."

"What do you call it when it's a lifetime sentence?"

10

"A very bad choice."

"I will be honored to accept this mission," Agatha interrupts before I can say anything else. Her eyes are troubled, an expression I've never seen on her face. The Adept glances at her and the expression is gone. *Distance and objectivity, benevolence to all,* I can almost hear her reminding herself. Distance? Objectivity? Agatha would gladly walk into hell for someone in need. So what's troubling her?

It isn't that dealing with the Salarians requires someone with keen and subtle negotiation skills. At the very least, someone who knows the Salarian language. That little detail wouldn't give Agatha a moment's pause.

"I am honored to be of service," Agatha repeats the words of obedience calmly, as calmly as my sister recited her vow to honor the roll of the Salarian die.

"What about the Select who are already there?" I stammer, gripped by a sudden fear. "Why can't they do whatever this mission is?"

Agatha looks at me. She was concerned they wouldn't give her another assignment after what happened on Malem, and now a vision!

A vision. An O.U.B. vision only occurs at times of great need, when something terrible is about to happen. This isn't about the slaves at all. That's just... how did he put it? Their "opportunity to weigh in."

I look at the Adept, feeling my eyes narrow and not caring that he can see it.

"You are a perceptive young woman," he says. "I assume that is why the vision included you." Ignoring what I know, what he knows I know, he adds formally: "We would like you to travel to Salaria with the Select, and interpret for her when necessary."

When necessary? They expect something significant to come

of this, something an e- translator can't handle. Only a human interpreter can get the nuances right, the colloquialisms and cultural connotations conveyed by word choice, gesture, and expression, all of which can change the meaning of a phrase completely. Detecting irony, appreciating humor, are crucial and no machine can do it.

"During the trip," he adds, "you will help her to improve her Central Ang."

Central Ang is the one language every human being knows. It's based on an Old Earth language, but it's been stripped of all complexity in order to make it accessible to everyone. There are no irregular verbs, no declensions, no masculine and feminine endings. It has clear, simple rules for plurals, possessives, and verb tense. There are no synonyms to choose between, no extra letters or alternate pronunciations. Its vocabulary is limited to the essentials, and that's all it's good for: a safety net tying the human worlds together at the most basic level of understanding. And it will be completely useless in negotiating with the proud and subtle Salarians for better treatment of their slaves.

"I already eat much Central Ang," Agatha says, in Central Ang.

I look at the Adept. "Your services are needed," he says.

It would get me to Salaria.

With Agatha, who will not survive there, let alone be able to help the slaves. Most likely she'll get us both killed. I start to shake my head. But what choice do I have? I have to get to Salaria. Especially if something terrible is about to happen. I have to get my sister out.

"Come to Salaria with me, Kia," Agatha says softly. "It will be all right. We can trust the vision."

Chapter Two

I barely notice the walk back down Prophet's Avenue. A few passengers glance at me curiously as I step up onto the transit strip; there's always a story when someone has come from Prophet's Avenue. I ignore them and move to the center of the strip as it picks up speed again. Usually I stand at the edge, my arm wrapped around one of the poles, where I can feel the wind and stare out at my city, pink and copper brick buildings racing by on either side. In the early evening like this, the sun shines brightly on the red clay tiles of the roofs, curved to deflect its heat, and turns the windows into rubies as we flash by. Today I barely notice.

Instead I'm remembering my sister's face as they led her away from the gaming table to two years of slavery in payment for her gambling debt. "Salarian Die." I whisper the name of the fatal game under my breath with the venom of a curse. It is a curse. How could Oghogho have been stupid enough to play Salarian Die? Why didn't she come to me? Or my brother Etin, why didn't he come when they thought they were going to lose our family tradeship, the *Homestar*?

Because they think I'm just a kid. What help can a sixteen-year-old offer? Oghogho most likely thought there was no point, and Etin would think he was sparing me. They'll never see me as anything but their little sister. "Bratty little sister," Oghogho would add. They know the O.U.B. is paying my university fees, but they probably think I spend whatever else they give me on myself. I slump into a transit seat. They're not far wrong. I learned to live cheap last year when I was on my own, and I still do, but even so there isn't much left over after I pay for my residence and food. Not anywhere near enough credits to pay off the *Homestar's* debt.

If I go to Salaria like the Adept wants me to, I'll make sure the O.U.B. takes care of that debt. But that won't help Oghogho. Two years of slavery in the mines on Salaria will kill her, no matter how 'humanely' she's being treated. Mining the Salarian crystals means exposing yourself to their slow poison, in the stifling heat of the mines. Maybe a year of it, if you can avoid an accident, a tear in your suit, maybe in time you could heal from a year of hard labor in the mines. But two years?

So. The question isn't whether I'm going, but whether I'm going on the Adept's terms. A little convenient for him, my needing to go just when he wants me to. I don't know how that relates, or if it really is just coincidence, but there it is. The Adept knew about my sister, I saw that when he mentioned finding Lady Celeste. More likely than not, my sister Oghogho went to the same mine as Lady Celeste, since they lost at the same gaming table and travelled to Salaria together. The Adept knew I would make that connection when he mentioned Lady Celeste. He was telling me I'll find my sister if I go along with their vision.

But he was also hiding something from me. Two things. Something about the mission, which is way bigger than reporting on the 'indentured servants' on Salaria, and something about Agatha. I picture the expression I saw on Agatha's face only for an instant, but I still can't make anything of it. She stayed behind to talk to the Adept after I was dismissed, so I didn't get a chance to talk to her. And all the Adept would say was, "The current task is to examine and report on the living conditions of Lady Celeste. You will know more if it becomes appropriate."

I mean to go to Salaria to find my sister, but I don't know what I'll be walking into if I go with Agatha. She might not know what she's walking into, either. What if I refuse, and go to Salaria on my own, and it turns out the Adept is right, that Agatha really does need me?

No, the Adept won't send her there without an interpreter. He might not send her at all without me, if that was their vision. And whatever's troubling Agatha—something she's afraid of?—won't happen. She'll stay here and be safe. From whatever they're each hiding.

The University of Translators and Interpreters slides past. I rush to the edge of the transit strip, balancing myself hand-over-hand on the poles. The tug of the wind increases. Ignoring the cord that will signal the strip to slow down, I lean against the cool curve of a pole and grab the looped strap hanging above my head. The strap is attached to a rotating disc at the top of the edge pole. Pushing off, I swing myself over the edge of the transit strip, dangle a half instant, then let go. I drop with my knees slightly bent onto the sidewalk. The entire manoeuvre takes only a second. It's so automatic I barely notice what I'm doing, because I'm busy berating myself for missing my street. Now I have to walk back two blocks as well as hike across campus. I glare at the transit strip and start walking.

I don't know how to make this decision: try to save Oghogho and put Agatha at risk, or try to keep Agatha safe, and possibly let my sister die?

One by one my family is being taken from me. I can't let Oghogho die. I can't do it, not even to save Agatha.

Agatha is my friend. No one but my brother Etin has ever cared about me as much as she does. I can't let her risk her life on Salaria, not even to save Oghogho.

Who do I think I am? How could I save either of them? I tried to help my parents, and they're both dead.

"What makes you think I can do anything for this vision of yours?" I asked the Adept.

At first he didn't answer. Adepts do not repeat themselves. Then he said, "The Select needs an interpreter." The half-second pause before he continued told me he knew what a huge understatement this is, and that it wasn't the real reason they want me to go. Who was he trying to fool—me or Agatha?

15

"There are better Salarian interpreters than me," I said. He still hadn't told me why Agatha is needed, with all the people they must already have there. "What about the Select on Salaria?"

Every planet has its own Prophet's Avenue, where the offices and homes of the O.U.B. who serve there are situated. Salaria is a large, well-populated planet, there will be plenty of Select on it. What would one more matter?

"The Salarians do not share our faith, although Salaria is in the Alliance," he said. Not repeating himself, but something almost as wasteful; he's telling me something he knows I already know. Which means I should be able to figure out the rest. Then he said, "We do not have many Select on Salaria."

"They're not very busy, then. They can interpret for her," I said. Insult and counter insult. Rude, I labeled myself. But then he's keeping secrets from me, important ones that will affect me if I do as he asks. So maybe not rude, but equal.

I remember the pause after I said that, the Adept looking at me without expression, Agatha stiff beside me. It's pretty hard to earn Agatha's disapproval, but I think I did it then.

"There has been a vision placing you in Salaria," the Adept finally said, actually repeating himself for the second time. The O.U.B. must really want me to do this, I thought. Which made me even more suspicious, because they're not particularly crazy about Agatha. She's one of theirs, but she embarrasses them a lot of the time. No, even worse: she surprises them. The O.U.B. hate to be surprised, they consider it a personal insult. Everything they do is geared toward seeing what's coming and steering it toward the best possible outcome. Agatha gets them an outcome they didn't anticipate but can't object to, using totally unexpected methods. I think they'd rather she failed.

So what outcome are they hoping for by putting Agatha and me on Salaria? They could check the living conditions of the slaves—excuse me, the indentured servants—and deliver their report without us. What is the problem this Adept didn't tell me about? Did he tell Agatha after I left? Does it have to do with that look on her face when he asked her to go to Salaria?

"What am I supposed to do there?" I asked, repeating myself, because you never know.

The Adept didn't fall for it, though. He won't influence my actions by telling me what they saw. If they saw anything. The whole thing could be made up. He probably read that thought on my face, too. Not that I was trying all that hard to hide it, there's only so long you can recite verb tenses when lives might be at stake—including mine.

When he told me, I got up and walked out.

I've reached my residence by now. The door recognizes my retina and slides open. It's quiet, it's simple, it's efficient; but right now I'd really like to have one of those heavy, swinging doors they have on Malem, that you could really slam—BAM!—as hard as you wanted. I'd like to rattle the whole building right now!

I will not do what he wants!

I'm still fuming when I get to my dorm room, but I've made up my mind: I'll go to Salaria my way, and after I find my sister, I'll look up Agatha, if they send her there, too. Agatha's pretty resourceful, she'll be okay till I show up. And if I'm right, and they won't send her without me, I'll find her and apologize when Oghogho and I get home.

I enter my room and go straight to my comp and wave it on. I may not have enough creds to get the *Homestar* back, but at least I have enough to buy passage to Salaria.

Broken glass. My comp screen lights up to display the image of broken glass. Or maybe it's supposed to be broken ice, because the comp is definitely still frozen.

I can't access my creds.

I don't have any doubt who's doing this, the image makes that clear enough, so there's no use calling in a tech, or trying to access my creds any other way.

Should I call my brother, Etin, and tell him the whole story? How Oghogho played Salarian Die, and lost, and now she's on Salaria working off a two-year debt, and I just stood there and watched, and could he come home from his trade mission piloting the *Montrealm III* so we can go to Salaria together and rescue her? And by the way, we'll have to make a slight detour afterward to pick up this Select I know. The Montcliff family won't mind him scuttling the trade deals they spend over a year setting up, will they?

Like that's going to happen. Oh, Etin would come. He'd come racing across the universe, dumber than me about it. Maybe we'd even get Oghogho and Agatha safely home—I'll be on Salaria just like the vision wants, after all. And when we get home I can watch Etin and Oghogho starve to death because no one will ever hire them to captain a tradeship again after the Montcliff family, who own the largest trading chain on Seraffa, lets everyone know what he did to them. They could get his trading license revoked so he couldn't even trade on the *Homestar* after that.

It's all I can do not to hurl my comp across the room.

So I'm back to a choice between Oghogho and Agatha.

Let's be honest. Even if I go, I probably won't be able to save either of them.

But if I don't go…

If I don't go, they'll probably both die anyway, but I'll never know if I could have prevented it. I'll never really know if I stayed here just so I could save myself.

I have to go: I know it in my gut. And I have to do it the way the O.U.B. wants. It makes me so angry I want to scream.

At least I'll make them pay for it.

I check my databud, my pocketcomp, my messenger, and just as I thought, every one of my connects is frozen. I rip a piece of paper from the sketch pad my roommate, who makes a hobby of antiquated art forms, draws in and hunt around for a pencil. I know I brought one back from Malem—a pencil! I wouldn't even know how to hold it if I hadn't been to backward Malem—and I start writing:

> Pay off all debt on the *Homestar*.
> Pay off Oghogho's debt to the Salarians.
> Ship to take us home <u>as soon as</u> Oghogho's freed and I've taught ~~Agatha~~ the Select to speak Central Ang.
> Reverse physical alterations <u>as soon as</u> I get back on Seraffa.
> Pay for the next two years of my university, during which time there will be <u>no more</u> ~~life-threatening~~ ANY trips off-planet.
> No more visions about me or anyone I know. <u>Ever</u>!!!

I fold the paper and tuck it into the pocket of my jumpsuit, then undress and go to bed. Let the Adept wait for my answer. I hope he's sweating it.

The idea of an Adept sweating something is so ridiculous I sigh and give up on that. The best I can hope for is he's starting to consider his alternatives, and even that's unlikely. He knows I'll be back. It's Agatha who's probably sweating.

The next morning I get up early, and take a little trip to the seamier side of town.

When I walk into his jewellery store, Messer Sodum takes one look at me and screams, "GET OUT!"

He takes some convincing, but I've come prepared, and I don't leave until I've got what I came for.

On my way back I check into the Traders' library to do some research on their datacomps. My family has an account which gives me access to the most recent info on all the human-settled planets open to traders—as well as a few that aren't; traders are an optimistic group. I return in time to attend all my classes. It's a little pointless since I'll be leaving soon, and will have to take the semester over again anyway. But it's something to do while the Adept waits. I find myself automatically relaxing in my first class. It's so ordinary, the dull beige walls of the room, the long lines of tables with their ports (no need to bring my databud to plug in today), the other students talking around me before class, ignoring me and me ignoring them back. Everything is so normal. I try to engrave it into my mind, even my prof's voice, going over everything in the resource file he sent us for today's lesson, nice and slow to make sure the other students get it. I lean back and fight to keep my eyes open. Perfectly normal. After Malem, I appreciate boredom. I'm pretty sure I'll miss it on Salaria.

I spot Jaro waiting outside the door after my last class. I look behind me to see if I can make it over to the side door against the crowd of students leaving the classroom, but before I can turn around, I hear him shout, "Kia!"

No way he'll believe I didn't hear him. I turn back and smile, a little grimly. Jaro was at the Kandaran embassy with me when my sister gambled away her freedom. We were both student interpreters. I should never have told him I was going to Salaria, but I wasn't thinking, and I trust Jaro, which made me sloppy. The worried look on his face now warms my heart, which is not a feeling I trust. For a minute, I think how great it would be to tell him everything. Then I consider just what everything includes, and drop that idea.

The forward momentum of the students around me carries me through the door toward Jaro. When I'm close enough, he says, "Kia, you're not—" He looks around, lowers his voice, "you're not going anywhere, are you?"

"Just leaving class, Jaro."

"You know what I mean." He frowns. "We need to talk. Why didn't you answer my messages?"

"I didn't get any messages. My comp's frozen."

He raises one eyebrow.

"Everything else is, too."

"Never mind."

That's what comes of being anti-social. No one believes you the one time you do have a good excuse.

"Let's go somewhere." He grabs my elbow—the only person I'd let do that—and steers me through the students toward the nearest caf. I have some time to kill, so I go along with him.

We sit at a little table at the edge of the caf. It happens to be the same one we usually sit at when I tutor Jaro. That's how we met; he needed tutoring, I needed money. He's a year ahead of me, but what can I say? I'm brilliant in languages. Jaro is pretty good in languages now I'm tutoring him, but he's really brilliant in getting along with people. I'm not entirely convinced it's worth the effort, but I'm trying to learn that from him. So I grimace briefly across the table.

Jaro taps in his order. He looks at me.

I shrug. "All my creds are frozen."

He rolls his eyes and taps in a frozen Lato, glances at me, then adds a chicken wrap.

This time, my smile is real. I can't help it. No one else, not even my brother, would know what I drink, what I like to eat, without even asking. "All that tutoring is paying off," I quip.

He smiles, but he doesn't get the joke. Jaro probably knows what everyone on campus likes and doesn't like, without even trying. He's naturally tuned in to people. It doesn't mean anything special.

"Kia, it's terrible what happened to your sister." He leans toward me, his entire attention on me. "I'm really sorry. If there was anything we could do, I'd help you do it. I would. But there isn't. So please tell me you're not going to Salaria."

I look away. With an ordinary person you can do that. At once I feel bad. It's not fair to compare Jaro to the Adept, even if this does feel a bit like a second inquisition. Even though, again, I have secrets to guard. But Jaro doesn't want anything from me, he just wants to help. He's being a friend. The problem is, I'm not used to friends. I don't know what to do with them.

Fortunately, the server arrives with my chicken wrap and our drinks. I haven't eaten all day and the wrap looks delicious. It tastes even better. "Thanks," I mumble around a mouthful.

"So your connects are all frozen?" Jaro asks, believing me now. "You need help with that?"

"Nope."

Jaro waits. I eat.

"You're going, aren't you?" he says, when it's obvious I'm not going to volunteer anything.

I shrug. "She's my sister."

"If I lend you the passage fare, will you promise to be careful?"

I swallow. Twice. Once for the half-chewed chicken in my mouth and the second for the emotion that catches in my throat. I don't look at him, because I don't want him to see it. The least I can do is keep him out of it. When I can speak, I say, casual-like, "I'm always careful. And thanks, but I don't need your money."

He glances at the chicken wrap I've been devouring like I haven't eaten in weeks. "You aren't going to do something stupid, or desperate, to get there, are you?"

I narrow my eyes. "I don't do that any—"

"Because you know a ship's captain is legally allowed to space a stowaway, right?"

I relax. He didn't mean what I thought. He doesn't know my past. I grin at him. "I won't stow. I'm getting my creds unlocked tomorrow."

"It isn't a joke, Kia. If the Salarians find out what you're up to, you'll be in more danger than your sister."

I think about my little errand this morning. If the Adept finds out about that, I'll be in danger from the O.U.B., as well. "I have to go." I stand up. "Thanks for dinner." I pause, getting my voice under control. He's right about the danger and I'm smart enough to be afraid, but no point admitting something you can't change. "Focus on the irregular verbs," I say instead, because I won't be here to tutor him this semester. "That's where most interpreters mess up."

My room-mate has come and gone when I get back to my dorm room. Her bed is unmade, her U of T & I jumpsuit and some dirty underclothes tossed on the floor beside it, her closet door left open. It would kill her to miss five minutes of a party to clean this stuff up? She invited me to go partying with her once. I told her I didn't see the point. She flounced off, thinking I meant to insult her, like she was wasting her time (which she was) but what I actually meant was, you go to a party to socialize. Like, hello, hermit here.

I check my comp. Still frozen. That's it, then. I'll be going to Prophet's Avenue first thing tomorrow morning, and I probably won't be able to come back here before I ship out. I grab one of my space bags from the shelf in my closet and stuff in a couple handfuls of clean underwear and bras, an extra jumpsuit, my lightest summer one, and a sleepshirt. I look around. Sandals, toiletries, language and vid discs for the trip, sunlenses, and my little box of thieves' tools with the small addition from my morning errand.

Chapter Three

"I bet you're surprised to see me again," I say when the porter opens the door to Number One Prophet's Avenue.

She maintains her cool silence, but I know it's killing her not to refute my greeting. I march past her with my half-inflated space-bag bobbing behind me and head for the waiting room. She has to wait till the spacebag's inside to wave the door shut, then hurry—yup, she has to hustle—to get ahead of me so she can appear to be leading me to the room.

"Oh, take your time, I know the way," I say, all friendly-like.

I am not offered so much as a glass of water this time, when I'm left to wait. No problem. I'm not as carefree as I sound by a long shot. This time, though, I'm angry as well as nervous. I'm tired of having the O.U.B. pull my strings. Sure, I deserved it the first time, but I paid off that debt on Malem.

So I'm all business when I'm ushered in to meet with the Adept. I re-wrote my list of demands (leaving out Agatha's name and the embargo on visions, which could be taken as sounding a little un-grateful at being so honored) on a second sheet of drawing paper, but I keep it in my pocket for now. It'll be awhile before we get to the real negotiations.

I don't look at the Adept as I take a seat. I'm completely out of my depth, going up against an Adept, and I know it. My first move is to try and level the field.

"If you look at me, if you try to compel me through my emo-tions, anything I say, any promise or confession, will be said under coercion, and is therefore null and void. Agree to that, or we're already finished." I speak slowly and clearly, for the official record. I've researched my rights and come prepared this time. It's his re-cord, on his implant. Doesn't matter. No member of the O.U.B.

would falsify a record or omit a significant part of one to change the meaning. It's the basis of their credibility. I'm still looking down so I can't see his face, not that that would tell me much, but I can feel the silence in the room like a palpable thing. Ah. I've done worse than insult him, I've surprised him. Not a good start, but necessary. I'm glad Agatha isn't here to witness my lack of respect.

"Agreed, and recorded," the Adept says.

I should feel relieved—first round to me—but now I'm really nervous. He's been alerted. There won't be any coercion, but there won't be any leniency, either. I've lost whatever goodwill or sympathy he might have felt for me.

Keeping my head bowed this way makes me look submissive or intimidated, neither impression I want to give, so I look up at him. His gaze is as focused and intense as ever, but has no whiplash edge to it. As I expected, I make myself think, so he will read in my face that I know he'll keep his commitment. Then I wait.

"Why make this difficult?" he asks.

"I don't like your plan."

"What does that matter?"

He says it so calmly, so matter-of-factly, I almost laugh. He isn't indifferent to my feelings, he's indifferent to feelings in general. Personal likes and dislikes aren't relevant to making decisions. It's actually a compliment that he expects me to rise above them. Well, we can start there.

"You want me to assume a false identity. I'm sure you're aware that each culture has a lower tolerance for certain actions over others. It's about losing face. Interpreters have a saying: 'Never challenge a Kandaran, laugh at a Gordian, or trick a Salarian.'"

"I know that saying. However, the O.U.B. does nothing without good reason."

"I believe entering Salaria under a false identity would increase my risk."

"Not in this case. We have run the probabilities. You are more at risk on Salaria as yourself."

"They might check the records. Salarians are very thorough. They'd see this girl died."

"Her mother became a Select shortly after the child was born. Under the Interplanetary Accord, the Select and the Adept, and their families, are visitors, not citizens, of any planet they live on. We have no allegiance except to the Order, and we keep our own records. We alone have access to them. There is no public record of the child's death."

"Alright, say I go. Say I use that girl's name. There's still no reason I have to change my appearance. They don't know what she'd look like. No one knows. You said she died in infancy." This is the real issue. This is what I do not want to do. I didn't mean to get to it so soon, but I do want him to know how repugnant it is to me, to change the way I look, to change my skin.

"I won't deny my race," I tell him.

"No one is asking you to deny your race. The girl you will claim to be had a paler complexioned mother. Her skin was lighter than yours. That is public record, she was born before her mother became a Select."

"What I look like is who I am. And I like who I am. Better than who anyone else is, anyway."

"You cannot go to Salaria looking like yourself. You were seen at the Salarian Nightgames."

"There were a lot of student interpreters there."

I realize, by his long look, what he's going to say. So he does know. I wait for him to say it, anyway.

"You were noticed. You made yourself noticed. Do I have to call in the Select who was at the Salarian Die game-table?"

I wince. There was a Select there, I remember now, making sure the players' oaths were freely given before they threw their dice.

I totally forgot her the moment I heard my sister swearing to be bound by the roll of her die. But she must have seen everything: me calling my sister's name, racing to her side, objecting to the outcome… There's no point denying any of it, or questioning her story. If a Select was in a position to hear a conversation, not a single word of the exchange can be in question. If their enhanced memory slips—highly unlikely—their video-audio scan implant won't.

"You have access to the Select's memory, but the Salarians don't."

"They will remember. They make note of friends or relatives who object when a player loses. You will have been watched, after that. Especially when you ran after your sister. We have no doubt they heard you tell your friend of your intention to go to Salaria. They will be waiting for you."

He doesn't look it or sound it, but I know he thinks I'm an idiot for being so obvious. He's right. I consider admitting as much, but there's nothing to gain by that.

"Which brings us to the problem of your sister."

I keep my face expressionless as I wait to hear what he has to say about Oghogho.

"Any move to find or rescue her while you're there would jeopardize your work for us."

"Alright," I say, reasonably. "You do it for me." I take out my piece of paper and hand it to him. He looks at it in my hand, like it's some prehistoric relic. I shrug. "You froze my comp."

He takes the paper and glances through my list of demands.

"Number two: buy out my sister's debt to the Salarians," I say helpfully.

"Yes, I can read. Although this barely qualifies as print. We cannot offer you that. The O.U.B. does not intervene in gambling debts. I made that clear last time we spoke." He pauses. It's as good as a facial expression. I am requiring a lot of repetition.

"I forbid you to try to find or free your sister. Do you understand?"

That catches me off-guard, the way he phrased it. Not, do I agree, but do I understand? Then I get it. "Yes, I understand," I say clearly.

"Number four is also inconvenient."

"Inconvenient how?" Number four says that any change in my appearance has to be reversible.

"The reversible methods available to lighten your skin would take longer than the permanent ones. Your departure, and the Select's, would be delayed."

I want to know more about the procedure, but it's apparent from the vagueness of his answer that he's not a medic. The fact that he has an answer at all tells me he was expecting my question.

"You guarantee any changes to my appearance will be reversible, and that they'll be reversed when I return, or I don't do this at all."

"I will, if that is your final decision."

"And how…" I swallow, not sure I want to hear this, but definitely I need to before I agree. "How will you make me look taller?" The O.U.B. are all quite tall. In fact, everyone is, compared to me. I take after a grandmother I never met.

"That will not be necessary."

My initial relief turns into alarm. "How old would this girl have been? If she'd lived?" They aren't going to make me impersonate a ten-year-old, are they? I try to remember myself at ten. A few unpleasant images come to mind. Nope, definitely not going there.

"Fifteen."

I sigh with relief. I was already cool by fifteen. Way ahead of my peers. Alright, nobody was actually attracted to my coolness, it was kind of a …well, a personal coolness only I appreciated. But I was smart enough by then to act like I didn't care, which is totally better than I was at ten. Too bad she wasn't seventeen. I'd be willing to upgrade. Then I remember this is someone who died, and never got to be ten or fifteen or seventeen, and I'm ashamed of my glibness. "It's too bad she died," I say. "I guess I should know a bit about her."

"She was only a few months old. It was infant apnea. Her name was Idaro."

"Idaro?" The name, which means watchful eyes, or one who notices, isn't a bad one for the child of a Select, whose mother probably hoped her daughter would also become a Select. But I'm surprised to hear an Edoan name. Most of the Select come from New Earth, or are born into the order, although officially they welcome anyone who wishes to dedicate their life to the O.U.B.

"The child's father was Edoan. You will learn more about her if you agree."

That explains why I only have to be a few shades lighter. "And the other things on my list?"

"We will agree to all except number two."

Right. The O.U.B. does not intervene when a choice has been freely made. No need for another repetition.

An Adept does not bluff. It's the best deal I'm going to get, and much as I hate to admit it, their plan is my best shot to get to Salaria. I'll find Oghogho myself, while I'm there. On the other hand, they're going to a lot of trouble and expense to get me there. That alone makes me suspicious.

"What do you expect me to do on Salaria?" Alright, I know I already asked this. But we're negotiating now, everything's on the table, including information.

"That is not yet clear," he says coolly. "We may never know. Our task is to get you there, along with the Select."

"There wouldn't have been a vision if Salaria wasn't facing a major turning point in their history, a crisis which could put universal benevolence at risk on their planet."

"That is true." He's reevaluating me, whether or not it shows on his face. And he's still underestimating, because I know something more than what I've just told him. "We cannot tell you more without a commitment. It may change your mind. If so, you must agree to a memory swipe."

That, I wasn't expecting. No way in this lifetime, I think. Then, remembering the Adept's persuasiveness, I say for the record, "I, Kia Ugiagbe do not give my consent to have any portion of my memories erased for any reason, at any time, by the Order of Universal Benevolence or by any person they delegate to do it." I look at the Adept. His expression is a little more expressionless than usual. I add, "No statement following this in which I retract my refusal to have a mind swipe may be taken as freely given."

We sit across the table looking at each other for some time. He's probably thinking I'm a complete heathen, beyond redemption, to insult an Adept this way. I'm thinking, have I missed anything?

Alright, I'm also thinking, if my mother were alive she'd disown me for showing such disrespect to a leader of her faith. Our faith.

The Adept is watching me. Waiting. I feel guilty, and it's my own feeling, not one he's imposed on me. I don't hate the O.U.B. I even agree with their goals. Who doesn't want a universe operated on truth, equality, and benevolence? It's the faith part that's difficult.

"I'm supposed to trust you to get me to Salaria, to create an identity they won't dispute, to reverse the disguise when I get back. You want me to interpret for the Select, but you won't tell me why we're even going? I swear on my honor as a Universal Interpreter in training (I can't wait till I don't have to add 'in training') that I won't tell anyone what you're about to tell me." That will have to satisfy him.

"I do not distrust you, child. I distrust your ability to resist questioning."

Questioning? Just how dangerous is the situation? This time I'm not rude. I don't repeat my refusal. But I don't say, 'Oh, in that case, sure, of course, go ahead and mess with my memories,' either. I just quietly sit there looking back at him.

Thinking: questioning?

"I'll tell you what I know," I say, ready to break our stalemate. "There are two distinct races on Salaria. The ones we know, those we call Salarians, the majority culture; and the desert people, a minority culture that keeps to itself. They live in the desert. Obviously."

I wait. His turn. Only he doesn't seem to get the 'taking turns' part.

"They have nothing to do with each other," I prompt him. I know all this from my language culture class when I was studying Salarian. There's something else I found in the Traders' library, an interesting note for traders that I might or might not bring up.

"The desert people live below ground, barely surviving, while the Salarians have more wealth than anyone needs."

The Adept listens, expressionless, even to this, which I know must offend him. The O.U.B. does not interfere in planetary issues like class systems or indentured servitude. I can almost hear him thinking it—no, waiting for me to think it. He knows I already know their answer. And I know why they don't interfere. I've studied Old Earth history. It's a required subject on every planet. One major aspect of that history is the way the old religions thought they had the right to force their beliefs on other cultures, and kill those who disagreed with them. All that fighting over who owns God. The O.U.B. combines the most altruistic, universal tenets of all the old religions and invites people, by example not by force, to embrace those tenets of their own will.

So I know the inequity between the people of Salaria is not why we're being sent there. That in itself is not a major turning point, a planetary crisis. It's just normal, nasty human behavior. It might distress the O.U.B., but they would never allow themselves to use it as an excuse for worse aggression on their part.

"Something's about to happen," I say again. I think I know what the spark is, that little side note I found in the Trader's library, but I want him to tell me. I need to know what it means, why it's important. How bad it could get. But if he doesn't want me to know, I guess he doesn't need a reason to think I have any ideas of my own.

What if, whatever the situation is, it's so terrible if I knew about it, I wouldn't go?

I think of the last time I saw my sister. "Don't tell Etin," she whispered, so low it barely disrupted the awful silence when her die rolled to a stop showing two years of slavery. Don't tell Etin because he'll come racing to rescue her and get himself killed. It never occurred to her that I would.

Come to her rescue, that is, not get killed.

And if I don't, what do I tell my brother when he gets home and there's no sign of Oghogho? When the days and weeks and months go by and she never reappears, and his search turns up nothing because Salarians are allowed to close the records on those who lose? What do I tell Etin when he comes to ask me if I know anything, anything at all?

"I'll go," I tell the Adept, without asking her any more questions, because the answers don't make any difference. I am going to Salaria.

He raises an eyebrow delicately.

"Freely and without coercion."

"I am sorry we have to involve you," he says. His face is expressionless. His shoulders, his hands—no single movement or intonation gives his feelings away, and yet I sense a depth of regret in that single, brief sentence. An unusual sentence for an Adept. They act with such certainty, always. A certainty, an unwavering moral confidence that we count on, all the human worlds, to keep us from straying too far. I am completely unnerved by this brief glimpse of vulnerability.

Just like that all my anger dissolves, because he is as bound to service in his faith as he is binding me. He can't see the end either, can't even try to achieve it himself, but has to send others out into that dark place of blind faith to reach beyond what we know, trusting in what we can't understand. He would so much rather walk into that unknown himself than put me in its path. What he is doing requires more faith than I will ever have.

"You know why I'm going," I say, because I'm not up to a task like that, to such high expectations, and also to let him off the hook for sending me.

He smiles, a very un-Adept expression. "Thank you."

"A little more information would be helpful, though."

"When you need it, I have no doubt you will receive it."

❧

The house assistant returns and leads me to the room I'll be staying in until I'm ready to go. There's a table with a notebud sitting on it, a bed, and a closet. I check out the notebud. It has a Salarian-Edoan dictionary and a batch of language lessons, as well as a short beginner's primer on the culture and history of Salaria. When I look in the closet, there are several blue jumpsuits in my size—which is even less coincidental than the programs on the 'tab, since I'm short and skinny. They're pretty sure of themselves, the O.U.B.

Sure of God's plan, Agatha's voice in my thoughts admonishes me. Right, I tell her. Get out of my mind. And before you go, you should know I don't think there's a vision at all. I feel better for saying that, even if it's all imaginary. It's going to be tough enough rescuing my sister without worrying about fulfilling some world-changing mission, too.

I take my own clothes out of my spacebag, deflate it, and stuff it at the back of the closet. I don't think anyone will go through my things, but there's nowhere to hide my little box of tools that's better than an empty-looking space-bag, anyway. I'm in trouble if they find it. I'm in worse trouble if it's found in my things by the Salarians. But most of all I'm in trouble if I find my sister locked up and I don't have what I need to free her. I lie down on the bed and fall asleep.

I waken to the smell of food and open my eyes to see a girl placing a tray on my desk. The scent of fried eggs, onions and cheese and a steaming Lato gets me off the bed quickly. I didn't have any creds to buy breakfast, and I'm famished. The girl smiles at me as she leaves, the first friendly expression I've seen here.

She comes back when I've finished my meal to collect the tray, followed by a man wearing a medic's badge sewn onto his left shoulder. Behind them, his assistant wheels in an IV trolley with a saline bag hanging from it.

"I will be in charge of your treatment," the medic says. "My name is Murdock."

"Murdock the medic?" I say.

He doesn't crack a smile. "No time for pleasantries. We have to get started right away. The treatment has been explained to you?"

"More or less." I wasn't expecting it to start so soon, but I take a breath and hold out my arm. "Mostly less." While the assistant prepares to insert the needle, Murdock explains my treatment. The med they're inserting through the IV is a combination of monobenzone, which will decrease the number and size of the melanin granules in my skin cells, and another agent that blocks Mc1r, the skin protein necessary for the production of melanin. Melanin, particularly eumelanin, is responsible for darker skin tone.

"It won't be permanent?" I ask, to make sure that got passed on.

"We've added an agent that limits the duration of its effect—prevents it from inhibiting the future production of melanin. Two months after your final treatment, your skin will begin reverting to its present color."

"That slows the lightening process down, though," he says. "So you'll also be having cryosurgery—liquid nitrogen applied topically to the visible areas of your skin, to destroy the surface skin cells. They'll naturally regenerate, but the excess melanin will come to the surface and peel off in a few days. You can expect a

little temporary redness, some discomfort, possibly a few blisters.
Nothing serious. Questions?"

It sounds serious enough to me, but I was the one who insisted a
temporary treatment be used, so I can't complain now. I shake my
head. He leaves me with his assistant.

"You're a brave girl," the assistant says, tapping the IV tube to
increase the flow of goop into me. I'm trying to decide whether
there's something about this treatment I don't know, or does she
know something about my trip to Salaria, or is she just a patron-
izing twit, but the moment passes to respond. After that we don't
say anything, just wait in silence watching that drip, drip, drip seep
into me with its promise of betrayal.

After the IV has finished, the medic's assistant leaves, saying
she'll be back at 1500 hours for the first cryosurgery treatment.
"Great, can't wait" I mutter._

I finally have some time alone. I check the notebud, skim-
ming through the lessons on Salarian for any topic I don't already know. I'm pretty thorough when I study a language, and
the University of Translators and Interpreters is thorough, too. I
wouldn't have been interpreting at the Salarian Nightgames if I
didn't know Salarian inside out and backwards, language and culture both. But the O.U.B. might have access to some social issues
I should know about that the University isn't privy to. Maybe I
should have agreed to the memory swipe, since I won't change
my mind anyway. I wonder what the Adept would have told me
if I had. But once I've agreed in theory to one, who knows when
they might play that card? Nope, better to go in blind and hope
I learn what I need in time, than to leave with a hole in my past.
A hole I wouldn't even know about. The very thought gives me
the creeps.

The door to my room beeps. It's way too early for the Cyrosurg.
Agatha, maybe? "Enter." I say, and the door slides open.

A Select of the O.U.B. is standing in the doorway. She looks to be somewhere in her mid-thirties, but she could be anything from twenty to forty—the Select are pretty good at hiding their age as well as everything else. I sit at the desk staring at her, too stunned to say anything, even to invite her in. The one thing she can't hide, without altering her appearance as much as I'm being forced to, is that she's Salarian. Creamy skin with a yellowish cast, like the sun, large, slanting brown eyes, perfect bow-shaped lips and high cheekbones, a frame as small and slight as mine under her blue and white robes. Beautiful. And every feature Salarian.

She raises one elegantly-shaped eyebrow.

"Come in," I stammer. I still don't believe what I'm seeing. Salarians don't emigrate from Salaria. They don't desert their triad. Ever. It would be akin to familial murder, and certainly not something that would look good on an application to join the O.U.B. It's all I can do not to ask her, "What are you doing here?" and I don't mean in my room.

"I am here to tell you about your alias." There's the tiniest hesitation before the word "alias", so small I wouldn't have noticed if I hadn't lived with a Select and become attuned to their fleeting tells. The fact that she answered my unspoken question confirms what I see—Salarian or not, she's a Select.

"Are you here to coach me on Salarian culture? Because—"

"I hope you already know most of what you need to about their culture."

Just what I was planning to say to her. She knows it, too, I see that in her eyes, the tiniest crinkle at the corners. "Because I'm always willing to learn from anyone," I say instead, a bit stiffly.

"If Idaro had lived, she would be about your age."

"A year younger," I clarify.

"And if she had decided to return to our people—"

"Your people? She was Salarian?" Oh no, I suddenly realize, "She was your—"

Now I know why my size doesn't matter, but I'm completely tongue-tied. I'm going to be impersonating this woman's dead daughter? She's going to teach me how to be the child she lost? I stand up, my mouth open, but nothing comes out.

"It was a long time ago," she says.

My father died a long time ago. Three years, two months and five days. I remember the way he looked at me, the way he talked and moved, his silences, his smile. My mother died six months and two days ago. I remember her face, her voice, every expression on her face. Death is never a long time ago. Death is yesterday.

"I… I'm sorry." It's totally inadequate. I'm sorry she died. I'm sorry they're using her death this way. I'm sorry for what I'm about to do to you, to her memory.

"Don't be sorry. Make it count," she says.

I swallow and nod. And I wish I hadn't so adamantly refused a mind swipe, because I'd like to lose those last three words. How can I ever make my trip to Salaria count enough for stealing the last memory she has of her daughter?

"Let us begin." Her voice, her whole demeanor, briskly sweeps that entire conversation behind us. "You need to know my history, what I would have told my daughter about her birth, what she could have expected on Salaria if she had turned from my path and returned to our people. What you can expect there."

It takes me a minute, but now I realize why the Adept wasn't concerned about my intent to rescue my sister. I won't even be able to look for her, not until I do what's expected of me first. They aren't just giving me an alias to get onto Salaria; they're giving me a script. And there's nothing I can do about it. I've already agreed. The first skin treatment has been started. I'm already moving, irrevocably, into their plan, without even knowing what I've agreed to.

Chapter Four

The Select, Idaro's mother, takes me with her to her quarters. It's three buildings down on Prophet's Avenue, on the second floor. Walking through the door to her unit, I see it faces the street, and I can't help wondering, when I glance out the front window, if she saw me walking past to Number One and knew what they wanted me to do. Did she hope I'd say no? I turn and sit in a straight-backed chair facing away from the window. The Select is in the kitchen dialing up two Latos for us.

"There are two living units on each level with two bedrooms. I would have had one if Idaro had lived."

I nod. She can't see me from the kitchen, but I still don't know how to deal with this situation. A nod is the best I have right now.

"I'm not sure I would have told Idaro why I left my home planet," she says, walking into the sitting room and handing me my Lato. I take a sip to cover my awkwardness at hearing her speak so casually about her dead daughter. The Select don't talk about personal things. They leave all that behind when they take their habit. She seems to be… not quite enjoying this, but something similar. I could be wrong, but maybe it's a relief to talk about it. The way Etin and I talked about our father last time Etin was home and came to see me, kind of keeping his memory alive.

I glance over the rim of my cup at the Select's expressionless face. I'm probably wrong.

"But if she decided not to join the Order, to return to Salaria instead, I would have told her certain things. The things I am going to tell you. They are my past. Mine, not yours."

I nod quickly. Maybe a bit too earnestly.

"My past, not my present."

"I understand," I say. "It's for the mission, not for me." The word "mission" sticks in my mouth, like someone else's words on my tongue. It sounds cold, impersonal. This is her daughter, not just a mission. I'm making everything worse. I won't say anything else. I won't even nod. It's not like it isn't apparent all over my face. She knows how I'm feeling.

She knows. But I don't know how she's feeling, what she's thinking. I haven't been trained in the O.U.B. skills, and that's going to be obvious to anyone.

"Would Idaro be able to read expressions? Would she have studied…?" Whatever it is they study.

"She would have chosen when she was fifteen. This month. I would have taught her to notice things, of course. She would have learned to hide her own feelings by watching me and her teachers. There's a school for our children in building twelve. She would have learned there what you learned in school. Maybe more of a universe-wide approach, a little less about Seraffa and the Edoan culture, but essentially the same basic knowledge: math, science, uni-net skills, languages, arts, human culture and history."

She stops. The silence between us grows. I take a breath. "What happened to your…?"

"Idaro's father? He left soon after she was born. She was a fretful baby, unhealthy from birth. Not all partnerships can survive something like that."

For the first time, I'm thinking maybe I was lucky. My father was strange, he was ill, he was usually absent even when he was right there, but none of that was by choice. He didn't want to abandon us. I grew up trying, usually in vain, to get his attention, but I didn't grow up wondering why he didn't want me.

"Tell me what you notice," she says.

As she would have said to Idaro. Is this the moment I start to become someone else? Or has it already begun?

"I notice you hesitate, just a little bit," a very, very little bit, it's true, "before you say her name. I notice you won't look at me when you say it. I notice when you talk about her, your eyes get…" what's the right word? They don't move, they don't narrow or widen or crinkle at the edges. Her eyebrows don't move. She doesn't display any clear emotion, really. Her eyes just get "…deeper."

"Deeper?"

"And a little colder."

She looks at me. This time I look away. She already dislikes me—how could she help it?—but do I always have to surprise them? I want to take it back, but I can't, she'd know I was lying if I tried. When she talks about her daughter, her eyes look like they've died, that kind of cold, not anger, or the sadness of a survivor remembering someone she's lost, but the dull cold of someone who died, too.

"The name suits you," she says. Her daughter's name suits me? One who watches, who notices? I'm not sure whether it's meant as a compliment or said with a Select's controlled anger.

"Your cryosurgery is scheduled to begin soon." She takes my empty glass, a sign that our session is over, and leads me to the door. But there she hesitates. "Try to imagine what it would be like to be Idaro, the child of a Salarian Select. To go to a school where no one looks like you, on a planet where you and your mother will always be foreigners. Notice things she would notice, think about them as she would have."

I don't nod, or smile, or agree. I just leave. The trouble is, I do know how she felt. Maybe the other kids in my schools looked like me, except that I was shorter, but no one else had a crazy father. No one else learned a foreign language in the hope that it would make her father look at her. I know what it's like to want to fit in so badly your teeth hurt, and not be able to, and pretend you don't care. I know what it's like to have a mother as cold as rock, as emotionally distant, for her own reasons, as a Select. Reasons you don't know, don't understand. Reasons that don't matter, because all that matters is how alone you are. I already know what it's like to be Idaro. At least I had my brother, Etin.

I've come to terms with my parents, with who they were, and with only understanding them after I lost them. It hurts to look back. This wasn't what I agreed to. Looking like someone else is one thing; becoming her is another. I don't want someone else inside my head, I have enough trouble sorting out my own thoughts. The truth is, I don't even want to look like this girl, let alone think like her.

I look down at my bare arms, and my feet in their open sandals, as I walk down the avenue back to Number One. I imagine the cold of the liquid nitrogen on my beautiful dark skin, and the way my skin will peel away afterward. They're going to freeze my race out of me, I think. Then I remember the Select's cool, slanting eyes under her blue and white hood, and I understand: they're not doing anything to me that they don't do to themselves.

❧

The room is warm, I tell myself, as I stand still, naked from the waist up, shivering. Small squares have been drawn onto my skin from my neck to my waist so that I look like I'm fashioned out of graph paper. Murdock slowly circles me, supervising five female assistants as they spray my skin in tiny spirals with the liquid nitrogen spray, maintaining each small ice field for exactly thirty seconds before moving on to the next area while it thaws. I'm not allowed to clutch my arms in front of me, either for warmth or modesty, but must leave them stretched out so they, too, can be sprayed. My face and ears they will do later, with sponge brushes, so as not to freeze away my hairline.

It doesn't hurt: another litany. The room is warm, it doesn't hurt, I tell myself, shaking so hard they tell me regularly to just stand still. I am cold all the way down to my bones. As soon as they finish, they'll redo each square, until every one has been frozen and thawed twice, for thirty seconds each time. I am already getting the beginning of a headache. I can feel my skin blistering on the finished areas, although they tell me I'm imagining that, the blisters won't begin forming for several hours, what I feel now is at most a sharp tingling.

"It doesn't t-t-tingle," I snap, my shivering turning the sharp retort into a childish stutter. I'd like to turn the spray on them.

I have a full-blown headache by the time they're finally finished. Murdock leaves last, adjusting the lights to low without being asked. He tells me he'll be back tomorrow to do the lower half of my body, unless I have a worse reaction than he anticipates. "Don't lie down for two hours, don't rub, and DO NOT scratch your skin," he says, just before the door slides shut. I check the timer so I'll know when I can take the next pain-killer, then close my eyes and wait for the one he gave me before he left to take effect.

By the end of the next day, my entire body is one continuous blister. I cannot bear to wear anything, no matter how loose. The bottom of my feet and palms were spared, so I stand until I'm exhausted, then sit as gingerly as possible, and finally, when I can't stay up any longer, I lie down, perfectly still, on my bed. The least movement tears open another blister, exposing raw skin. I would cry, but I know I'm being watched. I bear it silently, my teeth gritted until my jaw hurts, my hands clenched with the effort not to moan. The pain-killers cut the pain, they don't erase it, but I tell myself they are working, and I am religious about taking them exactly on time. That's the kind of faith I can manage. When Murdock examines me and asks how I'm doing, I tell him I've been through worse.

I haven't. Not worse physical pain, anyway. But I have endured worse, am enduring worse, when I think of Oghogho and the possibility that I may never see her again. Being wounded this way makes me feel vulnerable, ready to give in to my fears and imaginings. She'll be okay, I tell myself. I will get through this and find her. Then another blister breaks and optimism is beyond me.

Even if we're only talking physical pain, there's much worse than this, I know. I just hope I never experience it.

On the third day my skin begins to peel. The blisters were nothing compared to this. The emerging skin is maroon, bruised-looking. I've gone through all this for nothing, I think, but Murdock only hums and nods his head. The next day the red has faded, leaving new skin that is definitely lighter.

"You might only need one more treatment," Murdock says, smiling at me as though this is good news. I stare at him. Another treatment? He wants to do the whole thing again, this time to skin that's already sore? I open my mouth to ask if he's insane, or if he thinks I am.

Before I can speak, there's a ping at my door. I don't answer. Whoever it is should not enter now. Especially not if it's the Adept. If he thought I was rude before...

The assistant hands me my clothes and goes to the door. I haven't agreed to do this again, I think as I slowly, gingerly, put on my bra and panties and step into my lightest jumpsuit.

"There is a Select waiting to speak with you," the assistant says when she returns.

I seal the front panel of my jumpsuit closed, and nod. Immediately I wish I hadn't. Even my neck is raw and sore.

Idaro's mother enters as Murdock and his assistant leave. I haven't seen her in four days. Since then, I've had two more IV injections of the monobenzone mixture as well as the cryosurgery, a tuck at the corner of each of my eyes, and my hair has been straightened. She stops just inside the door and looks at me.

I'm still upset at learning I have to do the cryosurgery again and I wasn't expecting her, so I'm not doing as she suggested, I'm not noticing. In fact, I'm busy swearing under my breath in Salarian as I gingerly try to wriggle my feet into my sandals, until I decide it's not worth it.

I look up, realizing she hasn't spoken, and then I do notice her, the stillness of her, the way she's breathing. *I didn't swear out loud, did I?* is my first thought. I'm pretty sure I didn't.

She stands there, just looking at me, and I'm looking at her, and it's getting weird. Did I swear out loud?

"Sorry," I mutter, because maybe my lips did move, and they can all read lips and of course she speaks Salarian. I'm about to explain about the cryosurgery being done a second time, that I wasn't swearing at her, when she gives a tiny move of her head, like she's coming out of a dream. She says, "Your name... it's Kia, isn't it?"

I nod, just a small movement because of my skin, wondering why she would say that. The Select don't pay much attention to names. Then I get it. I flush, as though I've been caught doing something much worse than swearing.

"It was just... a surprise," she says. Then, all business again, "You've been thinking about her, trying to understand her, as I suggested?"

I nod again, still unable to speak.

"Have you had time to go through what's on your notebud?" She's looking away now, at the notebud on the desk, it's a relief for both of us, but she notices my nod anyway.

"Good. Any questions?"

"I don't understand the desert game. It's purpose." This seems a safe topic. At age fifteen, Salarian girls are sent into the desert. They're dropped off a hundred miles or more from any town or city, to fend for themselves. They stay there for a month, sometimes longer, and when they emerge eventually they're in triads, groups of three, bonded together. That was on this notebud. I'm not sure I believe it, I've never heard of it before, it wasn't in my Salarian culture class. On the other hand, the only mention made in my culture course of how Salarian women form triads was that it's a "secret selection process known only to Salarians". The desert game was briefly referred to as a coming-of-age ritual left over from the time of the early settlers.

"Its purpose," the Salarian Select says, still not quite looking at me, "is to separate childhood and adulthood. The girls enter the desert as children, attached to their families, unsure of themselves, still finding their strengths and their own unique skills. They return as women, aware of themselves and their abilities, no longer part of their childhood families but joined with two others they have chosen to share their thoughts and dreams with. They finish growing up together: university, choosing a profession, choosing their adult triad. They don't always choose each other for their adult triad, sometimes their goals take them in different directions, but they stay friends forever."

"So what happens in the desert?"

"I would not have told you that." She looks at me now, her nostrils flare a little as she draws in her breath. "Because, if you were Idaro, and you were going to Salaria at age fifteen, it would probably be to participate in the desert game. Each game is different. Girls are trained for survival, but the desert itself determines what they will face. They learn to rely on each other to survive; that's how they form their triads. Occasionally, if there's an odd number of girls, they may form a quad."

I have so many questions I don't know where to start. I want to say, I look like her, don't I? Because it's right there in the Select's eyes, in her silence, in the way she can't quite look at me, and can't quite not. I've never stolen anything as cruel as this.

The only thing crueler would be to acknowledge it. So instead I blurt out, suddenly realizing something, "You expect me to join the desert game, don't you? I'll have to do it, won't I, to maintain my alias?"

"Not necessarily. I don't believe city dwellers do it anymore. But the mining estates in the desert at the edge of the cities, they have to do it. My family sends their girls on the desert game, so if Idaro went to them, she'd participate with them."

"What happens to those who don't find a triad? What happens if I do?" How would I get out of that? A triad is for life, isn't it? If I faked it, what would it do to the other two girls when I left? Would they have to go back to the desert to find another third?

45

How am I supposed to accomplish whatever the Adept wants me to do if I'm stuck in the desert? This is a stupid disguise, what was he thinking?

"I'm supposed to be translating for A— the Select, she's going to report on the treatment of a sl—an indentured servant. I'm going there to interpret for her. That's my alias." And that's what I have to do, I can't find Oghogho if I'm wandering around in the desert.

"Maybe you have an ulterior reason for going to Salaria?"

I stare at her, wondering how she guessed, until I realize she's not talking to me, she means Idaro. Idaro has an ulterior motive. Idaro's using the pretext of interpreting for a Select in order to get to Salaria and claim her birthright, the desert game. It's beginning to feel creepy, how much I have in common with this kid we've resurrected. I shake my head. Of course she has a lot in common with me, I'm inventing her. She doesn't exist.

She doesn't. But still, I can't shake the feeling that someone else is creeping around inside my head.

"I'll answer your questions about the desert game," Idaro's mother says. "The ones I can, at least, but you have to be patient. I need to tell you as I would have told her. You need to hear it as my daughter would have heard it. If you're going to convince them, you have to be Idaro."

I'm noticing her now, I see the wince beneath her calm expression when she says I have to be her daughter. Did she see me wince when she said it? I'm not her daughter; I don't want to be her daughter. I have my own family. I need to go to Salaria to get my sister back, not to role-play the life of someone who died. I can't be Idaro, I want to tell her, if I could think of a way to put it that wouldn't increase the damage I've already done her.

"You can be whoever you want," she says, reading my expression as only a Select can, "while still being you. You are a sensitive person, a person of understanding beyond your years."

No one has ever called me sensitive or understanding. I wonder if she's thinking of someone else, or projecting what she hoped for her daughter onto me. But she's a Select. They don't make mistakes like that, they're trained to read people. It's possible she's just not very good at being a Select, like Agatha. I warm to her a little, thinking that, even though I don't want to. Liking her could be painful; having her like me even more so. I am not her daughter, and never will be. I am going to take her memory of Idaro and use it to save my sister, not to do whatever it is the O.U.B. wants, whatever they saw in that mystical vision. And she is going to hate me for it, so it's better she doesn't like me now.

"You're wrong," she says. "I don't know why you feel the way you do. I didn't like this idea at first, either. But I can see now that the Adept was right: you will make me proud that you bear my daughter's name."

It's a little much, this reading of expressions. I bet Idaro would have hated it. At least my mother stayed outside my head. Then again, at least Idaro's mother would have noticed her.

"I'm not Idaro." I don't go as far as to say she never existed, which is what I'm telling myself. I don't want to hurt this woman, any more than looking like her daughter already has. She knows I'm not Idaro, but her eyes tell her differently.

"She would have got darker as she got older," I say, hopefully, thinking of the cryo treatment still to come. It can't hurt to try.

The corners of her eyes crinkle slightly. "The medic has predicted what she would look like now. You're not quite light enough. If he can project it, the Salarians can."

"Why would they bother?"

"Before they allow you to participate in their rituals, to choose a youth triad from among their children, to infiltrate their society, of course they will make sure you are who you say you are."

This stops me. "And when I leave? When they learn the truth?" I can't believe the O.U.B. hasn't considered the repercussions of that. Then it occurs to me: what if the Salarians find out the truth before I leave?

"We will have to trust the Adept, and trust the vision we have been given," Idaro's mother says.

Right. She's not the one who might be caught tricking the most easily insulted people in the human universe. I keep my face carefully neutral, but I don't expect she has any trouble knowing my feelings. Next time I talk to the Adept, I'm going to make sure he has a back-up plan to get me out if I'm discovered. I hate relying on back-up, it's seldom reliable, but I'd like to know there's some back-up plan before I head into this insane, death-defying venture.

"This is not a good place for you. We should talk somewhere else." Before I can object, she adds, "I know you aren't allowed outside in the sun until your skin has healed, but we could go to the caf?"

I'd been about to refuse. I don't want anyone to see me like this, with my skin red and still peeling in places, walking a little funny because it hurts when anything rubs, but the thought of leaving this room is suddenly too tempting to resist. Besides, who cares if Adepts or Selects or porters or any of them see me? They're the ones who're doing this to me.

I haven't been allowed to leave this building since my physical alterations became noticeable. The fewer people who know, the safer I'll be on Salaria. I have nothing to fear from the Select or the Adept, and no one gets into Number One unescorted, but outside, there's always the possibility someone could walk by.

I follow her down three hallways, two stairways and an underground corridor past what I guess must be the kitchen, by the sounds I can hear through the closed doors, to a large room filled with long tables and straight-backed chairs. The walls are a natural shade of rusty-rose Salarian clay, the furniture as white as sunlight, giving the room a simple, functional elegance. I choose a spot to sit and tell her what I'd like. Might as well use this ugly red skin to get a Select to wait on me while I can. It's likely to be a one-off occurrence.

"I was nineteen when I left Salaria."

I set down the Lato she brought me, ready to listen. I'd rather ask questions, and get the answers plain and immediate, but I can see that's not going to happen.

"I'd gone through four years of university with my desert partners…" She pauses, looks at me. "You'll have to know their names, Idaro would, and they're likely to come see my daughter when they learn she's there."

"Will they be angry? Will they want to, I don't know," I do know what I want to ask, but I don't want to state it too baldly, "get back at you through me? For leaving, I mean."

"No, nothing like that. They didn't want me to go, but they understood why I left. We don't formalize a partnership until the age of twenty. I was under no obligation to them, except that of friendship."

"Why form triads at fifteen if it doesn't count till you're twenty?"

"Do you marry the first boy you like, here on Seraffa?"

"Is it a marriage?"

"More like a partnership. We take a spouse as well, those who want children. An ideal triad is actually a sextet, three couples forming an alliance to further everyone's goals. Most people don't know what their goals are at age fifteen. But we've found if young people wait much longer than that to practice being in a relationship, a partnership, where they have to consider each other's needs and goals when they make decisions or take actions… well, it's harder to learn certain things when you're older." She takes a drink from her cup. "I suppose you'll have to trust me on this."

"It's not easy to learn them when you're young, either." I'm thinking of Jaro, and my sister Oghogho. I can't imagine considering what Oghogho wanted before I did anything. I don't think I'll do very well on Salaria.

"What if I fail in the desert? What if no one will choose me for their triad?"

"Don't fail." I feel the sting behind her words. Don't risk failing the mission? Don't shame her when I'm carrying her daughter's image? Or is it a warning, that failure isn't a healthy option?

"I was nineteen when I left Salaria."

I know enough about the Select to blush at making her repeat herself, however calmly she does so. I close my mouth and tell myself to stop getting side-tracked, to shut up and listen, which is more effective than if she said it to me, as she well knows.

"My partners in our youth triad were named Kala and Nao. They were as their names implied: Kala was a beautiful person, and Nao was the soul of honesty. My name," she hesitates a heartbeat, "was Philana. It means lover of mankind."

I take a drink of my Lato to cover the awkwardness of the moment. Now I know the names of two Select. It's not like we're close. It's not like it means anything, I tell myself.

"I have a reason for telling you this. A name is important on Salaria. A name is who you are. We give that up when we join the order, we give up our own interests to dedicate ourselves to creating a benevolent human universe. But before I gave it up, I was already one who loved people. And if you love mankind, you cannot tolerate certain things. I left Salaria because I could not live in a society that condoned slavery."

I look up quickly. Slavery, not indentured servitude? She returns my look steadily. "I made my beliefs clear. Clear enough that I was no longer welcome on my home planet."

Does she know about my sister? Nothing in her face gives that away, which only means she's a Select. I can't ask her; I don't want to tell her if she doesn't know. She's committed to the O.U.B., committed enough to let me impersonate her daughter. How could she approve of me having my own agenda on Salaria, however sympathetic she may be if she learned about my sister? I don't care if my sister gambled and lost, I don't care if she agreed to her fate, I don't care if it's supposedly temporary, until she pays off her debt. My sister is a slave and there's nothing right about that.

"I would have raised my daughter to despise the way they use people to work in their mines. They will know that, when you arrive. So why would Idaro ever go back to Salaria?"

I wait, not realizing she expects me to answer that. When I do, when I start thinking about it, the obvious answer would definitely occur to the Salarians. Idaro wants to do what her mother ran away from: to agitate for freeing the slaves. They'd probably deport her before she got her second sentence out if she tried that. So what if her mother's cause is just that: her mother's cause? What if she simply wants to see her mother's home world? Check out her roots before she chooses her future? It doesn't feel right to me. It feels too… neutral for a fifteen-year-old. Anyway, the Salarians would still be suspicious, they'd be watching her every move. I wouldn't be able to do anything. And why now? Why at fifteen, when she knows she'll be sent out into the desert? She isn't prepared for that, she'd have to know that. And why would anyone who hasn't been raised to the custom want to be part of a triad?

"Grandparents?" I ask.

"My mother's triad owned a mine. They disowned me when I left Salaria. They won't make contact with you when you're on Salaria. If Idaro went to them, they'd probably send her away at once."

How am I supposed to know what this imaginary girl might do? And why is it up to me to fill in the details of their stupid plan, anyway? "This isn't my plan, it's the Adept's plan. Hasn't he thought of something?"

"I am asking you to."

"I don't know! I can't think of a reason that would work."

"Forget whatever the Adept told you about your purpose there. Forget your own purpose for going. Think like Idaro. Become Idaro. Tell me why she would go."

She's so calm, and yet behind her words the force of her will compels me to listen, to ignore the voice inside me crying: *she knows I have my own purpose?* Compels me to do as she says. How can you rebel against a Select? You can't even keep a secret from them. What would it be like to have this woman as your mother?

That's the moment when I know why Idaro's going to Salaria. But I don't want to tell her mother.

"Tell me why you're going," she insists.

"Because you messed everything up!" Once I start, the words pour out. Idaro's words. "Because you took her away from the only place where she might have been accepted, had friends. Because you never gave her any choice, your principles were always more important than she ever was. You couldn't even make her father stay. Look at you—you couldn't even love her! Did you ever hug her? Did you ever even smile at her?" Idaro's words, and my words, too. Only my mother can't hear them now, can't ever answer them for me. And this woman's daughter can't ever say them to her.

"You're going to Salaria because it's the one place I would never want you to go?" Her voice trembles. I've never heard the voice of a Select tremble.

"Yes." I hate to say it to her.

But that's why Idaro would go. I know it. This is what she would do, with a mother like this, with a life like hers would have been. I know it with complete certainty, because Malem was the one place my mother would never have wanted me to go.

Chapter Five

"Do you have a plan?"

I leave for Salaria tomorrow and she's asking me now about my plan? And not me, technically. Since the day I told Philana why her daughter would be going to Salaria, she has spoken to me as though I was Idaro. The one time I answered as myself, she looked directly at me and said, "In this moment, you are dead."

They wouldn't kill me, I thought. The O.U.B. would protect me, even on Salaria. But looking into her face I knew she believed it utterly. The Salarians are the most easily offended people in the human universe—I've said it myself often enough. They pride themselves on their subtlety. To find out I'd fooled them, that I was that much more subtle than they are, would be the worst insult I could give them. They would never allow that to become known. They'd pin a crime on me and I'd be dead before the O.U.B. even found out. That thought gave me a sleepless night.

Philana is waiting for Idaro's answer. I take a bite of my chicken to delay answering. She knows, of course, but she waits. We're having dinner together—my last dinner on Seraffa—in the caf in Number One. It's early, there's no one else in the caf but us, but still we keep our voices down. It's become a habit.

"I will keep your confidence," she says.

I glance up. Was that meant for Kia or Idaro? Her face, as always, tells me nothing. My answer will tell her a lot, however, especially if I lie.

I've been told I'll go to Prophet's Avenue with Agatha when we arrive on Salaria. My job is to continue translating for her while she's there. The Adept on Salaria will arrange for us to visit Lady Celeste and report on her living conditions. I tell Philana all this.

"That's their plan," she says.

Their plan? Like she's not one of the O.U.B.? But what she means is, I'm not. I take another bite of chicken. Then I'll find Oghogho, and figure out a way to free her and get her back home to Seraffa, is my plan...

Right. I don't have a plan. I have a goal, and a goal without a plan for achieving it is like a planet without a starship. That planet may look pretty sitting there in the sky, but you aren't ever going to get to it.

I'll need some allies. That's where Idaro will come in. I'm not about to tell Philana the real reason I'm going to Salaria, but I have to say something. She isn't asking me what my plan is, anyway; she's asking Idaro what her plan is. Only Idaro's answers matter to her. And if she's asking Idaro, she's asking as Idaro's mother. Stay in character, I remind myself.

"I'll keep my promise to interpret for the Select until she's done what she needs to do for her report, but after that I'm going to find my grandmother, and ask her to prepare me for the desert game. I'm going to join it. I have a right. I am Salarian."

"You'll be safer with the Select. They can protect you."

The Adept here already warned me they won't help free my sister. But that's Kia talking—what would Idaro say?

"I don't need protection from who I am. I need protection from who you've tried to make me. That's why I'm leaving. I'm not going to become a Select." Never in a hundred million years, I think. Kia and Idaro are in agreement on that one.

"Then go to my friends, take the city challenge instead."

"They're not my family. They're your friends, and you left them. That was your choice, but I never had a choice. Now I'm choosing to find my family."

"At least look them up. They'll help you. You'll find Kala and Nao in Tokosha. The main spacefield is there, that's where you'll be landing. They own a chain of restaurants called the Oasis Tree."

"And your mother, my grandmother? How will I find her?"

"What if my mother is dead?"

"Then I'll visit her grave. I'll find her triad and talk to them. I'll find my cousins, and aunts…" I stop myself in time from adding 'uncles'. Men don't count on female-centric Salaria.

After a cool silence, she says, "Her name is Ryo. They own a crystal mine, the Kicho-Ryo-Tomiko mine. It's outside the capitol city, Tokosha."

"Thank you."

"They're not an easy, open people. They're not welcoming or trustful. There's a reason they form triads as soon as they're out of childhood."

"I know. I'll be careful."

"Memorize this link."

I repeat it after her. She makes me say it five times before she's satisfied. "You can reach me anytime with that, if you need to."

This is sounding more and more like a mother-daughter leave-taking. It feels weird. I'm beginning to confuse Kia and Idaro. Which one is speaking now? On one level I'm alarmed, like it's getting out of control, but on another, I know this is what Philana wants, for me to lose myself in the part of Idaro, so I won't slip up on Salaria.

"I need to know about the desert girls."

"The desert people? What do you know about them?"

"I saw one once. Well, not actually saw her. She was on a holo transmitted from Salaria. Two of them, treading water, at the Salarian Nightgames. I was a student interpreter there."

"There isn't much to tell."

I know at once that there is a great deal to tell. Why would this woman, who so disliked her people she turned her back on them forever, not want to tell me about the other race living on her world? I say nothing, try to keep my face as composed as hers, and wait to hear what she will say. I'll learn more if she thinks I don't know she's holding something back.

"They don't form triads as we do, they live in tribes, men and women equal. They are white-skinned. They live underground, like the desert snakes. It's the only way to survive in the desert." She hesitates. "If you're seen with one of them, especially a male, you'll never be accepted into Salarian society."

I nod solemnly, but I notice the slip, the slight flaring of her nostrils despite her outward calm. I'm wondering why it's worse to love a free desert man from her own world than to reject her people forever, criticize their moral choice to use slave labor, and have a child with a man from an entirely different race on another planet. And I'm getting the "not much to tell" message loud and clear.

"Where did they come from?" I couldn't find anything about their past in the Traders' library.

"The original desert people came from Old Earth, as the Salarians did. They let us do the necessary terra-forming to make the planet habitable, then shipped down into the desert far from the early settlements, and stayed there, hidden in their underground tunnels, for one hundred years."

"Squatters," I say. I'm really thinking, land pirates. I learned about it in history. There were races on Earth in the early days of planet colonization that couldn't afford to search out, let alone make habitable, new planets for their people. They waited till one of the richer countries found a new home with a huge land mass, or better yet, several land masses, and put in all the expense to create a breathable atmosphere, then they hid their own small settlement there for one hundred years, after which time their descendants, having been born there and grown to legal age, were entitled to stay as full planetary citizens. Most of them were found and evicted early on, or allowed to stay and assimilated into the dominant culture. I can't believe that's the whole reason for the continuing bitter division between the two groups on Salaria.

"Why haven't they simply been assimilated?" I ask. The land mass on Salaria is huge. Surely they could accommodate a second group of settlers?

She looks at me, and once again her careful Select mask slips. "They have no right to be there."

"But you accept immigration. How are they any different? In fact, they're better, they're already acclimatized to the planet—"

"They are thieves! They didn't ask to immigrate, they brought nothing of value to our world. They just came and took the desert from us!"

Salarians are city dwellers. They don't want the desert. I don't argue any further, though, because first of all, I'm not really comfortable with talk about thieves, and second, I understand the issue now: the desert people were successful at squatting without being noticed, and to be successful, they had to be more subtle than the Salarians. Almost three centuries later, the Salarians are still ticked off about that.

I am definitely dead if my identity is blown. They'll only forgive me if they see through it themselves. I tuck that thought away for future reference.

"When the girls go on their desert game, do they ever meet the desert people?"

"Never!" She visibly takes a calming breath. "We give the girls knives, we teach them to defend themselves, but it has never been necessary. The desert people know if they ever harmed one of our daughters we would annihilate them."

"Harmed? The desert people would kill them?" I can't believe no one has mentioned this to me yet. 'Oh, go into the desert, Kia, all looking like sweet fifteen-year-old Idaro, and you'll come out with two new best friends. And by the way, here's a knife in case all you young girls are attacked by our bitter enemies, the desert people. Have fun, y'all.'

One stupid little knife?

Annihilate them?

Philana looks uncomfortable—she should!—but it's obvious she's not going to say anything more on the topic. It's not like I'm joining the desert game anyway, that's Idaro's cover story. So I let it go and get up to leave.

"Thanks for all your help."

I look her in the eyes as I say it. It's not what Idaro would say. I want this woman to remember, when I screw up the O.U.B.'s mission by freeing a slave—maybe a lot of slaves, as many as I can—and unleash all the harm their vision tried to prevent, and do it in her daughter's name—I want her to remember then that I went as Kia.

❧

Some things you never get over. I thought I made peace with my memories of my mother after she died. Even though I didn't get to say good-bye, even though we never talked, I thought I came to understand her. I thought I forgave her.

Now here I am, fifteen again, playing the part of a girl whose father left and whose mother was even more cold and unloving than mine. All my buried feelings about my own parents have been revived. At least Idaro didn't have to deal with my mother's anger. The Select control their emotions.

Do they? Is it even possible to wipe out all your emotions? Philana's mother disowned her at nineteen—only three years older than I am now. Her people's practices shamed her into leaving her home forever. Her partner abandoned her to raise their child alone. Angry? I'm surprised she can even function as a Select. Maybe that's all that keeps her going. If Idaro had lived, she couldn't help but sense that buried anger. She might have been the only one to see it.

I can't believe I've taken on a persona whose life was even worse than mine. Would have been worse than mine, if she hadn't died. That double sucks.

Until I revived her, and rubbed her mother's face in every mistake she didn't—but would have—made. No wonder Philana didn't come to see me at the spaceport when I left.

These are the thoughts I live with on my voyage to Salaria. These, and dreams of my mother, and the fear that this might be all in vain, that I won't rescue my sister or help free the slaves, or even survive this trip myself.

Survive it? I've already lost myself. Every time I look at the mirror on the back of my cabin door, a stranger stares back at me. Every time it startles me. I can call myself Idaro, answer for her, try to think like her—but seeing her when I look at myself, her lighter skin, her slanting eyes, her long, straight hair, it's always a shock. I feel like I'm being watched by someone else, like I'm disappearing. Finally, I hang a sheet over the mirror and learn to brush my teeth and hair by feel.

Listening to my Salarian culture and language discs brings no respite. This isn't a translation job. I'm not just here to teach Agatha Central Ang, and interpret for her on occasion. There's more going on that I don't know about, and I suspect it has to do with the desert people.

"So, what's your real mission on Salaria?" I ask Agatha during our first language lesson.

"To assess and report on the treatment of the indentured servant, Lady Celeste." She looks at me. "You like say that Central Ang?" she asks in her unique Central Ang.

"No, I'm just asking. That's really all you're going there to do?" I'm preparing my arguments, how anyone else could do that, and she can trust me with the truth, when she says, "No."

"No?"

"No, of course not. Any of the Select there could do that."

"So that's not our real mission?"

"Yes, that's our real mission. That, and how we do it, and what we do next, and how we respond to what they do or say in response to each thing we do and say. No one else can do what we will do, they can only do what they would do. If we don't act when we are called to, that action, the thing we would do, will never be done."

"Someone else could write a report—"

"Yes, but it wouldn't be our report."

"It might be better."

"Perhaps. Everyone is needed. But if we weren't needed, too, we wouldn't have been called here."

"You believe that vision?"

"I believe the feeling inside me that made me come here. I believe the voice in my mind, telling me this is the right thing to do."

"But you don't really know what you're going to do."

"Yes, I do. I am going to do my best. That's all I'm called to do. That's all you're called to do. Show up, and do your best."

Suddenly I'm angry. I did my best for my parents. Oghogho tried her best to keep the *Homestar*. "What about when your best isn't good enough? What if it takes more than you can do?"

"Then it's more than we can do. Others will have to show up and help us."

I huff disgustedly. I've never liked relying on backup.

"We are all each other's backup," Agatha says.

"And if they don't show up?"

"Then we will have done our best. It will be enough."

"It isn't always enough."

"Yes, it is. It just doesn't always produce the end we hoped for. That's disappointing, sometimes even heart-breaking, but it's not failure. Failure is not showing up."

Chapter Five

I completely disagree with her. If Oghogho dies, I will have failed. No qualifiers. And yet I find myself repeating her words when I lie down and try to sleep, and I feel better for them. Because here I am, rushing into I-don't-know-what-situation, without even a clue, let alone a plan, of what I should do, and still I can't shake the feeling I'm doing the right thing. I'm showing up.

For what that's worth.

The thing I like least is impersonating someone else. I thought it would be a bit like a game, but it's not. It's alienating. I look in the mirror and see someone else. I wake up from a dream of Idaro not knowing who I am, and when I wake up enough to know I'm Kia, I'm terrified I'll slip up.

I go to the mess hall in off hours and use the space-fit room in the middle of ship's night. I avoid everyone except Agatha when it's time for her lessons. Most of all I avoid mirrors. It's hard enough that this girl has taken over so much of my thoughts, without seeing her looking back at me when I look at myself. I even have to wear the blue jumpsuits the O.U.B. provided, they made me leave my own on Seraffa. This is what Idaro would wear. That's why I'm avoiding people—I can't stand to have them look at me and see someone else. To hear them say her name and have to look up. I don't want to respond to their questions with her answers. I'll have to do that soon enough, no need to start now. Let them think I'm just a moody teen. That thought, which would have annoyed me before, makes me smile.

I should be practicing on these people who don't matter, I know that. Agatha reminds me of it often enough. I should be embracing Idaro, doing all I can to forget Kia. My life will depend upon it, and Agatha's too, and maybe Oghogho's. If I have any chance of saving her, it will be as Idaro. Idaro is a moody teen right now, I tell myself, as I indulge in a little avoidance therapy in my room before Agatha's language lesson.

I'm not the only one practicing avoidance therapy on this ship.

"I don't need to learn Central Ang. I can learn Salarian," Agatha told me when she came for her first lesson. "Enough to say what I need to say, anyway. Listen," she switched to Salarian, "I need rest. Where is the room, please?" She beamed at me.

I stared at her until her smile faltered.

"Forget that your accent is terrible," I told her, "but if you say that, they'll take you to a bedroom."

"A bedroom? I asked for the restroom."

"It's not only what you say, it's how you say it." How can anyone be this bad at languages, especially when she's so good at understanding people, at making them feel they're understood? Even though no one, not even the O.U.B., can understand her.

What if she'd said "your" instead of "the" room? It's one thing to ask to wash your hands in someone's sink, quite a different thing to ask to sleep in their bed!

The thought made me look at her, see her as someone else would: her skin is too pale, almost translucent, but clear and soft, with a light blush in her cheeks; her eyes are a pure blue, the color of Old Earth sky—I prefer brown eyes, but hers are a beautiful shade; her hair, the part that shows around her face from under her hood, is white-blond and straight, not limp-looking, more soft, like clouds; her shape is hidden by the blue and white robe but she moves easily, like someone fit and healthy. I realized if she asked that question, whoever she asked would be only too quick to take her to his room for a 'rest'.

"Stick to Central Ang," I told her, a little desperately. "There's only one way to say anything in Central Ang. You can't go wrong. Promise me you'll only use Central Ang!" I won't be able to leave her alone there, I thought. I have a goal, one that doesn't include us sticking together, but how can I let her go off like this?

Fortunately, her Central Ang has improved. Slowly. And she's promised me never to try speaking Salarian. She agrees with me that after the report is made, Idaro might not stick with the Select on Prophet's Avenue, but would head off alone to find her relatives and her mother's old triad, the life she would have lived if she'd been raised here. That's when I'll go free Oghogho. Our cover is that Idaro paid her way here by agreeing to interpret for the new Select traveling on the same ship. That will enable us to meet up later, if it becomes necessary to get off-planet quickly. They know Idaro's the daughter of a Select so it shouldn't seem odd they offered her a way to pay her passage. But leaving her mother, deciding to come here—she wouldn't do all that, only to live with the Select on Prophet's Avenue the whole time, like the Adept wanted me to.

I look up my grandmother's name on my room comp, just in case I really do need to find her. Ryo: the word comes from an Old Earth language, and means 'dragon'. It takes me a while to find out what that is, but turns out it's an imaginary animal, huge and deadly, that breathes fire. Who would name their child that? It's worse than my father giving me the name Akhié, which means 'sorrow'. No one knows me by that any more; I shortened it to Kia when I left home.

My grandmother's triad mates have more practical names which mean 'valuable' and 'wealthy'. Not surprising the three of them have no qualms about owning a mine and using slave labor in it. I can't wait to meet them.

Agatha drags me to the portal when Salaria at last comes into view. I hate looking out at space. I hate being reminded I'm in a ship the size of a molecule in the vast nothingness of the universe. Who cares what the planet looks like from here? It looks like there's a lot of deadly vacuum between me and it, that's what it looks like.

Beside the portal, a comp screen shows images of Salaria, all city and desert, white buildings, white roadways, white sand everywhere, and hotter than Seraffa on its hottest summer day. You can practical-ly see the heat shimmering on the screen. Nothing grows there but a few desperate cacti. Nothing lives there that the settlers didn't bring with them and struggle to keep alive. Much of their food is shipped in. It cost a fortune to create a water cycle, and there's little to spare. They've made back that fortune a hundred times over. Salaria is rich in the special crystals they mine and cut, which are harder than diamonds and are so perfectly in resonance with the magnetic field of Salaria's sun that no matter how far they are, they always indicate the direction and distance back to that sun. They're used in the navigation systems of spaceships, and that's about as much as I understood of the article I read on them. I'm an interpreter, not a metallurgist or a space engineer. The important thing is that Salaria is one of only a few planets they've been found on.

"It's beautiful," Agatha says.

She likes space. She likes everything. It's all beautiful to her. Grey, overcast, freezing-cold Malem was beautiful, and now white, hotter-than-hell Salaria is. "It'll be more beautiful on the way home," I say, thinking, *if Oghogho's with us.* Out loud I add, "Unless it turns out that showing up wasn't enough." Okay, that's mean. Right away I wish I hadn't said it, even if we are alone here.

"You worry too much," Agatha tells me. "Everything doesn't depend on us. We're only here to do our part. Someone else will do what we can't."

"You worry too little." I stop myself from adding *I always have to rescue you.* It's true, but then, she's rescued me a few times. "I'd like to know what's really happening here. It's kind of hard to be part of the solution when you don't know what the problem is."

"The conflict between the Salarians and the desert people is escalating."

"They told you that?"

"Not intentionally."

I nod. They always underestimate her. It's easy to do. I look out at Salaria, white-hot in the black of space, and I think of Philana, so quick to sympathize with the slaves working the mines, like my sister, and so unmoved by the desert people, forever shut out of the life—and wealth—of their own planet. If someone who wanted to emancipate foreign slaves still dislikes the desert people, either there's something really terrible about them, or the prejudice is so ingrained it's second nature, an unconscious reflex even those who leave the culture can't escape.

The comp screen is now showing images of the desert people.

"Why aren't we looking into their quality of life and writing up a report about them?" Agatha murmurs.

I look at her, surprised. The O.U.B. doesn't intercede in planetary affairs. Agatha knows that better than I. She has an interfering nature when she thinks she's right, but there's something other than that in her voice. It sounds… distracted. Like she was talking to herself, not commenting on what I said. She moves closer to the comp screen.

"I read something in the Trader's library."

Agatha doesn't look at me, she's watching the comp screen, but I know she's listening.

"Just a note, nothing certain. That we may soon be trading for crystals with the desert people of Salaria, that's all. It said there's a rumor they've found a vein of crystals running through one of their tunnels."

Agatha breathes out. "God is good," she whispers.

"You think that's a good thing? You think if it's true, the Salarians will just let them? Welcome the competition? With crystals mined on their own planet?"

"It's our planet, too."

Our planet? The O.U.B. doesn't own land, let alone a planet. I'm trying to think how to ask her what she means when she turns and leaves, just like that, without saying anything.

I look at the comp screen she was staring at. There's a scene of some desert people, poor, underfed, the baby crying in its mother's arms. I'm not surprised it upset her. Something about the scene makes me look closer. There's a dignity about them, poor or not, the man standing by the woman and children, staring out over the desert. They wear loose white shirts and matching white pants, cut off at the ankle, males and females alike. Practical. Equal.

I glance at the portal again. Salaria completely fills it. In a matter of hours we'll be there, totally unready for whatever awaits us. I turn and head back to my cabin.

Nearly there, my legs begin to tremble. No, it's the ship. It's transferring from interstellar drive to its landing engines. I hurry the last few steps to my room.

We're slowing down, preparing to enter atmosphere. I take out of my spacebag the flowing white robe, as light as air, which Philana gave me, and strip out of my blue jumpsuit. The robe will cover me from neck to ankles, protecting my skin from the sun while the loose weave lets air through. The protection is doubly important for me. The treatments which decreased my level of melanin made my skin way more sensitive to the sun. I rub the sun block cream Murdock gave me everywhere over my body before donning the robe. The flowing cloth around me is comfortable and, I admit, pretty, with colorful embroidered symbols around its neck and down the sleeves, but I feel a little awkward in it, overly feminine. How will I run or scale a wall in it, if I have to?

I push that thought aside. I am not going to be chased here. Anyway, when on Salaria, dress like the Salarians.

"Strap in for landing!" the pilot's voice booms over the intercom.

I stuff my jumpsuit into my spacebag and strap myself onto my cot, taking a v-bag with me. Another reason I hate space. As soon as the ship settles and "all clear" is called, I unbuckle and rush to the sink to wash out my mouth. Then I wave open my cabin door.

Ready or not, Idaro is about to visit Salaria.

Chapter Five

Agatha meets me at the line-up to disembark. She doesn't say anything about her earlier abrupt departure, but stands beside me silently. When it's our turn, we hand our papers to the first officer to have our names entered on the list of departures, and wait before the raised hatch looking out at a blindingly bright, baking hot planet.

"The vision was right," Agatha murmurs beside me. "I am meant to be here. With my people."

Her people? I stare at her, open-mouthed. The pale skin, the white-blond hair, blue eyes so light they look like water... I thought she was from New Earth, where many blonds come from, but she's so fair...

The image of the desert family on the comp screen comes to me, their light blue eyes large in their faces, pale skin covering their thin bodies, as white as the moon, as white as Salarian desert sand—as white-skinned as Agatha!

"You're a desert girl!" Even as I say it, I can't believe it. I expect her to laugh, to deny it.

She doesn't.

"You never told me."

"I didn't know, for sure, until now."

Chapter Six

"Separate!" Agatha's whisper carries the command of a Select. I'm moving away from her before I've even processed what she said. A moment later I see two Salarian officials, weapons strapped to their hips, bearing down on her. I want to go back, I'm supposed to be translating for her, but the force of her whispered command still grips me. While I hesitate, fighting it, she glances quickly at me with the intensity of a Select. I turn at once and walk away.

"Come with us," I hear one of the port guards say.

I am sweating, as much with the effort of trying to disobey a Select's direct order as with the heat, when I stop my retreat and bend down to my sandal as if the strap has come undone.

The guards' arms are falling back to their sides. They tried to grab her, I realize, but she would not allow it. All this is so unlike Agatha, who rarely uses the persuasive powers of a Select—or at least, rarely used them on Malem, when I was with her. Her back is ramrod straight and her head high. "My people," I remember her saying as we left the ship. These men are here for her because she's a desert woman, an easy target, they think, and Agatha, who never insists on respect for herself, is demanding it for her people.

She won't understand a thing they say. I have to go back and interpret—but I can't take even a step closer. They'll recover from her refusal to allow them to touch her. They'll be all the more angry that a desert woman stood up to them, Select or not. I have to get to her!

"Can I help you?" a female voice asks. I look up to dismiss the stranger's intrusion, and find myself staring at a pale white face. Her lips are pursed in a way intended to convey concern, but their thinness turns it into a look of disapproval. I recognize her from somewhere, but can't place it. She's wearing the loose shirt and pants of the desert people, which makes me feel even sillier in my long dress, whether it's what everyone else is wearing or not. I shake my head, as much to clear it as to deny her offer, but when her hand reaches down I let her pull me to my feet.

"You were with her," she says quietly, leaning toward me. "A half-breed Salarian with a desert woman. Why?" There's an intensity to her voice that startles me. I glance at her, her pale blue eyes like Agatha's staring coldly into mine as though to rip my secrets out of me. I don't want this girl knowing anything. It's an instinctive response, I have no reason to distrust her, but I shrug and say, "We were on the same ship."

She smiles, a tight, unpleasant expression that doesn't warm her eyes. "Don't worry, she'll be okay. Help is already coming." The girl nods almost imperceptibly in Agatha's direction. I know I shouldn't look—what do I care?—but I turn, I have to, to see the blue-and-white habit of a Select striding across the terminal toward Agatha and the two guards.

"A desert girl in the O.U.B. Slumming it." The way she says it, I'm not sure whether she means the O.U.B. is slumming it by taking in a desert girl, or Agatha has degraded herself by becoming a Select, but my guess is the latter. I look back at her and find her watching me.

I shrug again. "They stick together."

"You know her."

Enough of this. I pull myself back into character and frown at her, scornful. "Who are you? What are you doing in the city?" I don't need to say more. I'm a Salarian female, half-breed or not, talking to a desert girl. She knows what I mean.

Her eyes narrow slightly. "I'll see you again." She nods for effect, as though she's been giving me directions or something, and walks off.

I don't watch her leave. She has been giving me directions, intentional or not. I don't know who she is or what's going on here, but my cover, interpreting for a Select who's come to write a report on the slaves, is over. Our cover. Agatha obviously dropped it when she saw the guards approaching her and ordered me away. I walk purposefully toward the line-up for customs, as though nothing has happened, but my mind is racing. Agatha's possibly about to be detained somewhere, and I've been threatened by some strange desert girl? That was never part of the plan we were given. How could it happen, without even a warning? The O.U.B. aren't prone to slip-ups like this. Understatement of the century. How fortunate a Select was right on hand, where she needed to be, to come to Agatha's assistance. And a desert girl, watching us both disembark. It looks like everyone was prepared for our arrival except us.

I want to run. It's real now, the danger I knew I was walking into, and my only cover is my disguise. I have to be Idaro, fully and convincingly. My life depends on a skill I've never studied: acting. I take a few calming breaths. Acting is just lying. I remember, years ago it seems, wondering how to lie to a Select. You have to convince yourself, first. You have to believe it's the truth. I am Idaro, I tell myself, as I join the line of people in front of the customs booths.

The customs officers at the port are all male. It's a clerical job, they'll pass me up to a female if they notice anything irregular. Which they won't, I tell myself. Even so, when it's my turn I can't help being nervous as I walk through the imaging gate and they take my holo. Their comp will compare it to the people they've flagged from the list they've been sent of those leaving the spaceship. Was the Adept right that I would be one of those? And if so, will my disguise be good enough?

"Identity and purpose of your visit," the official says, while the comp is clicking away over its holo of me.

"Idaro, daughter of Philana, daughter of Ryo, of the Kicho-Ryo-Tomiko triad," I say. "I've come to visit my grandmother, Ryo." He looks up at me with a frown as soon as I give my identity. Normally a Salarian wouldn't give two maternal generations, but since my mother doesn't have a triad I've had to give my grandmother's. That's not why he's frowning, though. I tell him I'm half Edoan, and stare him down. Prejudice is prejudice, and I won't participate. His lip curls into a sneer as he looks back down at his comps and clicks on something. He's assuming my mother disgraced herself, that's why she has no triad. She did disgrace herself, speaking out against slavery, and whether I'm Kia or Idaro, I'm proud of Philana for defying them with her ideological opinions.

"Is your grandmother expecting you?" he asks, still staring at his comp screen. "I don't see any record of a visitor's pass here."

"No. She doesn't know I'm here."

He laughs nastily. "Won't she be pleased," he says, as he presses something I can't see under the window of his booth. A door behind the booth—not the one I wanted to walk through—opens.

"You can go on upstairs," he says, shuffling my docs together and handing them back to me.

What about my spacebag, I want to ask, but I don't dare call attention to it. I did my best to disguise my tool-box as a jewelry box, even made a couple of the lock-picking tools look like pins and hair-clips, and sewed the palm-override into a glove, but none of that will pass a close inspection by someone who knows what he's looking at.

What an idiot I was to bring it! How could I have imagined I wouldn't be stopped and checked? I berate myself all the way up the float-tube. I've actually only been in a float tube once before, at a very wealthy embassy, and it takes a bit of concentration, standing straight up in the lowgrav field, so I can't beat myself up too much. In fact, it takes a lot of concentration; when the tube releases me three stories up, I trip and fall flat on my face in the entrance hall. The hall floor is cushioned, either to ease the dainty

feet of the Salarian officials here, or because they get a lot of inex-
perienced twits like me landing hard.

I pick myself up to face a smirking guard who asks me under his
breath as he leads me to the office of his superior, "More used to
walking on sand, are you?"

More used to walking through embassies than spaceports, I'd
like to tell him, but he'll remember a smart-mouth and I'd rather
he and the customs director I'm about to meet simply dismiss me
as a clumsy, tongue-tied girl unused to a wealthy city like Tokosha.

I bow, youth to elder, as soon as I enter the director's office. We
go through the identity-and-purpose routine once again, while the
guard stands just outside the door to her office, a glassed-in cubicle, watching me with one hand resting gently on his side weapon.

The customs director studies my docs, taps on her comp, and
stares at what comes up. I stand in front of her, trying to look only
moderately nervous, as Idaro would be.

"If I contact Matriarch Ryo of the Kicho-Ryo-Tomiko estate,
would she know who you are?" she asks.

I let myself squirm a little, not entirely acting. "Probably not," I
admit. "I was born after my mother left Salaria, and I don't think
she and my grandmother ever spoke after she went to Seraffa."

"And why is it that you want to see this grandmother who doesn't
know you exist?"

"I'm fifteen." I draw myself up as tall as I can. At fifteen I figured I pretty much knew what needed to be known. I let some
of that show in Idaro's face and voice. "I'm old enough to make
my own choices, and I don't want to enter the Order, like my
mother. I'm here to find out about the other side of my heritage."
I wait a moment before I declare proudly, "I'm going to join the
desert game."

She looks at me, the left corner of her mouth twitching upward,
making her look partly amused, partly exasperated. "Only Salarians

are allowed to participate in the desert game. Your mother should never have told you about it."

"I am Salarian!"

"You were born on Seraffa. That makes you Seraffan."

"The first mistake is thinking luck has anything to do with your life."

She looks surprised as I quote a Salarian proverb Philana said more than once to me.

"Where you're born is luck," I continue. "Who you are is a choice. In this case, my choice."

She shakes her head. "No grandmother should be denied the pleasure of your company. Especially not your grandmother." She feeds my entrance doc into her comp and moves her fingers over the screen. "You're under age. I'm giving you a twenty-day pass, conditional on finding a sponsor in two days to sign for you and record it with us." She looks at me. "Do you have anyone other than your grandmother to look up?"

I nod. "My mother's youth triad: Kala and Nao of the Oasis Tree Nourishment Centers. She said to start with them."

"So naturally you're going to start with your grandmother, who hasn't been on speaking terms with your mother since before you were born."

I think I've fully slipped into this role, because what she says makes perfect sense to me, even though I recognize she's being sarcastic. "I'll learn a lot more from my grandmother," I point out.

She laughs. "If you make it through the next twenty days and still want to join the desert game, come speak to me. With your sponsor," she adds firmly.

I stand up and bow the correct amount to convey my respect for an elder in a high position. She acknowledges my courtesy with an appropriate tilt of her head and hands over my docs. Her comp bleats out a sheet of paper, which she also hands me. On it, I see

73

my grandmother's name and an address, as well as an address for Kala and Nao. I bow again, a full inch lower, and back out of her office.

I'm free! All I have to do is get down the bloody float-tube without breaking my neck or humiliating myself again, pick up my spacebag, and figure out how to get to the address the director gave me for my grandmother.

⁓

I'm reaching for my spacebag on the baggage round when someone bumps into me from behind. I snatch my bag and glance around. What I see almost makes me drop it again: the blue and white habit of the O.U.B.

"My apologies," the Select says, bowing. "Left quad restroom one quarter hour," she murmurs while her head is bent.

"No harm done," I respond automatically, also bowing, since she's older than I am. What happened to the Select I came with, I'm about to ask as I come up, but she's already gone. I don't let myself look around.

Left quad restroom? Forget that. I'm not risking my cover identity as soon as I get here. Apparently Agatha's dropped the ruse that I'm here as her interpreter. She probably thinks any association with her now would put me in danger. I have to trust her and act on that. So if Idaro came here on her own, she wouldn't go near the O.U.B., unless she had no other choice. It's a little paranoid to think I might be being watched, but there are recorders everywhere here. At least I know there's a Select with Agatha; they have a better chance of keeping her safe than I do. I'll have to find a way to contact her later.

I walk away as though nothing has happened, toward the storage areas where I've decided to check my bag. I don't want to show up at my grandmother's carrying my spacebag, as if I expect to move in. Frankly, I'd like to see how well that fire-breathing image suits her before I commit to more than a short visit.

Idaro's grandmother. Already I'm calling her mine, I think, as I deflate my bag and stuff it into the smallest locker available for rent. I wave the locker closed and touch my cred-tab against the seal. There. The tool kit is safely hidden and there's nothing on me that I can't explain as something Idaro would have. It's smart to think of her life as mine, her relatives as my relatives, I decide. The further I tuck Kia away inside Idaro, the safer I'll be.

Next stop, the infocomp station, where I can look up the best method to travel outside the city to the Kicho-Ryo-Tomiko mine. The valuable-dragon-wealth mine: fire and money combined. Maybe if she's crazy rich she'll be more likely to help me out here. Not that I need money, or intend to take it if she offers. I'm not her real granddaughter. This isn't a scam. A little coaching and sponsorship so I can stay until I find Oghogho is all I need. And I admit I'm curious. Was Philana right about her mother? Has she mellowed with time? What's her side of the story? I never knew any of my own grandparents. I'm being drawn into Idaro's life more than I expected.

Until I find Oghogho. How is all this going effect our making a report on Lady Celeste? Because if we don't find Lady Celeste… I take a deep breath. First things first: Grandmother's house, like I told the custom's director—just in case they are monitoring me.

Something called a lightspeed station appears to have a line headed west which stops at several spots, all called Kicho-Ryo-Tomiko mine. How many mines does my grandmother's triad own? Wait, here's a stop that says Kicho-Ryo-Tomiko estate. That's what I want. Takes fifteen minutes, costs three creds. Fifteen minutes? To cover that distance? I grin and check out where it's located. In the spaceport's left quad.

Left quad restroom one quarter hour.

That Select knew where I'd be heading when I got here. A good guess, or did she know what was going to happen here? And how did they know I'd go to Idaro's grandmother? I told Philana I was going there, I remember. But that was just playing a character. Which I've been forced to fall back on. I wonder if this has all been orchestrated by the Adept, but I can't believe it. Surely he would have warned Agatha, at least. Maybe he just prepared for every possible hiccup, at least in the beginning. I feel a grudging respect for his ability to predict my responses. They've made it easy—I have to pass the restroom on my way to the lightspeed station, and it would appear natural for me to stop in there before going to meet my grandmother. I tap my cred-tab to check the time: I'll get there exactly when she said to meet her, and have a good half-hour before my transit arrives. Absolutely no excuse not to go hear what the woman has to say.

Three Salarians enter the restroom ahead of me. I take my time in front of the mirror, messing with my hair, using a flex-pick to clean my teeth, giving my face a quick sand-scrub with one of the brushes provided and then using a wet-wipe cleanser to remove the gritty feeling. I apply some of the make-up provided in tiny sampler sizes. Idaro would want to look her best to meet her extended family for the first time. Then I wait in a cubicle until I hear the Salarians leave. When I emerge, a woman in a blue and white jumpsuit is standing at the dry-sink, scrubbing her hands in the sterilized sand. Not a Select, but a member of the O.U.B. who serves them.

I walk over and dig my hands into the sand-scrub beside her.

"What's happened to the Select?" I murmur, in case anyone's in one of the cubicles.

"She's been detained. There was an explosion yesterday, in one of the mines—"

"In a mine? Was anyone hurt?"

She glances at me, a reminder to keep my voice down. "No, a warning was called in, they got everyone out, but the mine was destroyed. A group called Out of the Desert claimed responsibility."

"The desert people?"

She nods. "They've been agitating—" she shakes her head. Too much to go into. "So the sudden appearance the next day of a desert woman from off-planet, wearing the habit of a Select…" she trails off, pursing her lips. "This will make everything more difficult for us. I don't know what she's doing here."

"Nobody ever does," I tell her, commiserating.

She gives me a sharp look. I smile sympathetically, all sincere.

"Well, whatever you came here to do, you're on your own now." She shakes the sand off her hands and digs into her pocket. "Here." She holds out an e-bud. "It'll activate in five minutes. Find somewhere in the station where you're alone to listen to it. Then get it out of your ear—it's made to dissolve thirty seconds after it finishes."

I pull my hands out of the sand. She drops the e-bud into them.

"We've got someone at your grandmother's. Don't be proud, you'll need the help. So go on, put it in."

"Wait, what about the report?"

She looks blank.

"We're here to write a report on Lady Celeste. One of the indentured servants."

"I don't know anything about that."

"Someone here has to. That's why we were sent."

"We're taking too long in here. Put it in."

My heart's pounding as I press the e-bud into my ear. I have to know where Lady Celeste is, but I can't say anything more. I'm just an interpreter, she'll wonder why I care so much.

"We are here to pursue multiple goals."

"What?"

"That's the activating sentence. I didn't choose it." She leaves before I can answer.

Five minutes. I want to run, but force myself to walk out of the restroom casually, and stroll to the station just ahead. I touch my cred-tab to the gate, which opens with agonizing slowness to admit me. *Multiple goals?* I'm thinking. There, to the right, is a row of seats. It almost kills me to walk slowly over to them, looking around with feigned curiosity. I check the time on my tab—four minutes have passed—and choose the farthest seat.

"Kia, I am going to the desert people…"

I stumble and fall into the seat. Agatha! When did she record this?

I hold my breath, listening to her message. It's only six sentences long, and it changes everything.

Chapter Seven

"Kia, I am going to the desert people. I couldn't tell you until you got through customs, in case you were stopped and questioned. Find your own reason to join me, with the girls. If something happens to me, find the desert girl; you know who I mean. Trust your instincts. Remember what I told you on Malem."

I sit there reeling. Nothing in this message makes sense. When did Agatha create that message? Did she know more than she told me all along? Did the Adept expect me to be stopped and questioned, is that why he wanted me to agree to an auto memory swipe if he told me more? Was part of the plan that the Salarians would learn about a false mission from me? Writing the report about Lady Celeste? Or was that invented for me, to get me to come, because he knew I'd expect to find my sister with her?

I can't believe Agatha would betray me like that. Never mind that I was going to betray the O.U.B. It was for a good cause, to save my sister. Well, okay, I'll skip the good-cause argument, it works both ways. But not between friends. Not between Agatha and me.

I can't go there. It hurts too much to think she'd do that. I have to believe they wanted to tell me the truth, Agatha and the Adept, but I was the one who prevented them when I refused the memory swipe. The Adept told me then he was afraid I'd be questioned.

The crucial question now is, what's our real mission, and why do we have to go into the desert? It's got to do with the conflict between the Salarians and the desert people, the explosion yesterday points to that. That's not much to go on. I hope Agatha knows more. They wouldn't worry about a Select being questioned, only an Adept could get her to reveal something she didn't want known. Well, whatever she knows isn't going to help me now.

Then again, Agatha just realized her parents were desert people the morning we landed. Did she decide to go to the desert then, and record this message in her cabin? The Adept might have no idea about any of this. It would be completely like Agatha to follow an impulse like that.

Suddenly I remember the melting bit, and dig the e-bud out of my ear. Just in time. I watch it melt in my hand. I go over the message again in my mind with a sense of urgency.

Find your own reason to join me. What does that mean? Find a personal reason for coming here? Like to rescue my sister? Is she telling me that's what I should do now? Or does she mean find out the real reason we're here? It could be simply that she knew she was going to drop my interpreter role if she got detained, so I'm supposed to find another credible reason to contact her. Wait, is this about her going into the desert? Am I to find my own reason for going into the desert to meet her? And what does she mean by *with the girl?* Was it girls, or girl? Join her in the desert with what girl? The woman in the rest room told me there'd be someone at my grandmother's, is that who I'm to go with, to find Agatha in the desert? Anyway, she's not in the desert now, she's being detained in Tokosha.

I give up on that riddle and move on to the next: *if something happens to me.* Is she afraid of something? She must have thought she'd be in danger, when she made the message. Well, she was right, from what I saw at the port. But there has to be more to it than that. Was she half-expecting to have to flee as soon as she arrived, did she set up this message in case that happened? If she knew the danger was imminent, why would she ask me to come, putting me in danger, too? She wouldn't. So she didn't think she was in danger, at least not at first. Of course, Agatha never thinks she's in danger. Whatever happens, it's all part of God's plan as far as she's concerned. Which gets me back to zero on the what-was-she-afraid-of question.

Find the desert girl. I think I've got this one covered. She already found me, if it's the same desert girl. But why would Agatha want me to find her? I'd be more likely to believe that one set off yesterday's explosion than that she'll help us avert a crisis. So is there another desert girl?

You know who I mean. This one really ticks me off. I hate riddles. There is nothing that annoys me more than a deliberate mystery. Agatha used up five words there—she could easily have said something useful, like "white-skinned, blue eyes, blond." Well, maybe not those five words, they describe every desert girl, but she could have found five specific, helpful adjectives, none of this you-know-who-I-mean stuff! Agatha knows how I feel about riddles, she knows they set my teeth on edge!

That's right, she does. And Agatha is never deliberately annoying. (Unlike me). So she had a reason. Someone else might have had access to this message, and she didn't want them to understand it? The Salarians? Maybe she feared they might get it before she could pass it on to someone she trusted to give it to me? But I didn't see her passing it on, I only saw the Select hurrying toward her before the guards took her away. The Select? Did Agatha think she might listen to it? Or give it to someone else in the Order here on Salaria? No, that's got to be another dead end. Agatha reveres the Select and Adept of the O.U.B. She thinks she's not good enough to be one of them. And the Select she gave it to did pass it on to me. Without hearing it, since it only has one message life. But who else would she not want to hear this message?

Did I mention I HATE riddles?

Trust your instincts. My instincts. Hey, I get this one, I get it! Agatha trusts everyone, that's her instinct. But I don't trust anyone. She's telling me to trust that; or rather, she's telling me to go ahead and not trust anyone. Not anyone? That doesn't sound like Agatha.

But it does explain why the message is so vague. I'm sure I'm right on this one. And it's easy for me to do.

Remember what I told you on Malem. Not fair. We were there for months, and Agatha talks a lot. I'm sure she said something during that time that might be useful here, but as the Salarians say, "there's a lot of sand to sift through if you're looking for one particular grain." Maybe it'll come to me later. Probably like, five-minutes-too-late, later.

Agatha wants me to find her in the desert? Why? To translate? I don't even know what language the desert people speak. We both know there's only one way I can go into the desert without breaking my cover identity. But where in the desert? It covers more than half the land mass on this planet.

Something important is going on here, and in my experience with the O.U.B. that's not a good thing. I have no idea what I'm getting into, no clue what I should do, who I can trust, and who I should avoid. Maybe I shouldn't go to my grandmother's—Idaro's grandmother's, I mean. In fact, I should probably turn around and catch the first space flight back to Seraffa. I could die here. Not, like, in theory, but honestly get killed.

I look back the way I came. What if I am being watched, or somehow monitored? What if the customs director is monitoring everyone from Seraffa, looking for me, Kia Ugiagbe, like the Adept said they would be? Turning back now would look strange. They'd back up to see what changed my mind, and then they'd notice me being in the same place as the O.U.B. twice. The worst thing I can do—the very worst and probably fatal thing—is to make them wonder if I'm really who I say I am. So I guess I'm going to Grandma's house, fire-eating dragon and all. Just like everyone seems to want.

I don't like doing what people I barely know want. Especially when they won't say why they want it.

And I'm not convinced it's a good idea to go into the desert. Okay, I'm sorry for the desert people, they're getting a rough deal, and I'm sorry for the slaves in the mines as well, but after all that being sorry for people, I'm really here to find my sister.

I hear a kind of intake of air, and look up. Barreling toward me through the air is a huge bullet, big enough to take out half the station. It's silent, only the displacement of air as it whips straight for us can be heard. It's moving so fast it's almost a blur. I leap up, ready to run, but no one else on the station looks the least concerned.

The lightspeed.

I'm going to ride on that?

I hope everyone in there with me is prepared to get thrown up on.

The speeding bullet stops suddenly beside the platform and settles onto the ground. A rush of wind whooshes forward up the sides of the still-quivering bullet and over the platform, so hot I feel like cooking meat and almost cry out at the burn of it. No one else seems to find it painful, so either it's my overly-sensitive skin or they're used to this broiling heat.

The sides of the bullet roll up and a crowd of people swarm out. Everything happens so quickly I just stand there, staring. One instant the platform is half-empty, the next it's crawling with people, sweeping me away from the bullet along with them. I notice the Salarians who were waiting on the platform with me pushing their way through the exiting people, trying to get on board quickly. Really quickly.

I don't have to do anything. I can just be carried along with the crowd, let them sweep me back to the spaceport, back to a spaceship home…

No! I'm here. Oghogho needs me, and Agatha could probably use some help, too, wherever she is. I'll probably fail them both,

I'll probably get myself killed—I'm no secret agent, I've only just started a self-defense course for girls on campus, like that'll really help—but I am here. I am going to show up.

I shove myself against the bodies blocking my way, squirm between them, desperately aiming myself toward the open bullet. I'm almost there. Reaching out I grab a pole just inside the bullet, when I hear a clang. The press of bodies suddenly intensifies. With desperation born of terror I grab the pole and pull myself inside, just as the last person exits and the doors swoosh down with a terrible finality, so close I feel them at my back. I'm inside the bullet.

I brace myself. Nothing happens. No one else is holding a pole, or bracing themselves against the side of the bullet; let alone doing both, like me. A few people glance my way with amused smiles. Slowly I let myself relax. The bullet hasn't moved.

I leave one hand against the pole, casual-like, for when it does. But still it is motionless. Why did everyone rush to get off, and everyone at the station board so quickly, just to wait here, encased in a windowless machine going nowhere? The waiting gets on my nerves. If this thing is going to whip us through the air like a slingshot, I want to get it over with.

I'm about to finally say something, ask if anyone knows what the hold-up is, when I feel a little jar. More like a tremble. Good, the thing is starting. As unobtrusively as possible, I let my hand circle the pole, holding on.

Whoosh! The sides of the bullet spring up into the ceiling. We're stopped, still at the platform. A few people around me get off. I think they might be those who were too slow getting off when I got on, but then I recognize two of them who boarded at the same time I did. Have they given up waiting?

The warning clang goes off just as I realize what's happened. We're at the next station—the stop I want. And I have no idea how to get back here if I miss it! I duck under the door and leap! The sides slide down so close behind me I feel them brush my gown and grab it tight, terrified the skirt will be caught in the door and I'll be dragged to my death. What a stupid outfit!

Before I can do anything else, someone grabs my arm and yanks me forward, further onto the platform. Behind me the bullet takes off, creating a fierce rush of air into the spot it occupied a split-second ago. I would have followed that air suction like a leaf in the wind, except for the hand holding my arm. I gasp and look up into slanting brown eyes and a smiling face. The boy, who looks about my age or a year older, drops my arm and bows his head.

"Thank you," I say, breathing hard. I bow my head the same amount as his. The guy saved my life, who cares if I don't have to bow as low as him because I'm female?

"You're welcome," he says, his eyes serious now, like he's trying to figure me out.

Good luck on that one, I think, but since we're already talking I ask him if he knows how I can get to the Kicho-Ryo-Tomiko estate.

"I do," he says. "I am going there. I would be pleased to show you the way."

I've never spoken to a Salarian male before. Men don't have jobs in diplomacy or inter-planetary trade, and the few Salarian guards and staff don't talk much, especially not to females. I'm a little put off by this guy's formal way of speaking, but it's awkward walking through the station with him in silence. "Do you work at the mine?" I ask.

He hesitates a moment before answering. "No, I am a grandson of the founder."

I almost ask which one, before I remember that sons and grandsons are just generally part of the household—like servants, except they share the luxury of their masters—they're not likely to know which member of the triad is their female parent until they are offered in marriage. Even then, their intended spouse will be told, not them. They'll only be acknowledged by a mother or grandmother if they do something particularly worthy, or reach a high position of trust and usefulness. I doubt he's lived long enough for that.

It's awkward not answering this guy who might be—who is, in Salarian terms, where triad is family—my relative. But I don't know what to say. It's not like there's much need to teach interpreters how to have a conventional conversation with their cute Salarian male cousins.

"I hope it will be possible for me to speak to Ryo," I say, sidestepping the whole issue. I can't directly ask after her health, being a stranger. She must be alive, despite what Philana said to discourage me from seeing her, or the customs director wouldn't have given me her address and insisted I get her to sponsor me.

"It is possible." But I see the doubt in his eyes, which he is careful not to express.

To heck with it. Idaro wouldn't be hindered by knowing or caring about all these cultural taboos and verbal tiptoeing even if her mother did prepare her for the trip. What if my parents had had siblings, and I had cousins, how would I feel finally meeting one of them? I smile at this good-looking Salarian guy. "My name is Idaro." I bow my head, forcing him to respond in kind if he doesn't want to insult me.

"My name is Norio," he says, bowing lower than I did.

"I've come to meet Ryo. I'm her granddaughter. You and I must be cousins."

There's a moment of shocked silence. Or just silence. He doesn't look at me, so it's hard to tell. Kia the interpreter is embarrassed at making a cultural faux pas and causing this moment—I'm better than that—but Idaro is meeting for the first time a relation who isn't her mother. I go with that one, and look directly at him, curious and excited.

He takes a step backward. "I think you must be mistaken," he stammers, his eyes widening.

"I am the daughter of Philana, daughter of Ryo."

"Matriarch Ryo has only one daughter, named Chowa. Perhaps you have the wrong triad?"

I feel the heat rising to my face—and with my new lighter skin, he probably sees it—but his expression is concerned, rather than disdainful. I realize how thoroughly my grandmother disowned her daughter, if those born after she left don't even know she existed. I'm making a big mistake coming here, just as Philana predicted.

Kia or Idaro, I don't know which and it doesn't matter, we both respond to that thought the same way. My chin rises. I have every right to meet my grandmother, and I am not responsible for whatever happened between her and my mother. If she refuses to see me I'll go back to Tokosha without meeting her. Her rudeness will be an insult to her, not to me.

"There is no mistake," I say, walking through the door of the station.

The hot outside air hits me hard. I gasp, my throat telling me I am breathing in fire. It wasn't this hot in Tokosha, the brief times I was exposed to the outside air.

"What is it?" Norio says, catching my arm as I stumble.

"It... it's so hot," I gasp, my eyes stinging with sweat already. Everything is so white, so brilliant in the blinding sun, I can barely see even with my sunlenses on. I raise my hands, cupping my eyes to shade them.

"You're in the desert here," Norio says. He's too polite to add that he thought I'd be expecting it, but it's plain by the surprise in his voice.

"I've never been in the Salarian desert." I straighten, still shading my eyes, still nearly blind in the sun. "I need a moment to adjust." I hope my eyes will adjust, at least enough to see where I'm going. "Do we have to... to walk far in this?"

"Only to that building." He points. I take his word for it that the shape shimmering in the sunlight is indeed a building. Why would they ever build white structures in a white desert?

"The shuttles come there, including the one to the Kicho-Ryo-Tomiko estate." He hesitates. I imagine he wants to ask me again if I'm certain I want to go there.

"Good," I say, and strike out boldly in the general direction I think he pointed to.

He hurries after me and catches my arm once again, pulling me quickly to the left where the ground is firmer and my feet no longer sink into the burning sand.

"It's important to stay on the path," he says, sounding apologetic as he releases my arm. "There may be scorpions in the sand."

"Scorpions?" I stop dead.

"That's what we call them. Desert creatures, native to Salaria. Their sting is fatal if not treated."

"I thought there weren't any native creatures on Salaria."

He doesn't answer. I still can't open my eyes wide enough to decipher his expression, but I can guess.

"I'm not from Salaria," I tell him. "My mother left. She went to Seraffa. That's where I was born."

"Okay," he says, like he still has a million questions he's too polite to ask.

I look down. The path is white. The sand is white. They both shimmer like diamonds in the glaring sunlight. "And I can't see a *flickis* thing in this sunlight. You'll have to lead me to the shuttles." I hold out my arm. He doesn't know Kandarin, so 'flickis' won't mean anything to him, but I don't expect my voice leaves any doubt as to what kind of word it is. I hate feeling helpless.

"Okay," he says again. I feel his hand on my arm, and follow where it guides me.

Chapter Seven

He drops my arm as soon as we enter the shade provided by the shuttle building, and I can see again. The door opens and closes at once behind us. Fortunately by now I understand why doors work so quickly here, and I was ready to step through it the moment it opened.

Norio goes to a panel on the wall and taps some kind of message onto it. "The shuttle will be here soon," he says. "Would you like a drink?"

I look around. There isn't a caf in sight, just a small kiosk with holos on it of glasses of something white and liquid, and a narrow, indented shelf. We've arrived later than everyone else, thanks to my shuffling along the path blindly. Most of the other people waiting here are already sipping from small cups. "Sure, yes," I say.

Norio presses a spot above the shelf, and a small, clear drinking cup emerges onto the shelf. He brings it to me.

I look inside. Milk. I'm not crazy about milk, but after the blistering walk over here, I'm thirsty enough to drink anything. I lift it to my lips. A thin, sweet, slightly sticky liquid fills my mouth. I almost spit it out.

Norio coughs. "It is cactus milk," he says, his lips trembling with the effort not to laugh.

"You could have warned me."

"I... I didn't think in time. I apologize." His eyes glance quickly around.

I'm about to tell him not to be so formal, when I realize others are watching us. Watching him. Female Salarians, and they're frowning.

"Thank you for the drink," I say. Then, although it embarrasses me to have to, I add, "Please have one also."

He bows his head and gets one for himself as the other travelers waiting for shuttles look away, presumably satisfied.

I take another sip. Liquids are precious here, I remind myself. This time I'm not expecting animal milk, and the taste is actually

89

not bad, plus it's cool.

A shuttle arrives, an aircar with the single word "Estate" written on its side. It looks large enough to seat ten or twelve people, but we're the only ones waiting for this one. We step into the vehicle and Norio moves to the row behind me. I sigh. "Please sit beside me, Norio. Where I come from, males are as valuable as females, and have all the same rights."

He stops. "Where I come from," he says, not sitting down but not coming forward either, "men are respectful of women. Or else," he adds softly.

"I won't embarrass you in front of others. I understand. But there's no one here to see."

He comes forward and sits beside me gingerly, leaving an empty seat between us.

The aircar has shaded windows that cut the sun enough that I can bear to look out at this all-white world. As we ride, Norio tells me there are a number of mining triads in this area. Tokosha became the capital city of Salaria because of its closeness to a major discovery of crystal veins. The mines drew people, made them wealthy, and the city expanded to offer them ways to spend their wealth.

Good and bad, I think. If my sister is working in a mine as I expect, it'll likely be in this area where there's a concentration of mines. And many of them appear to belong to my grandmother's triad. With so many mines, how will I find the one where Oghogho is? Now that, apparently, we're not doing a report on Lady Celeste. Or not doing it yet. I don't know for sure that it's off the agenda. For all I know (which is nothing) Agatha was apprehended by the port guards because they don't want that report written. A little thing like local opposition won't stop the O.U.B. for long. But until I find Agatha, I won't know anything: what's changed, what hasn't, what was true, what was a lie. Maybe she doesn't know anymore, either. The further we go into this adventure, the more murky everything will become. That's the way these stupid visions work. For now, the best I can do is go along with what Idaro told the customs director.

We sail over a low ridge, or sand dune, whatever, and there before us is a white village, ten or eleven single-story buildings. The roofs shine in the sun like mirrors, I'm thinking, till I realize they're covered with solar panels. The estate is protected by a high wall that's guarded at the gate by an armed man. I turn to ask Norio what he's guarding it from, but Norio's moved back to the row behind me again.

I'm getting a good idea why Philana left this place, and I haven't even met her mother yet.

Chapter Eight

"I have come from Tokosha to speak to Matriarch Ryo," I tell the guard at the entrance to the estate when I leave the aircar. "My name is Idaro." Once again the sun is blinding me and the heat takes my breath away, but I stand up straight and try to look as self-possessed and in control as any Salarian female.

The guard lets me through the gate—Norio has already been admitted—and points to the largest building, a single-story structure spreading out over the ground more like a shopping concourse than a family home.

"I'll escort her," Norio offers.

As he guides me across the sand he reassures me that it's safe, there are no scorpions here. I'm relieved, but that's not all that's on my mind. Only I can't think how to say it. He's about to leave me at the door when I blurt out, "Norio—" and stop.

He waits, looking at me questioningly.

"Don't... don't tell anyone what I told you at the station, okay?"

He grins. "Not if you won't tell anyone I sat beside you in the aircar."

I smile back, but it's a little forced. I don't like being tied to someone by a secret, no matter how cute he is. It's better if it's mutual, but only marginally. I wish I hadn't told him who I am, but until I saw his reaction, I didn't know Philana's existence had been so thoroughly erased from her family. When Norio leaves, heading for one of the farther buildings, I wait a moment, looking around from the shade of the building. How many people live here, I wonder? I don't see anyone, but I'm not really surprised no one's outside in this manic heat. I'm just glad I made it all the way from the gate without tripping in my near-blindness. I take a breath and tap the door-pad, feeling like an unwelcome ghost.

Chapter Eight

The heat is making me dizzy; it seems like forever before the door slides open. A man about Philana's age stands there looking at me through eyes just like hers. If I had any doubts about coming to the right place, they are immediately dispelled. He motions me inside. I step gratefully into the cooler air.

"I've come from Tokosha to speak to Matriarch Ryo. My name is Idaro." I don't offer him any further identification. It's improper of me not to fully identify myself, but he's a male and can't demand it from me. He looks the right age to be her brother, or—cousin? What do they call them, the children of the other triad members? They must all be raised together. Whatever they were to each other, I expect he would know who I was referring to, unlike Norio. But I've reconsidered the straightforward approach. Obviously Ryo is as unforgiving of her daughter as Philana is of her mother. I don't want to tip my grandmother off so she can send me away without even seeing me.

"The matriarch is very busy," he says politely. "If you can tell me your business, I could suggest another family member who could assist you?"

"I have a personal message for Matriarch Ryo. It concerns her family."

He raises his eyebrows slightly.

I smile as sweetly as I know how.

"I cannot tell you when she may be able to see you, but you may wait if you wish."

At my nod he leads me to a small windowless sitting room immediately inside the entrance. I haven't even made it past the foyer doors. The room has three chairs, all made of a strong plastic material with padded seats and back. When I sit down in one it molds to my body and is the most comfortable chair I've ever sat in. He hands me a small white towel and leaves, motioning the door closed. Silence descends.

I wipe my hands and face on the towel. It's moistened with something sticky, maybe the cactus resin, which absorbs the sweat and grains of wind-blown sand from my skin and leaves me feeling remarkably refreshed. Time passes…

Is she keeping me waiting for a reason, or is she really too busy? More time passes…

Has she decided not to see me? Why doesn't she just tell me to go? Or is she hoping I'll give up and leave on my own, no need to explain anything to anyone? "Some stranger came but didn't stay." And more time…

Is she questioning Norio? What will he tell her? I shouldn't have said anything to him. Don't trust anyone—that was Agatha's advice, and I broke it with the first person I met. Norio: his name means 'man of principles'. How many people live up to their names?

I'm getting drowsy, sitting here in this incredibly comfortable chair. I close my eyes for a moment…

"—riarch Ryo has decided to see you."

I come awake suddenly through the second half of his sentence. The man who has Philana's eyes is waiting for me to follow him. I blink away my dream of being chased by a fire-breathing dragon and struggle out of the chair.

He's looking down at my feet. I glance at them. Well, of course they're sandy and dirty, it's hot outside, to understate the case, and I was walking through sand. The towel slides off my lap as I stand up. Oh.

He waits while I remove my sandals and wipe the sweat and sand from my feet, then from the sandals, before putting them back on. I don't know what to do with the towel, till I see a basket by the door. Should have noticed that earlier.

He bows his head respectfully when I'm done, ready to lead me into the mansion. I bow back—male or not, he's my elder—and follow him out of the room, and through the foyer door.

White. Walls, floor, ceiling. You'd think they'd get sick of the color. At least the upholstery on their furniture is in blues and greens, and there are holographs on their walls in vibrant colors. I don't get to see much because the room he leads me to is just down the hall.

This one has a window, a green rug, green cushions on the chairs. The holos on the walls are of Old Earth, woodland scenes. I've seen similar ones at the hololibrary. Do the Salarians still long for Old Earth, still find their idea of beauty in its landscapes? They should see the reds, rusts, and pinks of Seraffa, if they want to see beautiful. It strikes me as sad that they hunger for another planet's colors, rather than learning to love their own. Then again, who could love white on white on white?

Ryo sweeps in soon after the man—her son?—leaves. I rise and bow. She gives me a long, hard look, and not so much as a dip of her chin.

"You imagine you are my granddaughter."

Norio, I think, annoyed. More than a little annoyed, but there's no time for that now. "My mother says she is your child, and I know I am my mother's daughter. Unless Philana was misled...?"

"Philana." She says the name slowly, as one remembers something lost, but when she looks at me again there's no hint of affection in her eyes. "Yes, she was misled, but not by me. I might as well know the worst. Who is your father, child?"

"He was Edoan, from Seraffa." I raise my chin. Let her dare scorn my people.

"Was? Did he die, or leave her?"

I flush, and meet her gaze without answering.

"Ah, she drove him away, then."

I came hoping to find refuge here until Agatha's predicament was sorted out. Idaro came to meet her long-lost grandparent. But this is a low blow at Philana, which riles both of us. "Just as you drove her away," I reply coldly. "I guess she must be your daughter." I give her a curt bow—angry or not I can still be polite—and start for the door.

I hear a low rumble, and realize with surprise that she is laughing. "You have spirit," she says, as though she's judging the merits of something she might buy. "Sit down and tell me why you are here."

I hesitate. She is a dragon and I don't like her.

"Or leave," she says. "But that seems foolish after coming all this way."

For the second time since she's walked in, I flush. I'm tempted to leave, but that would mean walking out while she laughs. I sit down.

She raises an eyebrow, and seats herself. She has provoked me to rudeness after all.

"I came to see why my mother left her home," I say.

"And have you found an answer?"

There's an unmistakable gleam in her eye. She knows what she is. This time I laugh, I can't help it. "Maybe," I tell her.

"It was an expensive answer if that is all you came for." Then her eyes change, widen slightly. "Is your mother well?"

"Yes, she is," I say, liking the dragon a bit better for caring, although I suspect she'd deny it.

"Then tell me why you want to join the desert game?"

I didn't tell Norio that. I only told that to the customs director. I should have guessed my grandmother would check with the port authorities on someone who appeared suddenly at her door from off-planet. Salarians never go into a meeting until they know everything they can about everyone there. And the sarcastic director I spoke to this morning would be delighted to fill Matriarch Ryo in. Norio didn't betray me.

"I'm not sure I want to take it, yet."

"But you don't want to join the O.U.B., like your mother."

"I've been raised in the faith." I won't criticize what Idaro's mother, and my own, believed. What I sort of believe, in my own way. "But no, I don't intend to become a Select."

"So you think you'll try us out. The desert game is not child's play, girl. It's not something you try on to see if it fits. It is something you commit to."

"Not all Salarian girls join the desert game. What happens to those who do, but aren't successful?"

She shrugs. "Perhaps they become Select."

I feel my eyes narrow. "My mother joined the desert game and formed a youth triad. I believe that's considered a successful game. And if you think the Select are not committed, you don't know anything about commitment." I've gone too far. There's no greater insult to a Salarian than to say she doesn't know what she's talking about. I briefly consider apologizing, but I think of Philana and Agatha, and I can't take back a word.

"Your mother should have named you Ryo."

I know what she means. It's true. I remember how I spoke to Philana, not to mention my own mother. "I apologize, Grandmother." I bow my head. "You are right. I open my mouth and fire comes out, even when I don't mean it to."

"Oh, I think you meant it. I think you always mean it. Regretting it later is not the same thing at all."

I look up at her. She's not a typical Salarian, quick to take offense and nurse a grudge forever. She's quick to give offense, but she's let me get away with returning the favor. This woman I dislike may be the first to understand me. I still don't like her much. What does that say about me?

"You came here with a desert woman."

Her words catch me off guard—exactly what she intended, I suspect. "I came here with a Select of the O.U.B. They don't consult me when they're recruiting. And this isn't the only planet that breeds blue-eyed blonds. There's New Earth, Anglia, Nordicus—" I'm sounding defensive. Stick to the facts, I tell myself, since she probably already knows those. "I paid my transport by giving her language lessons. We parted when the ship docked."

"And what did you teach her?"

"They wanted me to teach her Salarian. She didn't know a word of it. Couldn't learn it, either. Salarian is a subtle language. The best I could do was teach her Central Ang."

My grandmother smiles. "And you? How did you learn it?"

"My mother has never forgotten that she is Salarian."

Again I have pleased her, although she doesn't let herself show it this time, except in a tiny crease at the corner of her eyes.

"You know, Idaro, dragons are considered lucky."

"For the dragon, maybe. Not so lucky for anyone who comes across one."

I hear the low rumble of her laughter again. "Then try to be more like your name," she says.

Watchful. Right. Would the real Idaro have been better at keeping her mouth shut and her eyes open? Well, I can be watchful, too. I can keep my thoughts to myself. In fact, I usually do. I realize now I knew exactly what this lucky, fire-breathing grandmother would respond to, because I understand her.

"I came to learn, Grandmother. Most Salarian girls have fifteen years to understand what it means to be Salarian, to be a member of a triad. I only have until this year's desert game begins, if I want to join it. And in that time I'll also have to learn how to survive the desert. I might not be ready in time. I can only tell you that I won't dishonor the desert game or those who participate in it. I won't pretend a commitment I don't feel."

She looks at me without speaking.

I'm busy thinking, what did I just say? How can I keep that promise? I came here to find my sister. Of course I can't commit to a desert game, let alone a Salarian triad! And now I've promised not to pretend to?

Fortunately, she isn't a Select or worse, an Adept. My face must be contradicting every word I just said, but she can't read it. I look up at her. She isn't even looking at me any more, but off into the air, thinking her own thoughts. She must sense my glance because she focuses on me again.

"I believe you," she says. "You may stay here for now. Report to the Master teachers for training, and do what they tell you while you decide. But I think we will drop the 'Grandmother' reference. You may call me 'Matriarch Ryo'. We will say you are the grandchild of a distant cousin. Very distant. If you agree, my son Ichiro will take you to your room."

"Thank you… Matriarch Ryo."

"I am told you have nothing other than what you are wearing?"

"I left my bag at the space station. I can—"

"We will supply what you need. I may not see you again. So—" She waits till I meet her eyes, "—remember, I expect you to keep your promise."

I nod.

She waits.

I clear my throat. "I will." That's it then. I can't go on this desert game and then disappear off on some mission for the O.U.B. If Agatha goes into the desert, I'll have to come up with some other way to join her. Or not. But at least I can learn how to survive the desert, which I now know has scorpions.

It doesn't make sense, the way I feel. This woman isn't my grandmother. She's a mine owner, a slave owner. This home and everything in it she got by working people like my sister to death. And maybe my sister too, right now. I don't owe her anything, least of all a debt of honor.

But I'm pretending to be her dead granddaughter, making her think Idaro is alive, making her like Idaro. I don't feel good about that. I shouldn't have come here. Philana warned me not to. It's too late to take it back, but I mean to keep my promise to this grandmother, even if I'm lying about everything else.

"There is something else?"

"Yes. I want to learn about Salaria, and the crystal mines which are the basis for the Salarian economy."

She raises an eyebrow.

"I can read. I wouldn't come this far in complete ignorance."

"Go on."

I should have heeded her tone, or at least the coolness in her eyes. But there's no other way to put this, and I'm short on time. "I'd like to see a Salarian mine. One of our family mines."

"Did your mother suggest this?"

She looks straight at me, and when I look into her eyes she lives up to her name, because they are the eyes I would imagine for the mythical monster she's named after, cold and deadly and alien.

"She told me not to come here."

"But you came anyway."

"Yes." I am in danger, those dragon eyes tell me. The wrong word will kill me. I've been trained in situations like this to say as little as possible. I've never needed that training till now.

"One thing," she says slowly, "must be clear. Your mother had certain ideas about our mines, and no doubt she shared them with you. If you have come with similar opinions, you would be best to leave now. I will not tolerate a single word, not so much as a whisper, against me and my way of life."

I nod, swallowing a sudden dryness in my throat. But she has not finished. She does not so much as blink those strange, cruel eyes.

"I do not mean leave here. I mean leave Salaria altogether, and leave quickly. I will not have another traitor crawl out of my nest, so do not think to shame me, and survive."

I nod again.

It's not enough, her eyes tell me.

"I... I won't." I croak. "That's why I came. Because I'm not my mother." The truth, only the truth. Who knows what those strange eyes can see? I am not like Philana. Don't even think of whether we share 'certain opinions'. And never, for one moment waking or sleeping, forget that I'm Idaro. She's a dragon, and if she knew who I really was, she would destroy me—I don't even want to think how.

"I will not bring shame on you." It isn't only fear that makes me say it. There's something else between us that I don't understand. That I don't want to understand.

She blinks. Slowly her expression thaws, becoming human again. "Good. We will not speak of that again." She nods a dismissal. "My son is waiting for you at the door."

I have no choice but to rise and bow and leave. Before I reach the door, she says, "Idaro?" I turn to her.

"This is not your family."

I bow again, without a word, and open the door.

Ichiro, Ryo's son, turns out to be the man with Philana's eyes. Her brother. I want to tell him his sister is well, but I've agreed to the story that I'm at most a distant relation. He takes me outside, across the hot sand. The sun is setting, I can see my way along the path, but I keep looking at the sand on either side.

"There are no scorpions inside the walls," he tells me. "The grounds inside the gates have been fully treated, they can't live in it."

"Outside the walls, in the desert?"

"Outside the walls, stay on the paths."

"What about the desert game? Are there paths?"

He laughs. "No, no paths. It's a desert game." He sees the look on my face and says, "There are ways to tell where they are. I'll have one of the boys take you outside tomorrow and show you what to look for."

I shudder. What a fun activity. "Thank you," I say, because it might save my life. "But I can't see in the sunlight. How do you stand it, it's so bright?"

"No one told you? We have implants once we reach adulthood."

"I'm wearing sunlenses. They barely make a difference."

"Did you buy them here?"

I shake my head.

"I'll get you a pair made for Salaria. It'll take you a few days to get used to them. You might have headaches at first." He says this proudly, as though enduring a blindingly bright, blistering hot sun is some test of fortitude. If I really were Idaro, I'd know right now I didn't want to stay here. "Thank you," I say again, for lenses that will give me headaches, another thing I don't really want but which might save my life.

He stops in front of one of the smaller buildings. "Place your hand here." He points to a pad beside the door. I put the palm of my right hand flat against it. He touches several spots in a line above my hand, in a quick sequence. "Now the left one."

"Okay, you're keyed in," he says. "Wave either palm over the pad and the door will open for you."

I wave my left palm in front of the pad, and wait for him to take me to my room.

"I can't go in there," he says. "This is the residence for girls in their last year before the desert game. The others share two to a room, but you'll have your own, number thirteen. It's a very lucky number."

Right, I think. Then why isn't it already taken? "The first mistake is thinking luck has anything to do with your life," I tell him.

I get my first smile from him. "I knew someone who lived by that old saying, once."

"Did it work for her?"

He looks at me.

"Or him," I add.

"I don't know. We've lost touch. You'll find clean clothes in your room. You've missed dinner, so I'll have a plate of food sent over for you. If you need anything else, ask the girl who brings your dinner."

Chapter Nine

"Who are you?"

"My name is Idaro." I don't bow, or even tilt my head. The girl accosting me in the hall outside our rooms is my age, and hasn't shown the courtesy required for greeting a stranger.

"Who are you?" I ask back.

She draws herself to her full height, about an inch or two taller than me. The dozen or so girls clustered around her straighten in imitation. For the first time, I'm looking at a group of my peers and every one of them is my height—some of them even shorter than I am. I almost grin, it's such a nice change. They're all wearing the same white, lightweight bodysuits, cropped just above the knees and sleeveless, like the ones I found in the bundle of clean clothes brought to my room for me to wear here. Way more practical than the dress.

"I am Kama, daughter of Chowa, of the Kicho-Ryo-Tomiko triad." She looks at me expectantly. Now I'm supposed to bow.

"Yes, I already figured out the triad." I recognize her mother's name: Philana's older sister, Chowa, the conciliatory one who probably hopes to take over running the mines one day. "I guess you're all going to the caf for breakfast. Mind if I come with you?"

They look confused, even Kama for a moment. "And who are you?" She asks, backing down only a little. They probably heard the girl who brought food and clothes to my room, and waited all evening for me to come out. The fact that I didn't makes me seem mysterious. Truth is, I crawled into bed and fell asleep half-way through eating.

"My name is Idaro. My grandmother was a cousin of Matriarch Ryo. I was born and grew up on Seraffa. Matriarch Ryo has graciously given me permission to stay here so I may learn Salarian ways." Then I bow my head two inches, at all of them. "And now I am hungry, but I don't know where the caf is."

They stare at me a moment with their mouths open. Kama gives me a look to say she still has questions, but the girls around her suddenly remember their manners and bow their heads, murmuring: of course, I must join them, be welcome. We leave the dorm together.

And almost run into Norio, standing outside the door with two other guys. Everyone bows. I'm going to get tired of all this bowing soon. As my head comes up, I notice Kama watching Norio. I know that look, and I glance at Norio to see if it's returned. He's smiling at me.

"I was told to give you these." He hands me a small box. Salarian sunlenses. "I'll take you outside after breakfast and show you a few things about the desert," he adds.

"You're kind to a stranger," I say formally. I do want the chance to talk to him alone, but I wish he hadn't done this in front of Kama. He's obviously unaware of her feelings for him.

"I'll wait while you put them on," he offers, waving at the two other guys to go on without him.

I look out into the shining sand beyond the circle of shadow cast by the dorm. I'll be blind the minute I step out of the shade.

"We'll all wait," Kama says, smiling at Norio. "Go ahead, Idaro."

I go back inside and run to my room. Kama is grilling him about me, I'm sure. If he tells her what he knows, Ryo will think I broke our agreement. I blink and pull at the corners of my eyes to remove the useless sunlenses I brought with me, and toss them into their case. The Salarian lenses are larger and thicker, a dark blue color. I pop one into my left eye. The room is suddenly cast into a deep shade. I pop in the other and I'm immersed in a dark, twilit gloom. Is this what they see all the time? How can they live in such darkness? Or do they only wear these lenses outside? No time to wonder, I have to get back to Kama and Norio as soon as possible.

When I emerge they are bunched close, their voices low and tense.

"We have to do something about her," one of the girls says.

"She's earned her right—" Norio objects.

"But she left," Kama interrupts him. Then she looks up and sees me, and hushes the others. "Hello cousin," she says with loud, false cheerfulness. "Ready for breakfast?"

I step out of the shade into the sunlight and everything brightens, about to the level of a sunny day on Seraffa. I'm too worried about what I heard to feel much relief about being able to see. There's nothing I can do about it now, though. I'll have to wait till Norio takes me outside the wall to find out what he told them. It didn't sound like they liked what they heard.

The caf is the central building in the compound. It accommodates everyone who lives here, except the founding triad and their chosen heirs. They dine in the main residence, discussing business, one of the girls tells me as we step into noisy chaos. It's nearly as bad as the university caf at noon, three or four hundred people all talking and eating, it's all I can do not to cover my ears. I usually eat at off hours, but I'm not sure that's possible here. I'll have to find out how long the caf stays open, if I'm here long enough.

We line up for food, which looks normal enough: eggs, some kind of cereal, bread, cactus milk and two choices of hot drink, some kind of tea and Lato. Kama gets her food and turns to check the tray of a chubby girl two places behind her. The kid has taken two slices of bread. Kama stares at her until she puts one back. Kama catches me watching and hisses, "None of us is risking our lives in the desert to carry her out. Not that we could carry her."

I respond with the expressionless face I learned from the Select.

I follow the girls to the only empty table. "It's reserved for the fifteens," the girl beside me says. "We do everything together this year." She grins smugly.

Oh, what fun, I think, though I don't let it show. If I'm supposed to be learning about the desert game and considering doing it with these girls, I'll have to join the pack. Kama just better not try taking anything off my tray.

I eat my meal as slowly as possible, watching to see how cohesive this group really is. Finally, Kama stands up. "We have training," she says, looking at me.

"Go ahead," I say in my friendliest voice. "I'll join you later."

"You're already starting late."

"I'll catch up."

She laughs. I would too, if I was her and some girl came to Seraffa without a clue, figuring she had nothing to learn. "We're not going to be responsible for you, too," she says.

"I don't expect it."

She shrugs and leads her tribe out of the caf.

I look around for Norio. His table is nearly empty but I don't know whether I'm allowed to join it, so I catch his eye and go back to finishing my meal. A minute later he's standing beside me. "Ready to check out the desert?"

The lenses help my eyes but they don't do anything about the heat. Just walking across the compound to the gate saps my energy. I'm not panting or tired so much as wilted. How can they stand it? I've heard people say that about Seraffa; next time I'll suggest they try Salaria.

"You'll get used to it," Norio encourages me when I lag behind him. "Just keep going and don't think about it."

I lean against the wall as he talks to the guard, who says something about boots. Norio shrugs.

Boots? I look down at my open sandals, and remember the scorpions. Boots, good idea. But I don't have any. Why weren't there any put in my room with the clean clothes? Norio's wearing boots, I notice.

Norio turns, sees me, and cries, "No!" He grabs my arm and pulls me away from the wall as the guard whips out his weapon and shoots, right where I was standing. Something long and thin and as white as a spray of sand falls from the wall to the ground.

"What is it?" I cry. But I can guess: another non-existent native species. "Poisonous?" I hear the rise in my voice and try unsuccessfully to control it.

"A desert snake," Norio says.

I glare at him. He was about to take me out there! "Desert scorpions, desert snakes—"

"They're not really. Those are just the closest names we can put to them."

"I don't care what they're called! It's what they do that bothers me!"

"You'll get used to—"

"Snakes and scorpions and who knows what else is out there? I don't think so!"

"So, should I open the gate or not?" the guard asks.

I stare at him, open-mouthed. Norio stares at me.

"What else is out there?" I ask.

"Nothing else. Just sn... those two. And a few flying things, but they're not poisonous."

"But they bite?"

"Well, yes, but only at night. And it's just itchy, not—"

"I know, not deadly." I take a shaky breath. My skin is crawling and it's not sweat, although there's plenty of that, too. They're probably drawn to moisture, those desert things. I look back at the compound, then at the gate. If I don't go out there I'll blow my cover. If I don't face this planet, I'll never rescue Oghogho. I might as well go home now.

That is the most intelligent thought I've had since I got here. It really burns that I can't do it. Why is doing the right thing always such a stupid idea? I ball my hands into fists at my sides. "Alright. Open the gate." I look at Norio. He's gazing at me like he thinks I'm amazing.

"You go first," I tell him.

"They're more afraid of you than you are of them," Norio says, leading the way. Behind us, the gate slides shut so fast there's a little intake of air, like a soft "Oh!" Norio doesn't seem to notice. We're walking on a wide path, to where the shuttle left us.

"When a scorpion stings someone, that's it. It dies."

"*It* dies?" I want to be sure I got that right.

"Without the serum in its tail, it can't digest food."

"So it's kind of an, 'I'm-taking-you-with-me' thing?"

"Yeah." He grins at me. I don't grin back. We're almost at the end of the path. "So they only sting if they think they're cornered. Or if you get too near their nest."

"What does their nest look like?" I look out over the sand. "I bet it's white."

"Actually, it's buried. But there's an indentation in the sand, with an air-hole in the middle of it, right above the nest. There." He points.

There's nothing to see but sand, blown into little waves and dips everywhere by the hot breeze. "You're kidding, right?"

"No, it's right there, you can see it."

I look. I walk to the edge of the path, looking exactly where he's pointing. Nothing.

He squats down. I squat beside him. He puts his head close to mine and points, his arm straight, directly in front of me. And I see it. "That dip, with the hole," I say, pointing.

"Yes, great!"

"I'd never in a million years see it on my own."

"Yes you will. We'll practice."

"Tell me about the snakes."

"They're not really snakes. They have tiny legs, more like Old Earth centipedes, if you've ever seen an image of those."

I haven't, but 'tiny legs' is pretty clear. "How fast do they run?"

"Slow. You can out-walk them, if you're walking fast. The trick is to see them."

"Yeah, I'm getting that."

"They burrow under the sand—"

"Everything here does."

"—and hear you coming by vibration. But they can't bite from underground. They have to come up, so they emerge at least a couple inches from you. And they're slow. If you're running, you're safe."

"If you're running, you can't watch out for the scorpion nests."

"There is that."

I stop at the end of the path. "This is impossible!"

"The thing is, just don't worry about it." He steps off into the untreated sand. "I brought some serum for you." He takes a little vial out of his pocket to show me. "After the third time you get stung—they're basically the same, same venom in both of them—you'll be immune."

"That's your solution? Go get stung a few times?"

"You've had needles, haven't you? Inoculations? A serum containing a weakened version of a virus so your body can build antibodies to it? Basically it's the same thing. A needle, a stinger…"

"It's *poisonous*." What about that doesn't he get?

He shrugs. "I brought the serum."

"You're crazy, you know that?"

"You coming or not?" He backs away from me into the white sand.

"You're not even looking where you're going!" I raise my voice as the distance between us lengthens. "Stop!" I take a tentative step into the sand. Nothing bad appears. I take another. "Come back for me!" He grins and comes to me.

"Why did you make such a big deal about the snake inside the compound if it's nothing?"

"I didn't want you to get stung before we got through the gate and out of sight."

I turn around. "You want me to get stung? You brought me out here so I would?" I scramble back toward the path. Norio reaches for my arm, but I swat his hand away.

"The guard won't let you in, Idaro. I told him to wait for me. You don't want to go back and cry at the gate for no reason, do you?"

. I hate this guy. I turn around and shove him, hard, into the sand. I hope he lands on a scorpion nest, on ten nests! He gets up quickly, but he's laughing, brushing the sand off, moving a few steps away from me.

I run toward him and shove him again, and when he gets up and tries to back away from me, I shove him down again. This time he stays down. I stand over him. "What did you tell Kama about me?" I ask, because now I don't trust him at all.

"Nothing." He stands up. "What makes you think I'd tell her anything?"

"I heard you talking when I came back with my lenses in. I heard one of them say, *We have to do something*, and Kama said I didn't have any rights because I left. So what did you tell them?" I glare at him. "I told you who I was in confidence. I didn't expect you to blab it to everyone."

"Wait a minute!" He frowns at me. "First, I didn't say anything. Kama and the other girls were talking, and it wasn't about you. They were talking about someone else, Nyah. All I said was that she had rights. That was the only comment I made, and it had nothing to do with you."

"So why did everyone stop talking when I arrived?"

"It wasn't... It's because you're not one of us. You're not Salarian. We don't talk about people like Nyah in front of foreigners."

"People like… who is she? Nyah?"

"She's a desert girl."

"The desert girl!" I stare at him. "Does she have thin lips?"

"Thin lips?" He frowns. "No. You're probably thinking of Malah. You'd remember Nyah if you saw her. She has green eyes."

"Green eyes?" We sound like idiots, repeating each other's words, but I'm remembering something… the Salarian Nightgames! Green-eyes and Thin-lips! "The desert girls!"

"You know about them?"

"Who are they?"

We both speak at the same time. He looks at me strangely. "They're just two girls, desert people, that's all. They did something… and won some money for doing it, and received Salarian citizenship."

Nyah and Malah. "They did the water survival game."

"You know?"

"I heard about it. Someone was talking about it in the spaceport. I overheard," I lie quickly. Now I know their names. If they're the same girls. Others might have taken the water challenge, or some other game, to get their citizenship, too. "They stayed in the water five hours? Together, and they both survived? The one with green eyes saved the other, holding her head up?"

He nods at each of my questions. "That was a pretty specific conversation you overheard."

You know who I mean, Agatha said in the e-bud. But Agatha couldn't have known I saw them at the Salarian Nightgames. What if she didn't mean these desert girls? And I thought she said 'the desert girl'. As in one, not two. Nyah or Malah? Or someone else entirely?

"What about Nyah?" I demand, hoping for some clue.

"What, 'what about her'?"

"What did they say about her? Kama and the others?"

"Why do you care?"

"Because…" I think fast, "she's a foreigner in your society, too. If they can take away her rights, they could take away mine. I want to know what she did."

"They won't take away yours. She's a desert girl. That's enough." His face goes still and cold. I feel my own face stiffening, too, until he adds, "for them."

"But not for you?"

"I'm male. It doesn't matter what I think." His face does that momentary coldness thing again. "But it's Malah that's the problem, for them. Malah goes around talking about all the desert people getting citizenship. How it's their planet, too. She's the one whose citizenship they want to revoke."

"And Nyah's, too, because they were granted citizenship together?"

"Everyone's. All the desert people who've done something to earn their citizenship. It's a mess."

"It's a mess because people are listening to her? Agreeing with her?" *It's our planet, too*, Agatha said. I thought she meant the O.U.B.

"Forget about her. Look around, Idaro. Where are you?"

He looks uncomfortable. Why would talking about the desert people make him nervous? But I do as he says, and look around. I'm standing in the dessert, at least fifty yards away from the treated path. I swallow, my throat suddenly dry. He kept backing up, and I kept following, caught up in our argument. I look down at my feet, searching for holes in the sand. I don't think there are any.

"The snakes hear vibrations," I whisper.

"That's right," Norio agrees.

"So if I don't move, they won't know I'm here?"

"Right again. But you know, it'll get dark in about ten more hours. And the scorpions come out to feed on the night flyers."

Chapter Nine

"I hate you."

He laughs. "Honestly, Idaro, I'm not trying to get you hurt. I wouldn't. This is the best way for you to acclimatize to the desert. You told me you wanted to join the desert game. I'm helping you. I promise it'll be okay. Unless you're allergic, that is. Only one way to find out."

"I do hate you." I grit my teeth and start walking carefully back toward the path. Halfway there, a Salarian snake pops out of the sand, I see it just as it reaches my foot, and feel its teeth sink into my heel. I scream and kick it off me, falling backward—oh no, is it underneath me? I leap up still screaming.

Norio grabs me, holds the serum to my mouth and orders me to drink. I stop screaming long enough to gulp it down. He picks me up and carries me to the path, murmuring, "You're okay, it's over, you're fine," and when that doesn't work, "Stop whimpering, you'll be fine!"

He lowers me onto the path and kneels beside me, fumbling in the pack at his side. My foot is burning. I look down. The poison is spreading, my whole foot is red and swelling. "It's not working," I cry. "The serum—"

"Quiet!" he hisses, pulling a roll of bandage from his pack and wrapping it around my foot. "The serum will work." His face looks tense.

"I'm allergic! What if I'm allergic?"

"Then you'll die. And I'll be charged with reckless behavior endangering a female." He ties the ends of the bandage around my ankle. "Don't tell anyone about this. Don't ever mention the serum. You fell and twisted your ankle, and I bound it for you. The guard saw you fall. That's all he needs to know. Or anyone needs to know."

Something in his expression makes me pause. But my foot is in agony, I've never felt such pain. I'm going to pass out.

"Trust me!"

Trust your instincts, Agatha said. I don't trust Norio. But I trust everyone else here even less. "I won't tell," I whisper. Leaning forward, I throw up into the sand beside the path.

"That's okay. That's normal," he says, his voice an octave higher, like he's trying to convince us both. He helps me to my feet and half-carries me as I hobble toward the gate which is magically opening.

"Sprained her ankle. I'll help her to her room," he calls to the guard, steering me toward my dorm. I should see a medic, but I'm too dizzy to insist. I let him half-carry, half-drag me to the girls dorm. My left foot is on fire. What is it with this planet, even pain is hot here.

"Don't tell anyone about the snake bite, or the serum," he warns me again, as he lowers me onto my bed.

Chapter Ten

I wake up alive: that's my first thought. I'm so relieved I want to laugh. Then I feel my foot, hot and throbbing. It wasn't a dream.

PING. I realize I've been hearing that sound for a while. It takes a moment to identify it as my door. "Enter," I croak. The room is shadowed in the dusk of early evening. I must have slept all day.

PING. Either the door isn't voice activated or it hasn't been set to my voice. I sit up. And gasp as the pain in my foot escalates to unbearable! I can't move. I can't get out of bed. I don't care who's at the door. I can't even lie down again without moving my foot, and every movement sends searing stabs of pain all the way up my leg.

PING.

"Go Away!" My voice is weak with the effort of bearing the searing pain, but the door doesn't chime again. Slowly, agonizingly slowly, gasping with every movement, I lie down again.

&

It's still dusk when I wake up. My eyes feel dry and I have a splitting headache, but my foot feels better. I wriggle it very carefully. It throbs, but I can bear it. The headache is worse. I rub my forehead, squinting. Even my eyes hurt. I can't have slept long the second time, it's still early evening.

Then I remember the sunlenses. I slept in them. Didn't someone warn me not to? One of the girls—they all competed to give me advice this morning. I crawl out of bed, careful with my foot, no pressure on it, and get the lens container. I pop out the lenses. It isn't evening, the sun's bright outside the window. Did I sleep all night?

My head still aches brutally, and my foot is worse for moving. I hop back to bed and sit, with my eyes shut and my foot still, enduring the pain at either end of my body. My stomach rumbles. I haven't eaten since breakfast. Maybe since yesterday. I'm starving. I think of the caf, the noise, the blinding sunlight I'll have to walk through to get there... My eyes hurt. My foot throbs. Forget it.

PING. The door again. I hobble over and pass my palm in front of the pad.

It's the chubby girl. She told me her name... Kayo. It means beautiful, poor kid. "Hi Kayo."

She holds up the tray she's carrying. A wonderful smell makes my mouth water. "I heard you fell and twisted your ankle. You missed lunch, so I thought you wouldn't want to go without dinner, too..." her tentative voice trails off. She looks embarrassed.

"Kayo, that's great." I wince. Even looking at her hurts my sore eyes. "Are you okay?"

"I fell asleep with my lenses in." Now I remember, she's the one who warned me. I raise my hand to rub my forehead, waiting to hear her told-you-so.

"Oh, I can help with that. I do it myself all the time," she gives a small, embarrassed laugh. "I've got some drops in my room." She looks down at the tray. "You probably don't—"

"Yes I do, I'm starving. Thanks." I hobble back a step, minimal pressure on the left foot, and look around the room. No table. But Kayo's already stepping around me to put the tray on top of the low dresser beside the bed, like she's done this before. "I'll get the drops." She hurries back out.

I check out the tray while I'm waiting: chicken, some kind of grain and some fried white veg stalks. One thing I like about this planet: no fish. They take too much water.

I hear a cough behind me at the door, which I left open. "Enter," I mumble around a mouthful of the grain, before I remember that's a door command, not how you talk to people. Kayo bounces in happily, holding up a small bottle.

"You want me to put them in for you?"

The relief is almost instantaneous. "Ohhh," I sigh.

She giggles. "Yeah, I know, right?"

"Oh look, the two losers together." Kama stands at my door, surrounded by the other girls.

"Hello, Kama," Kayo says in a small voice.

Oh look, it's the silly sheep and the mangy dog that herds them. I almost say it. It's on the tip of my tongue. Kama deserves it, but I'm not sure yet about the others. This morning I would have included Kayo in with them.

"One can't stop eating; the other can't even stand up on a sand path. You two are a real asset to this year's desert game. Why don't you go to the city, and join a little girl's club? Find yourself a safe little teen triad there."

"Go back to your nest, scorpion. There's nothing but poison in you."

A couple of the girls crowded around Kama gasp or look shocked. Kama's face goes red. All I'd have to do is stand up, for her to leap at me. I would if I could. I started taking self-defense as soon as I got back from Malem, and I'm pretty good by now. I'd like to flip her on her head, knock some respect into her…

The thought shocks me. I'll have enough trouble finding Oghogho and getting her home, without starting a stupid fight with the granddaughter of a wealthy triad. My anger disappears as quickly as it came up. I turn my back on Kama and continue eating my meal. The room is dead silent for two… three… five minutes. Then with a *huff!* I hear Kama stomp away, the others following after her in a muted chorus of "she doesn't matter," "she won't make it anyway," "who cares about her?" that sounds more like relief than scorn. I wink at Kayo.

Her eyes go wide. She claps her hand over her mouth to stifle a giggle.

I'm not sure it'll work at this distance, but I wave my palm toward the door pad. The door slides shut. I wish I'd known that earlier, I'd have closed the door in their faces. But I didn't want to look like an idiot if it failed with them all watching.

"These are delicious." I point to the fried white stalks on my plate.

"Salarian cactus." She looks at them wistfully.

"Help yourself."

"Really?"

"Sure. You can tell me about the desert game while we eat."

Her hand freezes above my plate. I look up. Her face has drained of color. "I'm going to die out there," she whispers. Her eyes fill up.

"Hey, sit down, Kayo. Have a veg stick." I wait till she calms down a little. "So, why are you going if you don't want to?"

"I do want to," she says quickly. "Everyone here does the desert game. Grandmothers Ryo, Kicho, and Tomiko insist."

"I thought it was a choice?"

"Well, some girls, maybe, in other families…" She looks wistful, then rallies, "But we're mine-owners. In our family we all have to join the game. Better to die with honor than live with shame."

"Really? Is that what you'd rather?"

She looks aside. Her lower lip trembles. I'm afraid she's going to cry, so I say the first thing I think of. The thing I've been thinking about since I got here, actually. "Have you ever been to a mine?"

"A mine?"

"A crystal mine, like the ones your family owns."

"I know what we mine. I don't know why you think I'd go there?"

"Well, your family owns some of them. It's, like, your family business."

"But why would I need to see one?"

"I'd think they'd be at least as interested in teaching the heirs to run the family business as in teaching them to eat cacti in the desert."

"Heirs? I'm never going to inherit the mines. Maybe Kama's and Norio's older sisters, someday. They're studying mining and business in university."

"What if you wanted to see one? Would you be able to?"

"The boys have gone there. Those who are training to be guards, anyway. And I'll have to see one. At least, if I survive the desert game I will. That's when we decide what we want to study for." She frowns. "Probably I won't get to the mines."

"What if I wanted to see one?"

She looks at me. "Why? They're dark and dirty, and the people who work in them..." she shudders.

I shrug. "Just curious. It's not important. Tell me what you learn in training.

"Well, we learn how to catch the scorpions and snakes—"

"How to catch them?"

"Yeah. If you cut off the scorpions' tails and the snakes' throat pouches, you can eat them."

I make a face and push my plate away. She giggles. "They're awful. They made us eat some and I threw it all up. Master was furious. But the cactus is good. If you can avoid the thorns. If they prick you, they can get under your skin and cause an infection..."

I'm getting ready with a pep talk in case she goes teary again, but she jumps up, blinking hard, and grabs the empty tray: "I'll take this back now." Before I can answer she's gone.

My foot is better the next morning. I get out of bed gingerly, but I can walk on it, limping a little. At breakfast I pass Norio when I line up for food. He smiles at me. I look right through him.

The other fifteens don't talk to me in the caf. Kayo sits beside me but she's too cowed to speak. I'm fine with that. I'm thinking how I'll get to see the mines. It's a long shot, but what if my sister's in one of them? And even if she isn't, knowing what they look like, where the workers go, how they're assigned jobs, it all might help. There wasn't much info, even in the Traders' library, about what happens to those who come here as debt-workers. First I'll visit a mine, and if that doesn't give me anything to go on, I'll say I'm interested in the gambling trade, I'd like to check that out. Someone there will know what happens to off-worlders who gamble away their freedom. If that doesn't work I'll make up an excuse to go to Prophet's Avenue and ask about Lady Celeste and the report.

For now, though, I'm stuck pretending an interest in the desert game. Apparently, it's the gate to everything here. So after breakfast I limp off with the rest of the fifteens to training. We walk between the buildings to the end of the compound. A large area, about a hundred feet square, is marked off, backing onto the wall. Two adults, a male and a female, are waiting for us. They don't look surprised to see me.

"We expected you yesterday," the woman says.

"I fell and sprained my ankle…"

"You may call me Master. He is Teacher." She points to the man, then looks down, frowning, at my foot. "You may be excused from the physical training today."

I'm already sweating and half-suffocated from the heat; I can't imagine exercising in it, but that's exactly what the others do. There's a circular track in the sand around the perimeter of our training area, and after a series of limbering stretches, they hit it at a run. Not a fast run, but by the third lap I'm sure someone's going to die. Teacher has me do more stretches while they run the first lap; sit-ups during the second, and push-ups from my knees, to avoid putting pressure on my ankle, while the third and final lap is being run. I think I'm going to pass out. How must they feel?

After a short break, Master sets the fifteens to practicing self-defense maneuvers on each other: throws and rolling falls, holds and ways to escape holds. I've done similar things in my self-defense class back on Seraffa. Kama is strong, and the most aggressive. No one can hold her, and few can escape her hold as Teacher counts out the time and Master rails at the trapped girl to free herself. When Kama throws a girl, I can tell it hurts. I watch her carefully, mentally supplying the defensive move I'd make for each hold or throw. She isn't very imaginative—none of the girls are—they simply do the moves as they've been taught. It's an exercise for them, they don't really think they'll use these holds and escapes. I felt the same way before I went to Malem.

There are some moves I've been taught that aren't being used here, and a few new moves I haven't seen that I'd like to try when my foot is better. I run through each of them several times in my mind, imagining myself performing them, and thinking what I'd do to counteract each one, particularly if I was struggling with someone stronger than me. Surprise them, that's the key, with a twist or lunge they aren't expecting. I'm going to toss my classmates around like sacks of red Seraffan flour with these new moves when I get home.

"Enough," Master calls. The girls collapse onto the sand. Master looks at me. "Your turn." She turns to the fifteens. "Who will work with our new girl?"

"I'm… my ankle…" I protest.

She turns on me. "Do you imagine you'll walk through the desert and not get hurt? Will you be given time off to recover there? Do you think the desert game we're training you for is child's play? A little stroll across the sand?"

I press my lips together and get up. From among the girls, Kama rises. "I don't mind showing her a few things," she says, walking over in front of the teachers.

She's not going to give me any slack because of my foot. In fact, from what I've seen, I expect she'll use it, deliberately hurt me there, making it appear unintentional. The only thing I have on her is a couple of moves she hasn't learned, and responses she isn't expecting. She thinks I've never done any of this before. Well, she's almost right; I haven't done it with a snake-bitten foot and sun-lenses that make my eyes burn and water. I move forward, into the circle Teacher drew in the sand. When Kama drops into a half-crouch, ready position, I crouch also, as though I'm just copying her as best I can.

Why are we doing this anyway? We're not expected to fight each other. From what I gather, we're supposed to help each other during the game. So who do they think will attack us in the desert? The answer is so obvious I straighten up. That's when Kama runs at me.

I try to dodge but I was caught off-guard and my foot slows me further. She grabs me. I prepare to break her hold, but her intent isn't to hold. Her foot 'accidentally' kicks my left ankle, hard, before she throws me to the ground.

If I had a twisted ankle rather than a bite on the heel, that kick would cripple me. It's pretty bad as it is, throbbing badly from the jar and the fall, but I can still get to my feet. I emphasize my limp, making it worse than it is. She doesn't grin, the teachers are watching, but I'm closer; I see the gleam in her eyes that's just as telling. We circle each other, slowly. This time when she lunges I'm prepared. I feint sideways and stick out my right foot, tripping her as she passes. It's put too much weight on my left foot, though, we both go down.

My foot is really throbbing now. I'll have to end this quickly if I want to win. So as we're getting up I turn a little, my back to her. She's supposed to wait till we're both up, but I know she won't. No surprise when I feel her grab me from behind. It's a weak hold because I was only half-turned. When I feel her hands grab me I straighten suddenly, tucking my head and thrusting up, my elbows digging into the inside of her elbows, releasing her hold. She flies over me, into the sand.

I reach a hand to help her up, and predictably she tries to pull me down as she rises, but again I'm ready, I saw her do this to another girl earlier. I twist, trying to flip her over my hip as I imagined my counter-move, but my weak foot gives out and we both go down again.

It's all ridiculous. We're both sweating so hard our hands slip, and gasping for air in the unbearable heat, falling over each other onto the sand. I can't help laughing, lying there beside her.

It's the complete wrong thing to do. She thinks I'm laughing at her. In a second she's on top of me, reaching for her knife, the one they all carry at their sides.

"None of that," Master roars, pulling her off me just as the knife touches my throat. She slaps the knife out of Kama's hand. It falls on the dirt, dishonored. For the second time I see Kama flush red, and once again, I'm the cause.

"You would attack a games companion from your own family, with your knife?" It isn't Master's voice, or Teacher's. I look up startled, as does Kama. Matriarch Ryo walks toward us. She holds out her hand to Kama. "Your sheath."

Kama unbuckles the sheath for her knife from her belt and hands it over. "I apologize, Matriarch Ryo," she says in a choked voice. "I forgot myself. The heat... the fight..."

"Forget yourself if you want, but don't forget your family. Ever." Matriarch Ryo's voice shakes with suppressed rage. "Do not imagine I will hesitate one minute to turn a traitor out of my house. I have done so before."

I keep my head averted, eyes down. I know who that's meant for.

"You'll go into the desert without a knife," Matriarch says. "And if one girl from this house doesn't come back—one girl!—you don't come back either."

I look up quickly. She's looking at Kama now, but what is she thinking? One girl *from this house* echoes in my mind. Quickly I unbuckle my belt, removing my sheath and knife I received with my clothes. I hold it out to Matriarch, with my head bowed. "I won't forget my family again, Matriarch Ryo. Forgive me." And then, even though it ticks me to do it, I add for good measure, "Forgive me Kama, for fighting you instead of learning from you."

I don't look up, but I can feel the dragon examining me. I hold my breath, forcing my hand to stay steady as I hold the knife out to her. When she takes it, I let my breath out slowly. Glancing sideways, I catch the quick flash of anger in Kama's eyes, as quickly hidden. I have an enemy here, but she's not the one I'm afraid of.

Nobody moves until Matriarch Ryo has left. Then Master looks at Kama and me, still on our knees in the sand circle. "I charge you both with each other's safety. Either you both survive the desert game, or neither of you comes back."

I look up, surprised that she heard what I heard, and equally surprised she would countermand her Matriarch. She looks from Kama to me. "Yes, Master," we say together. I glance around quickly; none of the other fifteens has noticed the shift in message.

If I was going on the walk, I'd be delighted. No one would dare question Master's interpretation of Matriarch Ryo's words. But in this case, it could work against me. Kama wants me out of commission, now more than ever. I thought I'd be safe here at least until the desert game, which I have no intention of actually joining, but now that Kama can't come back from it without me, she has to do something to prevent me from going. I'll have to be on guard every moment.

Lunch is an unpleasant affair. I sit at the table with them pretending nothing's off, we're the fifteens, a team. Norio tries to catch my eye twice, but I ignore him. On the way out, I see him talking quietly to Kayo. He looks at Kama and frowns.

After lunch Master supervises the other girls as they practice their survival skills, and Teacher takes me over to a small crop of cacti. It's fenced in, to prevent younger children from going near the thorns, I imagine. We go inside the enclosure. Up close, there appear to be several different types of cacti here.

Teacher squats down and points to a small one. "This little, pinkish variety is what we call Salarian cactus. It's the most tender for eating. You've probably already tasted it, the fried veg sticks?" He continues without waiting for my answer. "Their needles are almost invisible, they look more like fuzz, yes?"

I see small and fuzzy, but pink? It looks white to me, like everything else. How can he tell it apart from a younger example of one of the larger varieties? I squat down, shading it from the sun, and look at it closely. Now I can see a streak of the faintest color which, with a little imagination, looks pinkish. I reach out to touch it. Teacher slaps my hand back.

"That 'fuzz' is a million tiny needles. Touch them and they spring free, embedding themselves in your skin. It's nearly impossible to extract them without surgical instruments. Leave them in for two days and they'll fester and become infected; three days and you'll lose your hand."

"How do you get inside them?"

"Cut the stem with a knife, leave them to dry in the sun. By sunset, the needles will fall off harmlessly. Try it." He hands me his knife.

Very carefully I saw through the stem of a small branch until it falls from the plant. I spear it with the tip of the knife and place it in the direct sun.

"Good." He stands up. I rise too. "This one," he points to a huge white cactus as tall as I am, with bulbous growths, "is good for its sap. We call it desert doctor, or D-doc." He smiles briefly. "Not too imaginative, our ancestors. It can be used on your skin to heal a wound or a rash. Cut into one of the bulbs. Careful, its spines are less dangerous but they're jagged-edged, they hurt coming out."

I jab the tip of the knife into the closest bulb, avoiding the two-inch-long thorns, and saw a little before pulling it out. Drops of liquid form along the edges of the cut. Teacher reaches into the pouch at his side and hands me a small container. In a few minutes it's half-full, and the dripping has stopped.

"Rub some of that on your ankle tonight, it's good for easing pain, too. Just a thin layer. It'll make the area feel numb, and speed up healing. Keep the extra in case you need it again. Don't drink it, though. One swallow is enough to stop your heart. Now this one," he steps around the large cacti to stand in front of a shiny, globe-shaped cacti with even longer needles, three to four inches at least. "These are the most useful. Keep your eyes open for one of these. You can use the needles to sew with or pin things together, and its sap is thin and sweet, drinkable and very healthy. You could live on it for days. No, don't prick it, you've got the idea. We don't waste any of these. They're called sweetwater cactus, no doubt you've already tasted their milk." He waves his hand, indicating all the cacti. "They grow better outside the gates, where the soil isn't treated. That's where our real gardens are."

We walk past several rows of the cacti globes until we come to a tall, splotchy-white cacti, growing in the shade of the wall.

"Wood cactus," he says, pointing to the rough-looking plants. "We use these for building. They also make long-burning firewood. Snakes and scorpions won't come anywhere near a fire, the smell drives them away. Burn them with the thorns still on and the smoke keeps the night flyers away, too," he says. "They grow in the shadow of the taller one I showed you earlier." He catches my expression, peers into my face. "What is it?"

I shrug. "Nothing."

"Say it."

"You think this'll keep us alive? Eating dried cactus around a smoky fire?"

"I do. And Kama will make sure of it." He grins at me.

I laugh sarcastically. "You're sending us out there to face the desert people."

All trace of humor leaves his face. "What makes you think that?"

I hand him back his knife. "We're not learning self-defense to fight off cacti and snakes."

"The desert people have never attacked girls on a desert game." I might believe him, except that I've spent too long with the O.U.B. Every muscle in his face is screaming: lie. I just don't know what he's lying about.

"Okay, sure," I say.

"We're training you in self-defense to give you confidence. Every girl should know how to defend herself. Haven't you ever studied history?"

"This is a, what, a feminist thing here?"

"This is a practical thing. But I assure you, the desert people have more reason to fear us than you have to fear them."

Something about the way he says it, or in his expression, makes me pause. Kama could say the same words, or Matriarch Ryo, and mean something entirely different. "What did you do, before you became a teacher?" I ask him.

"A Master teacher. And what I did before is none of your business. Keeping you alive, on the other hand, is my business, so you will be successful in the desert. You've missed a lot of training. Use that sap you collected on your foot tonight, and come tomorrow prepared for a full day's training."

I nod and limp off. The others have already been dismissed. I'm the last to leave, and he thinks today wasn't a "full" training day. I'm hot and tired, my foot is throbbing, my eyes and head ache, I'd give anything for a shower and all I'm going to get is a bowl-and-cloth rinse. Why am I even training for the desert game? I have no intention of joining it.

Because this is a desert planet, a white, hot, deadly planet, and I have things to do here before I can leave. Like it or not, I need to know how to survive here. I turn to look back. Teacher is standing at the edge of the training grounds, watching me. I raise my hand: "Thanks."

He bows his head. I bow from the waist. I think I see the corners of his lips twitch upwards, but I'm too far away to be sure.

Supper is nearly over by the time I've wiped the sweat and sand from my skin, applied the sap to my heel and wrapped a clean bandage around my foot and ankle. I collect a tray of food and head for our table. Kama, passing me as she leaves, "accidentally" knocks my tray, splattering my dinner across the floor. "Sorry," she says, to a chorus of smothered laughter.

She bends beside me as I try to wipe up the mess, picks up my fork and puts it on my tray. "Don't join the desert game," she warns me, her voice so low only I can hear it. She rises and walks off with the other fifteens, laughing.

Chapter Eleven

Thwack.

I open my eyes. The room is dark and quiet. I've been dreaming of the desert, of something dangerous coming for me, breathing heat. I'm sweating, even though the air is a comfortable temperature inside the dorm.

Thwack. The noise that woke me repeats itself. I listen hard, my heart pounding, but there's no sign of anyone in my room other than me.

Thwack. This time I see the sand hit my window. I get out of bed and walk over, keeping to the side, peeking out from behind the shutter. It's late at night, but even here in the desert it's light enough, thanks to Salaria's twin moons, to see the figure standing just outside my window. It bends down, grabbing another handful of sand. He straightens, arm rising—it's Norio. I step into sight before he throws his sand.

What's he doing here? It's got to be against some rule, for a guy to come to the girl's dorm in the night, even if he hasn't come inside. Yup, I'm right—he puts his finger across his mouth, warning me to silence.

I fold my hands together up beside my head like a pillow. I'm going back to bed. I didn't want to talk to him in the daytime, why would I want to at night?

The guy can't take a clear message, forget about a hint. He raises his arm, still holding the sand.

I shake my head. I don't want him getting into trouble. Also, who would believe I wasn't encouraging this idiotic behavior?

He points urgently to the door.

I shake my head again, feeling along the window frame for a latch or lever.

He shakes his head—the windows don't open.

I shrug, but before I can turn to go back to bed he raises his hand full of sand again. *Flick is* annoying twerp. I glare out the window.

He stands there, hand raised, sand ready to launch. And then he grins.

Despite myself, I laugh. I hold up five fingers and close the shutters.

Norio is waiting at the door when I come out. "What do you want?" I whisper. I'm not used to good-looking guys paying any attention to me.

"You have to come with me. I made a promise." He turns and starts walking away.

"What kind of promise? Norio!" I hiss. He keeps walking, so I have to follow.

"I promised to help you," he says when I catch up.

"Who did you promise?"

"I'll explain later. Did you have to wear white?" He's keeping us in the shadows of the buildings, pausing to look around before he moves between them.

"It's all they gave me. Believe me, I'm sick of white." I follow him exactly, keeping my head down. He's awfully nervous about getting caught. I don't know whether to be pleased he's taking such a risk to be with me, or suspicious. I settle on a combination of both.

"Where are we going?" We're almost at the gate. "Norio, where are you taking me?"

He slides up to the gate and knocks once, quietly. It opens without a sound. I stand my ground. I am not going out there at night. He waves frantically. I don't move.

"At least get out of the open," he whispers.

I move into the shadow of the wall. "I'm not going out there till you tell me what's going on."

"How's your foot?"

Chapter Eleven

I realize with surprise that I'm not limping. "It's okay," I say. "It's better."

"You see? Just trust me. I promise I'll explain."

I'm tempted. I want to just go with him. But it's just not in my nature. "Explain now."

"We have to get through the gate. It's never left open, someone will notice soon. I'll explain on the other side."

I need boots. Everyone else wears boots when they go into the desert, even Norio. Why wasn't I given any boots? Didn't they think I'd ever go outside the gate?

Norio walks through the open gate. It starts to close…

I race through just in time. "Okay, tell me," I say, panting, on the other side.

"You won't like it."

That tells me all I need to know. I feel sick, mostly at my own stupidity. "Tell him to open the gate. I'm going back." I was an idiot to trust Norio again. I'm usually not so easy to fool, but I just don't get bad vibes from him. Well, fooled twice is once too often. Twice too often, actually. Something flies past me. I swat it. I feel something crawling on my arm, and something else tickling my ear. "I'm going back now!"

"They're just night flyers." He swats one away from his own face. "Look, the sooner you step off the path into the desert, the quicker we'll get back."

"You want me to get bitten again?" I can't believe this guy.

"Or stung. It doesn't matter which, the venom is basically the same."

"I'm not stepping off this path!"

"Okay. I can wait."

"They come on the path? They come on the path at night?" I look down, turning around quickly to see the ground near my feet. Nothing. I run back to the gate, on my tiptoes, and hit it hard.

"Quiet!" Norio whispers. "You want to get us both in trouble?"

"I'm in trouble just being out here with you," I whisper back.

"Believe me, a scorpion has nothing on Matriarch Ryo."

I believe him, but that just means we have even more reason to go back now. "Why are you doing this to me?"

"So you'll be immune, you idiot. I'm not sure you're worth it, but I'm trying to keep you alive!"

That stops me. It hurts, the comment that I might not be worth it. There I was thinking he liked me. Why try to keep me alive if he doesn't? "I don't see you dragging the others out here. Why should you care about me?"

"I don't. Okay, I do. But I'm not out here risking my future because I like you. You're important somehow. That's all I've been told."

"Oh great! They told you about the vision. And you believe that?"

"What vision?"

"Nothing. Forget it."

"You believe in visions?"

"No! Stop it. You just want to distract me, to keep me out here. If you think this is such a good idea, how come you're wearing boots?"

He doesn't answer.

"Right. You want me to let myself get bitten, but you won't do it."

"There isn't enough serum for both of us."

"Why don't they just immunize all their kids? If there's a serum, they must have a vaccine. I want that."

"There isn't a vaccine. Not for Salarians. We're allergic to the venom. The first time, if we take the antidote right away, we'll likely survive. The second time, probably not."

"What do the desert people do? I've seen holos of them, they don't wear boots."

"How should I know about the desert people?" He doesn't look at me.

"Norio, what do they do? They must get bitten all the time."

"They're not Salarian."

That's right, they're a different race. Some northern Old Earth race. Squatters. And turns out they're better adapted to this planet than the rightful owners. That must really burn the Salarians. "So every girl who takes the desert game…"

"Is risking her life." He nods.

But he doesn't want me to risk my life. Or somebody doesn't want me to. Who? And why? He's already dodged that question twice, no use trying again. "What makes you think the serum will work on me?"

"Because it worked last time."

"You said it works the first time on Salarians."

"That's not this serum. This isn't an antidote, it works with the poison to build up your immunity."

"Where did you get it?"

"I think you can guess. If you tell anyone, I'm dead."

"If it doesn't work, I'm dead." But my mind is buzzing. It's not the antidote the Salarians use. It's not something that works on them…

Is Norio somehow connected to the desert people?

"We can't stay here. We can't be caught out here," he whispers urgently.

With this serum, he means. He's trusted me with his life. So why can't I trust him with mine?

Because two idiots don't make one intelligent human being.

Unless I'd be an idiot not to accept his help? I walk to the edge of the path. There's a movement in the sand, and another beside it. Scorpions. They come out at night to eat the night flyers, I remember. I raise my right foot in its flimsy open sandal. And lower it back onto the path. I can't do it.

"You can't die in the desert," Norio says. "You're important. I don't know why, but she says you are."

"She?"

"The woman who works for the Select." He sighs. "I know, it sounds crazy. But listen. She said if you refuse, I'm to give you something, but you have to sit down before I do. Just sit on the path. You're safe on the path."

I search his face, trying to figure out what this is, what trick he's up to now.

"Just sit down!" He hisses.

I look down. There's nothing moving on the path. Of course not, I know it's treated. I sit down. He crouches beside me.

"Here." He holds out an e-bud.

I don't make any move to take it. The last one wasn't exactly helpful. Also, I'm thinking. Norio's the person the woman from the O.U.B. meant, when she said she had someone at my grandmother's? But he's done nothing but hurt me! *Don't be proud, you'll need the help,* she said. I don't want this kind of help.

"Take it," Norio says impatiently, grabbing my hand and dropping it into my palm. "You've seen one of these before, haven't you? You put it in your ear."

"I know what to do with it."

"Then do it! We haven't got all night."

He'll probably keep me out here till I do, so I press it into my ear.

"Sleep with one eye open in the dragon's den."

I look at him, alarmed. "What's that supposed to mean?"

"I don't know. How would I know? It's the activating sentence. I didn't choose it. It's supposed to mean something to you."

"'Sleep with one eye open in the dragon's den?' That's supposed to mean something to me? What, you're telling me I'm in danger in my bedroom? I'm not in danger there. I'm in danger right here, with you, that's when I'm in—"

Agatha's voice floats into my head. "Kia, if someone is giving this to you, it means I can't reach you. It means you're in danger. Trust the person who activated this message. Do whatever he is asking

134

you to do. If you find the desert girl, do whatever you can to make her trust you, confide in you. We may need her help. That's all I can tell you now."

The second message. Just as infuriatingly vague as the first!

"What? Idaro, what is it?" Norio shakes my shoulder, peering into my face. "Are you alright?"

"I'm fine," I snap.

"Do you know what the message means?"

"You said the woman who works for the Select told you to say those words? And she's the one supplying the serum, getting you to bring me out here?" I don't wait for Norio to answer, I know I'm right. The O.U.B. must have developed the serum for their people. "Why don't they give the serum to the Salarians, and make them immune?"

"It doesn't work for us. We can't produce antibodies to the poison. The serum would just make us sick, or kill us. I don't know why it works for you. Maybe because you're only half Salarian."

Agatha must have told someone she trusted what to tell Norio to say when he gave me the e-bud. There's no other way he would know how to activate her message. If I trust Agatha, I have to trust Norio.

You can't die, Norio said. He's right, because if I die, Oghogho will die.

Before I can change my mind, I stand up, take a deep breath, and step off the path.

It happens almost at once. The scorpion stinger is worse than the snake's bite. I stumble back onto the path; it's all I can do not to scream. I taste blood in my mouth and let up on my bottom lip. Norio already has the serum out, pressing it to my lips. I swallow it convulsively, as though it will stop the fire in my right foot.

"Sit down. I have to take the stinger out," Norio whispers. I let him ease me to the ground, feel a light pulling at the center of the pain. I sit with my head bent as he bandages my right foot, fighting nausea, fighting the urge to faint, the ringing in my ears, the flashing pinpoints of light and a gathering darkness deeper than the night.

"It won't be as bad the second time?" I mumble, my words slurred. "Because I'm already becoming immune, right?"

"Actually, it'll probably be worse. But you are becoming immune."

"Okay…" I slump forward, barely aware of him lifting me, carrying me back to the gate. How will I explain another sprained ankle? I wonder, at the edge of consciousness.

The last thing I hear is the sound of the gate opening and Norio's voice coming from a distance: "Maybe you are worth it."

Chapter Twelve

I wake up in my bed the next morning. What a nightmare, I think. Then I move my foot.

When the pain recedes enough that I can breathe and all my energy isn't needed just to stop myself from screaming, I lie there thinking of every nasty word I know in all six languages I'm fluent in, and a couple more I'm still learning, and direct them all at this rotten planet.

The cactus sap I got yesterday is sitting on the table, but I would have to move to get it. Desert doctor, Teacher called it. D-doc, for short. I remember the immediate relief in my left foot as the sap numbed the site of the snakebite.

But I would have to move to get it. And then I'd have to remove the bandage, and touch the fiery, throbbing, agonizingly painful underside of my right foot to apply it, and wrap the bandage around my foot again... I close my eyes.

PING. I wake up slowly, trying to place the noise that intruded on my sleep. I was dreaming a dragon with a preference for barbeque was cooking my foot with his breath. It's well past rare, verging on medium-well, when the timer goes off again: PING.

No, that's not a cooking timer. It's my door. I frown at it. "I'm sick." I call out. Maybe.

My whole body feels hot. On Seraffa, that means fever. On Malem, if it weren't a fever, it would be a miracle. Here, it could just mean the air cooler is overtaxed and failing.

PING. I give up and wave my palm at the door. It hesitates a moment—my thinking is a little fuzzy—and opens. Kayo walks in with a tray of food. The smell alone is enough to make me want to throw up.

"I can't eat," I groan. "I'm sick."

"Really?"

I close my eyes.

"Because Master is furious with you. She told Kama to drag you out there if she had to."

I wave urgently at the door until it slides shut.

"You sure you don't want these?" Kayo starts in on the veg sticks.

"I'm sick," I say tersely, because even speaking increases the torture in my foot.

"You look kind of red."

"Fever." Doesn't she get it? I could be contagious. If we were on Malem, she'd be out the door already, not dawdling closer as if she's going to touch—

She puts her hand on my forehead. "You're really hot. Maybe I should call a medic?"

"No. I'll be okay. I get this sometimes." Like whenever I go into the desert with Norio. "I just need to sleep."

"You're sure?"

"Kayo, please. Just say... say I have a headache." I glance at the tray. "And leave the drinks."

"Okay," she says slowly. "Do you want a pain-deadener? I have some in my room."

I drift off to sleep after gulping down a capsule of relief, wondering why Kayo needs pain-blocks, but glad, in a totally selfish way, that she does.

When I return to training two days later, both Master and Teacher stand in front of me and berate me for, among other things, my lack of commitment, motivation and general intelligence (the last is untrue). Master tells me it would be suicide for me to participate in the desert game, which is only a week off. Teacher looks away when I glance at him.

"Do I still have to make sure she comes back alive?" Kama says.

Chapter Twelve

"Until I tell you I have changed my mind about anything, you may assume I have not." Master snaps. "Back to your exercises!"

I do the full round of push-ups with everyone else. Thanks to the D-doc cactus sap and two days' rest, my right foot looks normal. It's still tender, but I'm not limping. Which means no questions as to how the sprain in my left ankle migrated to my right foot. It also means I have no excuse not to exercise hard in this killing heat. Long before Master finally calls a break, I wish the scorpion sting had killed me.

When she pairs us off for the defensive wrestling, I'm paired with Kayo. I let her throw me as often as I throw her, and loosen my hold twice so she can escape it. Kayo beams. Master looks at me levelly and raises one eyebrow.

After lunch, I check out the desert survival stations I missed last time I was here, while Teacher was showing me the different cacti. I practice throwing Teacher's knife at targets in the sand, presumably to kill a snake or scorpion for food (gag), using thorn-needles to repair a tear in an old tent similar to the ones we'll be using, and using one of the compasses we'll each be given.

"You may each bring one extra thing with you," Master tells us at the end of the day. "Choose something that's an indication of your greatest skill or talent, that will make you valuable to others so you're chosen for a triad, and that will help the triad you form to survive the desert game. You have one week to make your choice before the desert game begins. Come to me if you need some suggestions."

A week? I didn't know it was only seven days off! I have to get away from here before they make me do this stupid game. Learning to survive the desert is one thing—for all I know the vision showed me in the desert—but forming a triad? I'm not here for that. I don't know why Agatha said to join her in the desert, but it's a big desert and it's pretty unlikely she'll just happen to be wherever the walk takes place. I don't even know if she's in the desert, for that matter. She might still be detained by the port authorities.

I wait till everyone's left but Master and Teacher. Just to make sure no suspicion falls on Teacher when I disappear, I approach Master.

"I need to go to Tokosha to get my one item. I left my bag in a locker at the spaceport before I came here," I tell her.

"What is it? Maybe you can pick up whatever it is here. You can't afford to miss any more training."

"I won't. I'll go now, or tomorrow right after training." I'm pretty sure they won't have a box of thief's tools lying around here.

"Tomorrow. I'll set it up."

Teacher clears his throat. "My son could escort her. He can make sure she doesn't get lost in the city."

"Good idea," Master says, and I'm stuck with an escort I don't want.

I get the best night's sleep I've had since I came here. No painful swelling of fresh bites on my feet, no poison fever, just the solid, deep sleep of exhaustion. When I wake up, I've come to a decision: I will not take the desert game. I don't care if Agatha or the O.U.B. want me to; if so, they haven't told me why. They haven't told me anything except lies. I came here to find my sister, and she's almost certainly working in a mine, and definitely not roaming the desert. I promised to teach Agatha Central Ang on the trip here, and I did. At least, as much as it's possible to teach Agatha a language, I did. The Select in Tokosha can help her now.

When I get to the city today, I'm going to find a way to escape my escort and look up the Select. If there was any truth to the story of reporting on Lady Celeste, she'll be able to tell me where to find her, and that will lead me to my sister. If not, I'll go to Philana's friends. They might share her feelings about slavery. I can't risk telling them who I really am, or why I'm here, but they might be willing to tell me more about what happens to the indentured servants who come here, where they go, where the records are kept, something that will help me find Oghogho.

One thing's certain: I am NOT going to let Norio talk me into getting a third sting of poison.

First I have to get through one last day of training. I roll out of bed, wishing it was already over.

Before we leave, Master makes us all sit in the sand for a pep-talk. I'm anxious to get away, I have to change out of this sweaty bodysuit, sponge myself off as best I can with a small bowl of water, get dressed, probably wait for my escort to arrive, and then for the air transit to pick us up...

She's handing out drinks. I sip the cactus milk, enjoying its slight sweetness and the way it makes me feel cooler and more alert already. They should export this stuff, if they didn't need for themselves as much as they can produce here. I must be getting stronger, because even before the drink I didn't feel as totally wiped as I did at first, brain-fried and body-fried from exercising in the scorching heat.

"Some of you," Master looks right at me, "are not as committed to this training as you should be. You're not giving it everything you've got. You're getting by." She says this like it's a swear word, as she looks around at all of us. I'm certain she looks longest at me.

Beside me, Kayo whispers, "Did you see? She looked right at me when she said that. I am trying, I swear! I'm just not athletic, I can't help that."

I nod, relieved that everyone else feels the way I do. Master would make a good Select.

"Getting by is not good enough. The desert won't let you get by. The desert will show you no mercy. You'll have to be alert, focused, every minute. One instant of inattention could kill you. And while your body and your instincts are focused on staying alive, on *keeping each other alive*," she stresses the last words, looking directly at Kama and me, "your mind should be reflecting on what your strengths and weaknesses are, what skills you have that you can count on, that you can offer to others. You'll have to learn to work as a team. Who's fast and sharp-eyed? Those are your scouts. Who's good with a knife? They are your hunters."

"Who's not good at anything? That's our dead weight," Kama mutters, glancing at Kayo and me.

Master stops. She looks at Kama. "Who's good at getting people to pull together, and who isn't? That's your potential problem."

"The desert will focus you; the self-reflection will sharpen your mind; all this is so you can get to know the girls you'll meet, quickly and thoroughly. Those are the girls you'll choose your triad from. This is the most important decision of your life. Who will you choose for your friends, your companions? Your youth triad will change you for the rest of your life.

"There is a reason we hold onto the desert game. It isn't to teach you to survive in the desert. Most of you will never go into the desert again. You'll choose a profession that takes you to the city, or to the stars, or to other planets." She doesn't look at me, but I know she included that because of my mother. Idaro's mother.

"It isn't only because we have to. You all know," she glances at me, "the daughters of mine-owning and gaming triads must by law participate in the desert game. How can we be permitted to gamble with the lives of others unless we are willing to gamble with our own? It's a just law, and we are proud each year when our fifteens honor it. But that's not why we do it."

Whoa, I think. The other girls are drinking in everything she's saying, but this stuns me. I tuck it away to think about later, and listen to the rest of her pep-talk.

"We send you into the desert to make you aware of the choices you're going to be making. To make you pay attention to those choices. To make you focus on them, on what they mean and what they will make you into.

Chapter Twelve

"There's a reason we send you out now, half-way through your teenage years, when you're still a child, on the verge of being a woman. We send you to the desert now because this is the time in your life when you will naturally be making those choices. Every young person on every human planet all through time has made similar choices on the verge of adulthood. Most of them haven't even been aware of making them. We want you to be aware. We want you to make the best decisions you can. The best decisions for you.

"You have to make those choices on your own. We have prepared you as best we can. Your teachers, your parents, your family, have taught you and loved you and guided you for fifteen years. Now it's up to you. Now we have to step aside, send you away from our influence, so you can choose for yourselves.

"Will you choose girls who are studious, earnest, reliable? Will you choose creative, artistic friends? Will you choose adventurers? Will you choose dishonorable friends, who will lead you down dangerous paths? Foolish or lazy friends who won't encourage you to become better than you are now? It's your choice. In many ways this is a more important choice than your adult triad. You will be forever changed by the triad you choose and the experiences you have in these next five years. Choose wisely."

As we get up to go, Master says, quietly, "Idaro."

I walk over to her.

"Join the desert game," she tells me. "Whether or not you plan to stay on Salaria, and even if you don't choose a triad. You are a person who makes a lot of choices. Participate in the game."

"Matriarch Ryo made me promise not to if I couldn't commit to it."

"She's right. But commit to the game, Idaro, not to what other people think the outcome of it should be."

I have something else I'm committed to, but I can't tell her that.

She nods, a brisk dip of her head. "Think about it, anyway. Teacher's son will meet you at the gate as soon as you're ready. I expect to see you at training tomorrow morning."

I bow and leave her.

I almost wish I was Salarian. Despite my initial cynicism, what she said about making choices makes sense. I've made decisions since I was fifteen, some of them made quickly and badly, and I can never take them back. And I made even worse choices when I was younger, choices that changed me forever, just like she said. That wouldn't happen here, where children are supervised more closely than I was. Kayo was sorry for me, I saw it in her face, when I told her I was raised by one set of parents. "What happens when one mother is away, or one of them is angry at you?" She asked. My father was distant, locked in his illness and his memories, all through my childhood, and my mother was angry, usually at me it seemed. I didn't tell Kayo that, but it made me wonder what it would be like to be Salarian. Even though they're prickly, and they live on the shady side of subtle, and they own slaves, none of which is excusable, I don't pity Kayo. Right now, I envy her.

Until I remember why she's risking her life in the desert game. It isn't because she wants to make new friends, or learn to make good choices—this isn't a good choice for someone like Kayo. It's because her family wants to be rich mine-owners, and she's just a pawn they have to forfeit to do that. Maybe she was loved, maybe she still is, but they're willing to gamble with her life, nonetheless. My mother didn't love me as much as I wish she had, but she didn't use me.

Norio is waiting for me at the gate. "Don't even talk to me," I tell him. "I'm waiting for someone, or I'd leave."

"Teacher's son?"

I look at him, taking that in. "Keeping you alive is my business, so you'll be successful in the desert," Teacher told me. And Norio's his son. Is Teacher the one supplying the serum, not the Select? Or maybe he's getting it from the Select? How much does he know, I wonder. Then, how much does Norio know?

"Alright, let's go," I say, as though it's no big surprise to me. I walk toward the gate.

We're alone in the aircar to the lightspeed, but Norio sits in the row behind me. As though the autopilot would know.

"You're here to make sure I come back," I say.

"Yup. But you'd have an escort anyway; Master has taken an interest in you. So it's better to have someone you can trust."

"That would be nice," I agree. We travel the rest of the way in silence.

When we get to the port, we have to push our way through a crowd of people trying to get on the westbound lightspeed. I wriggle between them, zig-zagging my way through the crowd, trying to lose Norio without intentionally appearing to be doing so, but he somehow manages to stay close. Then we're through the crowds on the platform and in the open port, with strategically-placed vids catching everything, and it's just as well I'm with someone from my grandmother's estate, since she's sponsored me.

Nevertheless I get nervous as we approach the lockers where I stashed my airbag. I make Norio wait at the end of the row of lockers. "You don't need to see my lock-code." I tell him, but it's actually the stuff I'm getting out I don't want him seeing. I wrap my "jewelry box" and gloves in one of the jumpsuits and jam it into the satchel I brought along, returning my spacebag with the rest of my things to the locker. I tap my handtab to the meter to pay for another week.

"Where to now?" he asks, not even suggesting we go straight back.

"Let's go eat. Not here, though. I'd like to see a little of Tokosha."

He grins. "You picked the right guide." I roll my eyes.

We take a short, packed aircar ride into the city. It stops at a busy intersection where the streets are lined with hotels and restaurants offering every kind of food imaginable. The streets are wide,

pedestrian only, so it doesn't feel crowded even with the aircar's load
of people spilling onto the already busy walkways. Norio leads me
to a chicken burger place. I check the menu and tap my order into
the table-com. Too bad I won't get to eat it. Norio's still ordering
when I excuse myself to go to the restroom. It's down a little hallway which also leads to the back door. I slip outside into an alley.
Too easy, really, and not a minute wasted. Now I just have to get
some distance between me and this restaurant. It's dark and quiet
and the heat wraps around me like a blanket as I jog to the end of
the alley.

Where Norio's leaning against the wall, waiting for me. "Ready
to eat?" he asks.

"Working up an appetite."

"Worked for me," he says cheerfully, following me around the
corner, back to the front door. "I'm starved." He holds the door
open so I can go in first.

"Want to tell me why you're trying to ditch me?" he asks, when
we're seated again. "I'm supposed to bring you back, but, you
know, it's not like you're male. You can leave any time. Matriarch
Ryo will let Customs know she's no longer sponsoring you."

"You could just not tell her."

"Okay, I won't tell her. I'll just come back alone. I think she'll
figure it out."

The boy arrives with our orders. Norio takes a big bite of his
chicken burger. "Or you could trust me," he mumbles around a
mouthful of food.

I take a bite of mine, thinking of what he said. *It's not like
you're male.* It strikes me, with shame, that I've never thought
about the males in this society. They're well-treated, they live,
for the most part, in wealth—at least as much as the females
they're related to do. The slaves are worked to death and the
desert people are outcasts, living in poverty in the desert;

compared to them, male Salarians have nothing to complain about. Do they? I glance at Norio, over my chicken burger. I don't have to go where they tell me, because I'm not male. But he does. Reckless behavior endangering a female: that's what he told me he'd be charged with if I died of a bite outside the gate with him. What's the punishment for that? I think I can guess, but I don't want to know. Sitting in the back seat of the aircar—every day, every minute it's shoved in his face that he isn't important, the poorest, or stupidest, or nastiest female is more valued than he will ever be. What's the difference between a slave and a pampered slave? What's the difference between being an outcast in the desert and being outcast in your own society? In your own family?

What will happen to Norio if I don't go back with him?

"I'll go back with you," I say. "But first I want to—"

"Let's go for a walk," Norio interrupts. "I'd like to show you the city, a little of it, at least." He touches the medallion at his neck, and nods when my eyes widen. Then he shrugs, letting me know he isn't happy about it, and stands up.

I think of everything we've said, how it would sound if someone overheard it as I chug down the last of my Lato. "I wasn't trying to ditch you," I say. "I just wanted to be alone for awhile. It's Kama. She makes things pretty unpleasant for me."

He nods at me, smiling. I've guessed right. "Don't take it personally. She makes things unpleasant for everyone."

"They all like her. They agree with her. She's their leader."

"They don't like her. They'd just rather laugh with her than have her laughing at them.

I stand up. That's enough for whatever device they made him wear. Like I care about Kama's opinion of me. "Let's forget them," I say. "I'd like to see your city."

Chapter Thirteen

The paved streets are warm under my sandals, but still cooler than the desert sand. Days are long here. The sun has descended behind the tall white buildings, but is still bright enough to bathe the city in daylight: a softer glow than it casts from above. The buildings aren't squared off; they curve and appear to flow into one another, in layered tiers accentuated by the darkened windows. They cast odd shadows on the ground, shading the walkways and yet not blocking the air flow, but rather strengthening it with clever wind-tunnels, so the breeze fans us as we walk. There must be hidden fans filling the streets with cooled air as well, because this is the most comfortable outside temperature I've felt on this planet. Everywhere I look, the city is clean and white and light. A splash of color on the buildings, to highlight the white, is all it would need to be stunningly beautiful.

The area around the aircar stop is primarily a hotel and restaurant district. The street is full of tourists, wearing every kind of outfit imaginable. Or at least, parts of their home-world's outfits. Even in this artificially-cooled district, people are sweating in the unaccustomed heat, and clothing has been pared down to the essentials. If the Salarians didn't have strict minimum-clothing laws, I bet most of these people would go naked.

As we walk, we pass street after street of architecturally-striking buildings, their fronts lit up with holos depicting smiling people enjoying every kind of game available on this wealthy planet known across the universe for its love of gaming. I recognize half-a-dozen games I saw at the Nightgames on Seraffa, including Salarian Die. I don't even want to go down those streets, but they're crazy popular with the laughing tourists.

Norio must sense my aversion, because he guides us to a quieter area. We pass a park and walk through it on firm sand pathways past sandstone statues of famous Salarians and cacti that have been trained to grow into exotic shapes. It's quiet and soothing after the busy tourist section. We stop to sit on a bench. The awkwardness of male-female relations here makes it difficult to talk with any kind of familiarity, but sitting beside Norio, feeling his arm on the back of the bench brushing my shoulders, the heat of his thigh close to mine, gives me a queasy but excited feeling in the pit of my stomach. Neither of us says anything. Neither of us moves. Finally I look up into his beautiful Salarian eyes, and he leans down and kisses me.

I have never been kissed before. It is a serious oversight, because this kiss gives me the softest, warmest, thrilling-but-absolutely-safe feeling I have ever had. When our lips part I still sit with my head tilted up to his, glowing foolishly as he smiles down at me. I can still feel his sun-warmed lips on mine, taste the clean desert wind on them. We don't move, just sit there looking at each other, until we hear people approaching on the path.

Norio jumps up, reminding me that we are on Salaria. I'm about to say something to put him at ease, but he places his finger on his lips and winks at me, reminding me that we can be heard. This time, I love being tied to him by a shared secret.

We haven't been walking long when we come to Prophet's Avenue. "Let's turn down this street," Norio says, touching the medallion again.

There are only four buildings on Prophet's Avenue—the O.U.B. are barely a presence here. The door to Number One opens when we stop in front of it. Norio nods at my questioning look.

"You may speak freely here," the porter says as soon as the door closes behind us. "Whoever is listening will only hear silence while you are inside."

"I want to talk to the Select I came to Salaria with," I say at once. This should be news to Norio, but he doesn't look startled. Alone, I'd like to add, but it would sound bad after the park.

"Come in and sit down. Would you like some tea?"

Norio accepts, but my interpreter's training kicks in: never let someone you don't know serve you food or drink. "I've just had a Lato, thanks," I say politely.

She leads us to a small sitting room off the grand hall, where I imagine formal events take place. This small room is for private negotiations mediated by the Select. Its intended use reminds me this is not a social event, despite what she may be trying to make it seem like. The porter leaves, and a Select walks in. We wait in silence for our tea. I try to distract myself, looking around. The chairs are comfortable, relaxing, very good quality, but there are no unnecessary pieces of furniture, and no decorations on the functional tables or the walls. The O.U.B. does not flaunt its wealth; what it does flaunt is its neutrality. Decorations make a statement; so do bare white walls and comfortable seating.

"The Select you want is not here," this Select says when our tea has finally been served and we three are alone.

"She's still in detention?"

"No, of course not. The Select are never detained." She takes a sip of tea. "I believe you received a message from her?"

Norio nods. So he's in their confidence. That explains why he's been allowed to stay. I can talk freely, then.

"If she's not here, where is she? When can I talk to her?"

The Select hesitates. "At the moment, she is... out of touch with us."

Agatha is 'out of touch'? She means they don't know where she is. How could they lose contact with her? The only way a Select could disappear—

I remember the swamp on Malem, and the body of the Select I found in it. But this isn't Malem. Salaria is part of the Alliance, they're not opposed to the O.U.B. I close my eyes. The vision. I don't want to know what it was, now. Surely not that.

"I am not telling you the Select is dead. Her transmitter is still live."

For the first time I appreciate their skill, which has saved me from asking a question I couldn't bear to put into words. But how can Agatha be missing? "Have you looked for her?"

"That would be… awkward. It would involve admitting we do not know where she is, or what she is up to. The Salarians already distrust her because of her race. Our admission might put her in danger."

I almost laugh, as much in relief as at the thought that they don't know what Agatha's up to. There probably isn't a single other Select they could say that about.

"We think she may be in the desert."

"But you don't even know that for sure?" I'm rubbing it in a little. I try to look innocent.

"Her locator has been disabled."

I pause a beat. A transmitter, and now a locator. They are telling me things not commonly known about the Select. Not that it comes as a great surprise that their people would be monitored while they're watching and recording everyone else, but the Select wouldn't be telling me this without a reason.

Are they going to insist on putting a transmitter and a locator into me—is that why the Select let me know about them? Likely she thinks it would reassure me, but what it means is I won't be able to abandon my mission for them and search for my sister, and when I find her, it'll be a lot more difficult setting her free.

Right now, I'm more concerned about Agatha, though. She wouldn't break contact for no reason. Whatever she's up to, she's probably okay. When she decides to use it, she's quite good with the mental control of a Select.

In fact, I doubt she's missing at all. I wouldn't be surprised if she disabled the locator herself and went AWOL, following one of her stupid intuitions. Suddenly it makes sense that Agatha is missing. This is the kind of trouble she just can't resist. Whatever's going on, she'll be in the thick of it, I have no doubt, hopelessly over her head in a complicated language she doesn't understand a word of.

"But why would she go into the desert?" I ask. I know she thinks they're her people, but she's a Select. She's dedicated to the Order. It's not like she's going to run off and live in the desert.

Why aren't we looking into their quality of life and writing up a report about them? I remember her asking when we stood at the portal looking at scenes of the desert people. "You sent her to talk to the desert people?" I glance at Norio. He probably already knows I came here for a reason, what's one more secret between us? "That's not our mission. We weren't sent here to interfere with the desert people." I deliberately use the word 'interfere', to provoke her, but she doesn't answer. I'm going to have to say it all. She'd better be right about Norio's device not working here.

"We did not send her to talk to the desert people." Nothing about the Select's expressionless face indicates she's annoyed, but I have no doubt that it's not there by intention. "We deal with the ruling government of a planet, no one else."

I wait. No more is volunteered. "We were sent here to report on the living conditions of an indentured servant, Lady Celeste, on behalf of her family. You must have been told."

"That is no longer the Select's task here."

No longer her task? Says who? It doesn't matter, I only know I have to get the location of Lady Celeste from this woman, even if it means stretching the truth a little. I banish that thought at once and tell the Select, speaking calmly but firmly like they do: "I agreed to go to the mine where Lady Celeste is paying off her debt, to report whether she's being treated according to the interplanetary laws on the treatment of foreign servants. Until the Adept who sent me tells me otherwise, I must do it."

I want to go on, to insist, but I stop myself. I have my orders, I tell myself, hoping that's what will show on my face. They mustn't suspect there's anything more involved than obedience to the Adept who sent me here, and maybe some wounded pride at not being kept updated. It isn't anything personal.

She observes me silently for a moment. What can she see in my face? I'm about to conjugate some verbs, just to be on the safe side, when she says, "You are aware of the group, Out of the Desert?"

I frown. "They set off an explosion the day before we arrived. Are you saying the Select has gone to meet with them?" Without speaking a word of their language, I'm thinking. Just like Agatha.

"The Select was on her way to the mine where we believe Lady Celeste was interned. We know she boarded the lightspeed, and that it stopped at the platform before the mine she was going to. It did not continue because of the incident. Shortly after she left the lightspeed, her locator stopped broadcasting. We believe the Select may have gone to convince the desert people to publicly disassociate themselves with Out of the Desert, to condemn their actions, and the recent deaths."

"The deaths?"

"You haven't heard." She takes a breath. "There was a second explosion, in another mine."

"But they called it in, like the last one? They got everyone out?"

"The call came in too late, or else the explosion went off prematurely. The casualties were extensive."

"What mine?" I can barely form the words. I know why she took that breath. I know what she's going to tell me. *Oghogho!* I think. "What mine?" I whisper. I don't want to know. I have to know.

"The mine the Select was on her way to visit, where we believe Lady Celeste was working. It happened last night. We do not have a list of casualties yet."

It *is* personal. I can't hide it, I can't even try. I bend, holding my gut, gritting my teeth to keep silent.

"Idaro, what is it?" Norio asks. He rushes to my side, but doesn't touch me, a well-trained Salarian male. Instead, he kneels beside my chair. "Tell me Idaro, please."

I can't answer. If I make a noise, any noise at all, it'll all come out, and I'll be howling on the floor. *Oghogho isn't dead, she isn't dead, she isn't dead,* I tell myself over and over.

"The Select was not harmed by the explosion," this Select says. "It went off early, and the lightspeed stopped short of the mine. We will let you know as soon as we hear from her, but we have no reason to fear for her safety." Her voice comforts me, reassures me...

I look up. "Get... out...!"

"Very well," she says. "If you do not want comfort, stop groveling for it."

"What mine?" I force myself to straighten, to look at her. I don't care what she sees in my face. I am beyond caring about that now.

"What good will it do you to know?"

"What mine!"

"The Kicho-Ryo-Tomiko Number Four mine. You'll find it on any newsreel covering the explosion." She looks me in the eyes. I realize what she's about to do too late to look away. "You will not go there. I will let you know the minute we hear whether Lady Celeste has been harmed," she says in the authoritative voice of command.

I nod, unable to speak.

"Give me your handtab. I'll have a direct line wired into it."

I hand it over reluctantly.

"I'd like you to wear a locator." When I don't answer, she says, "I need to have your agreement."

I know that. I let her see it in my face. I can't go to the Number Four mine, no one is immune to the direct order of a Select. But I won't agree to wear a locator, and she can't legally place one inside me without my freely-given consent. She doesn't want it out of concern for me, anyway; she thinks I'll lead her to Agatha.

"Very well." She stands. "Your handtab will be returned shortly. Leave as soon as you have it, before they begin to wonder about the silence from Norio's device." She pauses at the door. "I was not aware you knew Lady Celeste personally. I promise I will get in touch with you as soon as I know about her."

All of them, I want to say. A woman named Oghogho, I really want to say. But Lady Celeste is the only one I can admit to. At least I'll know when the death list has been released.

&

"Tokosha's a beautiful city," Norio says as soon as we're back outside on Prophet's Avenue. He looks apologetic and gestures toward the medallion he wears round his neck.

I don't want to talk. I can barely make myself walk. But someone is listening to us, and will be reporting to the dragon. "It is. I'm enjoying our walk." I force myself to sound cheerful. I don't quite make it, especially when I choke a little on the word 'enjoying'. I clear my throat.

"Sorry for not talking much. I'm tired. Training for the desert game all day, it's ...tiring." I don't have the energy to think of a second adjective. I am tired. Bone-weary, heart-weary. I've done my best. I showed up. And it wasn't enough.

Norio takes my hand. A remarkable gesture for a male to initiate. "Don't be discouraged," he says quietly. "I know how you feel. But... nothing's certain. Things might turn out better than you think now. I know you'll be successful... in the desert game." I know what he's really trying to say, and I'm grateful, even if I can't bring myself to believe him. I can't bring myself to hope. I hoped my father's fever spells would stop, I hoped my mother's surgery would heal her. Hope is too hard.

But Norio's hand encircling mine is a comfort. He continues to hold my hand, and I hold onto his.

When we reach the nearest westbound lightspeed station, I'm surprised by the size of the crowd waiting to board. I remember there was a crowd heading west earlier, too, when we arrived. I didn't look closely then, but now I notice they're all adults, and mostly men.

"They're probably going to help clear out the mine we saw on the newsreel, where the explosion occurred yesterday," Norio says. "It's one of our triad's mines. It's on this line, three stops further after ours. The 'reel said there'd be shifts night and day, trying to find any…"

"Survivors," I say, when he stops awkwardly.

Three stops further, I'm thinking. I look at Norio. He gives his head a quick, sharp shake.

He's right, it would be foolish. Dangerous. *If I hear so much as a whisper,* Matriarch Ryo warned me, meaning, of my being interested or concerned about the slaves who work the mines. But I have to go. I know I could learn something if I was there, if I could talk to the rescue organizers, the reporters. Someone *has* to know who's died and who hasn't.

If I go, Norio will go. He'd never let me go alone. Besides, he's not supposed to return without me. And if we both go, at the least he'll be guilty of exposing a female to danger; at worst, my enquiries will make Grandmother Ryo suspect him of being sympathetic to the slaves, too. If only he wasn't wearing that stupid medallion.

I hear the distant *Whoosh!* that indicates the lightspeed is approaching, and move a step back with everyone else to avoid the rush of hot air when it arrives. I'm still unnerved by the sight of it whipping toward us in a blur of motion, and its sudden complete stop to settle on the ground beside the platform.

The sides roll up. A crowd of men, filthy from clearing rubble from the caved-in mine, swarm out. Their eyes are dull, their faces slack with exhaustion—or despair?

Chapter Thirteen

Is anyone alive? I want to shout, but then what? Name my sister? Even if I could, how would these men know the names of the slaves and Salarian supervisors they're digging out of the rubble?

It's suddenly real, the death, the bodies. My knees cave, Norio has to grab me to stop me from falling to the ground. The Salarians waiting on the platform to replace these tired men swarm around us, pushing their way onto the lightspeed. Norio pulls me back, out of their way.

I stumble, regain my footing, resist him. "No, we have to get on, we have to—"

"We'll catch the next one."

"No, this one, I'm okay." I struggle forward, but the crowd of men leaving pushes me back, I've lost the momentum of those getting on, they've moved ahead of us, and Norio is urging me back, too, placing himself between me and the open door, "You need to rest, sit down, there'll be another lightspeed soon—"

BOOM!

Norio throws out his arms, shielding me, as the blast knocks us backward, onto the ground. We fall together in what seems like slow motion, deafened by the noise, as the explosion burns upward, a roar of heat and light against the evening sky.

The men ahead of us, leaving the lightspeed, have taken the brunt of the explosion. My sight is partially obstructed by Norio's body covering mine, but I see people behind him being flung left and right. Sparks fall around us, burning my arms and legs, while the platform under me shudders with the impact of pieces of the aircar and soft, wet pieces of human bodies....

I scream, the sound muted by the after-effects of the explosion. I try to get up, to scramble away, but my arms and legs won't obey me. A siren sounds, far away. People rush toward us, lean over us, but there are so many of us, so many bodies. Their clean, white city is streaked with red...

"Are you alright?" "Are you hurt?" Their voices, like the siren, are distant and dim.

No, I think. It's not them, it's my ears. I open my mouth. The men on the lightspeed, I try to say, but nothing comes out.

"Don't try to talk, medics are coming." A woman kneels beside me, takes my hand, tears on her cheeks. Why is she crying? I'm okay, don't cry, I want to tell her. Norio should tell her. Norio's still half-covering me. Why doesn't Norio reassure her?

The woman stands up, letting the medic through. Gently the medic moves Norio aside, but doesn't examine him. *Norio,* I struggle to say. *Norio...*

The medic straps a cuff around my neck, forcing my head straight. I stare up, into the sun, and close my eyes. I can feel the medic's hands on me, checking for damage. Why isn't she doing the same for Norio?

"Move her," she says, motioning with her arm at the edge of my sight. "Gently, carefully." I feel people taking hold of my arms, my legs, their arms sliding under me, all distant, dulled. I lie in their arms, limp and numb to their touch, as they lift me onto a waiting stretcher and carry me away from the station.

Norio...

Chapter Fourteen

I wake up in bed in a med center.

"Where's Norio?" I croak, as soon as someone comes in, but he's just a nurse, he wasn't there. "There were too many bodies," he tells me. "They haven't all been identified yet."

"He was with me, on top of me…" shielding me, his arms flung out to protect my face, the second he heard the explosion.

The nurse shrugs regretfully. He takes out his notebud. "Tell me his name. I'll see what I can find out."

"Norio—" I don't know his last name. "From the Kicho-Ryo-Tomiko triad, a grandson, about my age."

"I'll look into it," he says. "How are you feeling? Is there any pain?" He checks the IV monitor.

"He saved my life." I start to cry. Streaks of red against white, blood on the ground, burning embers falling from the sky, bodies… I close my eyes to shut out the images, but they're still there, faces I don't remember seeing, their mouths wide in screams I don't remember hearing. "Stop it! Please make it stop!" I cry, twisting in my bed.

I feel a prick my arm. The images begin to fade.

～

There's relief, at first, when they put me to sleep, but the effect wears off. In the darkness I'm vulnerable; in sleep I have no defense against the images in my brain. There's nothing to distract me then, only the terrible pull back to the explosion, a roaring vacuum dragging me back there time and again. The brilliant light and deafening noise of the explosion, the terrified faces and mouths open in silent screams, and Norio's body, Norio's arms flung out, Norio still and silent on top of me. I wake up screaming, I wake up sobbing, and always my head is pounding, a concussion headache even the meds can't alleviate.

"It'll go away," they say. "A few days, a week at most. You're almost healed, nothing broken. A miracle, really." They look at me like I should be grateful, like I don't think about the real victims, the broken people they're trying to put back together in the other rooms. The real victims are always there, in their eyes, when they look at me and tell me I'm lucky.

The next time I wake up the Select from Prophet's Avenue is sitting beside my bed. "Your sister is alive," she tells me. "She wasn't in the mine that morning. At the last moment they changed her to a later shift, to fill in for someone who was ill."

I look at her, my thoughts sluggish.

"She's fine," she repeats. "She's been transferred to another mine. All the indentured servants who weren't… in the mine at the time, have been moved somewhere else."

She waits for me to say something. How does she know about my sister? She didn't the last time we spoke. And who else knows now?

"What mine?" I finally ask. It'll have to be one of my grandmother's. If she owned the mine that was bombed, she owned the slaves working it.

"I don't know. Only the records of those who are dead have been released. Unfortunately, Lady Celeste was killed in the explosion. Your mission here is over."

Lost and found and lost, I think. But Oghogho is alive. Not one of the real victims, either. It's Lady Celeste who is now part of the blood, red streaks on white, another of the silent screamers in my nightmares. I remember her at the gambling table, her face tense as she threw the die. I remember her face when she lost.

A splash of color to highlight the white would make this city beautiful, I thought, when Norio was showing me around Tokosha. A splash of red?

"They are going to round up all the desert people who live in Tokosha. They're passing a bill to rescind their citizenship right now. They mean to question them, find the perpetrators."

I don't answer. I don't know why she's telling me this, but I don't want to know what 'round up' means, what 'question' means. I feel my heart pounding.

"The Select you came here with. You know her? You care about her?" this Select asks. She waits for me to respond.

I nod, slowly, fighting a rising panic. The people I care for die. "Norio is dead?" My throat tightens.

"The boy who was with you. Yes. I am sorry."

I close my eyes.

"He was an unusual boy. An idealist. He wanted the desert people granted full rights as citizens, he wanted the indentured servants to have their debts forgiven, he wanted males to have equal rights to females. He saw a better world than he lived in."

Did he see the bombs they would use to achieve that world? I wonder. Out of the Desert, they call themselves. Did he know they would walk out of the desert on a path of blood?

"The Select is not dead. She has gone to the desert, as we thought. She sent us a message. And one for you."

I open my eyes. The Select holds out an e-bud for me.

I have enough noises in my head: the roar of the explosion, the sounds and sights that followed... I swallow, trying to push them away. I don't want another voice inside my head.

The desert will kill her. "Does she know there are scorpions? And snakes?"

"She is with the desert people. She's one of them. She was born with natural antibodies in her blood."

Blood. I turn my head away, fighting down the swell of panic. The medic told me there would be triggers—words, sounds, sights, scents that would remind me, take me back there. Streaks of red blood on the white platform… No. I am here, in a room in the med center. I am safe, I tell the terror that howls inside me.

"I'll leave it here," she says, placing the e-bud on the table beside my bed. She puts her hand on my forehead, cool and firm, drawing my gaze back to her. "Rest. Heal," she says with calm authority. I feel the fear receding. My eyelids are getting heavy.

"You are safe, you are needed, you are loved."

Looking into her eyes, I believe it. For the first time since the explosion, the sounds are quieted, the images gone. The pounding in my head diminishes. A soothing calm fills me.

"Sleep and be well," she says. My eyes flutter shut, heavy with sleep.

I awake much later. Someone else is in my room. I glance sideways and freeze. Sitting in my chair, white hair, white skin, white shirt and pants…

"Ahh, ahh…!" I recoil, the cry of fear strangled in my tight throat.

She looks up, green eyes staring at me.

I scream!

"Stop, stop!" she whispers urgently as I cringe away from her. "I just want to talk to you. Please!"

I stop screaming just as a nurse runs in. "What is it, what hurts?" He looks at me, my back pressed against the railing of the bed as far as I can get from the desert girl in the chair by my bed. His face darkens in a scowl.

"I haven't touched her," Green-eyes protests.

Her fear alleviates mine. I breathe. *Trigger,* I tell myself. I'm here in the med center, I'm safe.

The nurse grabs the girl, lifts her roughly from the chair. "Out! You've done enough here, you and your kind!"

"No!" It comes out a squawk. "No, it… it was a nightmare. She hasn't done anything," I protest weakly.

"She's done enough. Come to see your handiwork, have you?" he demands, shaking the girl.

"I didn't do this," she says fiercely.

"Let her go. She hasn't done anything. I had a nightmare." My voice is shaking, it's all I can do not to weep. I can't help it. The nurse's rage terrifies me. Leave, I think at him, go away. My whole body is trembling. Anger is dangerous. Anger kills. *Go away!*

The nurse lets go of the desert girl. She falls back against the chair. "Five minutes," he growls at her. "And if I see you here again, you'll look like the patient in the next room." He glances at me, the lucky one, cowering in my bed, and stalks out of the room.

I edge back to the middle of the bed, not too close to her, and try to relax. Every part of my body hurts. My head throbs so fiercely I wish I could lose consciousness. I want to close my eyes, but I'm afraid to.

"My name is Nyah," the desert girl says, her voice little more than a whisper.

I don't say anything. It would hurt too much to speak, and she already knows who I am or she wouldn't be here.

"I'm sorry about this."

"You didn't do it." I speak without moving a single unnecessary muscle. The stabbing agony in my head is beginning to recede. I wish I had asked the nurse for something, but it wasn't very good timing for that.

"I didn't stop it." Her voice is so low it takes a second to register, and then another to realize I heard her right. She could have stopped it?

I open my eyes a fraction wider. "You know them? The Out of the Desert group, you know who they are?"

"My sister Malah knows them."

Malah? Thin-lips? The girl who tried to drown her in the Water Game is her sister? I remember that girl. "She's one of them," I say. It's not a question. Thin-lips, Malah, would join that group. She would lead a group like that.

"I can't say that."

"I saw you gain your freedom." I saw your sister try to push you under so she would win, is what I'm telling her.

"Did you win?" Her eyes flash.

"I didn't bet. I wasn't there by choice." Nevertheless I flush, feeling the shame I felt then for being there at all, for saying nothing, just doing my job, interpreting, while her and her sisters' imminent deaths were made into a game of sport. She sees my flush, and nods.

"My people have been persecuted for generations, left to starve in the desert of an indecently wealthy planet. They used us, Malah and me, they would have happily watched us die for their sport. They have killed others, countless others of us, just for trying to survive. If Malah... Whatever Malah does, it isn't half as bad as what's been done to her, to our people."

"This is as bad." I close my eyes. My head pounds. I can't endure much longer. I need a pain block now.

"Can I get you something?"

"Better not."

"You see? That's how it is for us. We can't even ask a nurse for medications, we can't help our family, our friends..."

"I'm not your friend."

She is silent. I lie still, my eyes closed, thinking about what she said, and getting angry.

"Norio is dead. A boy who tried to help you, who wanted to improve things for your people. He died in the explosion."

"I knew him. He was a good person." Her voice is sad.

I open my eyes. She's looking down at her hands, twisting them in her lap. I believe her, that she didn't do this, that she didn't want it. Any more than I wanted her to drown, when I didn't say anything at the Salarian Nightgames. I couldn't have stopped it, but I didn't object, either.

"The government's going to rescind your citizenship, all the desert people in Tokosha. They're going to round you up and question all of you until they find the radicals."

She doesn't answer. I don't know if I should have told her, even if, as I now suspect, that's why the Select told me. I want them stopped. But I saw her in the water, her and her sister, struggling for their lives. That should be stopped, too. Just not this way. Not Out Of the Desert's way. There are too many wrongs here, and no clear right.

I close my eyes again. Even the low lighting in my room is too much for my headache. I'll have to tell her to leave soon, so I can call the nurse to bring pain killers.

"You have to go home." She says this in a low, urgent voice that startles me into opening my eyes and staring at her. "Back to the planet you came from," she says, while I'm wondering what she means by the word *home*.

"I am Salarian." Does she know? I can't let anyone even suspect. "My mother was—"

"That doesn't matter. You have to leave. You're in danger here."

Her words, her intensity, cause a surge of panic. I struggle to force it back. "I can't. I can't leave yet."

"I can't protect you, then."

I stare at her. "What are you saying?"

"Nothing. I'm saying you should leave, that's all."

"The explosion on the lightspeed…" I stop. She didn't mean that. I have to be wrong. Please, let me be wrong. "It was meant for me?"

She stands up. "Leave Salaria. You're in danger here."

❧

If I was having panic attacks before, they're nothing to what I feel now. I'm the cause of all those deaths? I was the target? How did they know where I'd be? And why? Why would they target me? Idaro's not even a full Salarian. Why not the Ruling Triad? Or members of their council? Idara's nobody here, even her grandmother isn't willing to claim her. Why would anyone want me d—

I can't say it. I can't think it. I grip my call cuff with such force I can hear the alarm all the way down the hall at the nurse's station.

"Pain block," I gasp, when he arrives on the run. "Sleep med."

"Which?" He looks exasperated. *Heart attack*, he was probably thinking. Even more likely, *the desert girl did something to her.* He wouldn't have run for a headache, is what he's thinking now.

"Both!"

He raises an eyebrow.

"I should have let you throw her out!" Then I wince, tears forming at the corners of my eyes, because shouting kills my concussion headache.

He nods. "I'll get them right away. And you don't have to worry about any more visitors of her kind upsetting you. They won't get past me."

‿๑

I dream I am racing across the desert, being chased by Agatha. She is wearing the white top and loose pants of a desert woman, and she holds a small explosive above her head, ready to lob it at me. The sand burns my feet in my light sandals as I dig them into it, trying to run faster. I am sobbing, *why? Why are you doing this?* But Agatha, silently intent, does not answer. I glance behind. She's gaining on me! Then she morphs into Malah, grinning fiercely as she throws the hand explosive. My legs tremble with the effort of running in the heat as the grenade whizzes toward me. In the air, it transforms into a writhing mass of snakes and scorpions just before it hits, knocking me down. I thrash wildly in the burning sand, slapping and scratching at my face, my arms and legs and body, trying to pull the biting, stinging, poisonous creatures off of me!

I wake, sweating and whimpering with terror, pulling at the bed sheet twisted around me. Even when the dream has faded, the horror lingers. Why do they hate me? Why do they want me dead? What have I done, what has Idaro done, or her mother, to make them want her dead? I can imagine the dragon being on someone's hate list, but I'm nothing to her, she won't even acknowledge me as family. No one even knows Idaro's related to Ryo, so no one would think they'd hurt her by hurting me.

The only people who think I matter at all are the O.U.B., because of a stupid vision, and they don't exactly advertise those. They didn't even tell their people here about it—the Select who talked to me at the port had no idea why I had come, she told me I was on my own here. The Select I met with on Prophet's Avenue didn't know my real identity either, when I spoke to her two days ago—just two days ago? Norio was alive two days ago? I blink hard.

She considered me of little importance then; she didn't offer me refuge on Prophet's Avenue, she didn't press me when I refused the implant. But today she knew my real identity, she told me about my sister. Even so, she still thinks I'm unimportant, she didn't offer me her protection, or suggest I go to Prophet's Avenue.

Am I being paranoid? Is it possible for a Select to be so wrong? Nyah never said I was the target of the bomb, she said it was dangerous here. She thinks I'm Idaro, nothing she said indicates otherwise, at least nothing I remember. I must have misinterpreted what she said. I *am* being paranoid. Triggers, I think, breathing deeply. I'm wrong. They are not coming after me.

I reach for a drink, and there's the e-bud the Select left, with Agatha's message, sitting on my bedside table beside the glass of water. Then I hear Master's voice, arguing with the nurse as they walk down the hall toward my room. I whip the e-bud into my ear and close my eyes.

"I've come to take you back with me, Idaro," Master's voice announces as they enter my room. I keep my eyes closed and focus on breathing, slow and deep like I'm asleep, and on not rubbing my ear, which is itching from the e-bud inside it.

"She was given a pain block and a sleep tab an hour ago. You won't wake her for another half hour, at least."

"A sleep tab in the daytime?"

"She was upset. She's suffering from post-traumatic stress. Let her sleep. Come back in half an hour."

I hear Master *huff*, she's used to being the one who gives the orders. "You told me she was all right."

"Nothing's broken. She's been shaken up and badly bruised, but by some miracle no bones snapped. A concussion headache that we've been treating. Should be gone in another day or so."

"Good. Here are some clothes for her. Have her dressed when I return," Master says. I wait until I hear two pairs of footsteps leave my room and retreat down the hallway.

What I don't hear, is anything from the e-bud. There's no one to say the activating sentence. I need to hear Agatha's message and dispose of it within the next half-hour. The Select knew I couldn't access the message without it. She must have given me the sentence, somehow. She wouldn't leave it lying around in print, someone else might find it. Bad enough the e-bud was sitting there in plain sight. But it's small, and she tucked it behind my glass. I think back to her visit, trying to remember anything she said that sounded out of place. "Sleep and heal," something like that, just before I fell asleep. I try saying it, and a few variations. Nothing. It was just a command to make me sleep deeply. As it did.

What else did she say? There was something, just before that. Two or three phrases. They sounded a bit odd, but I was upset, I thought she was reassuring me. What were they?

You are safe, that was the first one. Then something like, you are valued? No, needed. *You are needed.* This has to be the activating sentence, the Select would never willingly say that to me. And one more. It reminded me of Agatha when she said it, something Agatha would say. *You are loved.* That's it.

"You are safe, you are needed, you are loved," I whisper. I feel a little foolish saying that out loud to myself, I'm glad no one can hear m—

"Kia," Agatha's voice fills my mind. "I've learned the Salarians are planning some kind of retaliation against the desert people for what Out of the Desert has done. I've gone to meet with their leader, Sven, to try to talk him into a meeting with the Ruling Triad of Tokosha, before that happens. I need you to interpret for me. Join the girl's desert game, I will find you there. Also, I told the Select here about the vision, and who you really are, so she will protect you until you can get to me. Be careful. You can trust Teacher and his son, Norio."

I dig the e-bud out of my ear and watch it melt. I didn't trust Norio. I told him I hated him. I open my mouth and fire comes out; that's what I told Grandmother Ryo. I hope he knew—I have to believe he knew how I felt when he kissed me. And that nothing I said to him before that mattered.

I drop the melted plastic into the recycler beside my bed. No puzzles this time. Agatha trusted the Select to get it to me unread. She must be sure of this Select. Except that the Select didn't mention the vision or offer me protection, when she visited me.

So what now? I still have to find my sister, only now I don't have an excuse to look for her. At least I still have the satchel with my box of tools inside; I was carrying it across my body, the strap over my left shoulder and the satchel under my right arm, and it came that way to the med center with me. So if I find her, I might be able to free her.

Agatha believes she can convince the rulers of the desert people and the Salarian Ruling Triad to settle their differences peacefully. Right now, I'm not sure I care if the Salarians retaliate. Did the desert people care about Norio? Or about Lady Celeste and the other slaves they killed? I know what they wanted; they wanted to create an interplanetary incident. Something that would make their situation more than just an in-planet strife. Something that would force the O.U.B. to call in the Interplanetary Council to sort things out. So they killed a lot of helpless foreign slaves—Lady Celeste probably *was* a target—and Agatha and Oghogho and I almost got killed in the fallout.

I don't want to believe Agatha and I were targets, too, but it's possible.

I don't care about any of them anymore. All I want to do is find Oghogho and leave.

The nurse comes running into my room. "Get up! Get up and get dressed!" He throws a clean Salarian dress at me. Down the hall, I hear Master's voice approaching.

Chapter Fifteen

"His cremation was yesterday," Master tells me when I ask about Norio. "It was good of you to mention him when the city guards took down your testimony about the explosion. He was awarded a posthumous ACSF." She glances at me. "A medal for an Act of Courage which Saved a Female. I'm sure it was a comfort to his father."

I'm not so sure. I think Teacher would rather have his son than a medal, and I'm certain Norio would rather have had equal status than acknowledgement that he put a female first. He didn't. He put me first. He expected something of me, and now he has a right to expect it, just like Philana does. I've taken something from both of them. You can't take without giving back. Only I have nothing to give them.

Just show up, Agatha said. Here I am, getting everyone killed. Hey, you're welcome, think nothing of it. Glad to show up and do my part.

Up ahead I spot a lightspeed station. I stop cold. Master takes a few more steps, notices I'm not with her, and looks back.

"What?" she asks.

"I... I can't..." I stare at the station, fighting down panic. It wins. I can't move a single step closer.

"Look at all the guards." Master says with steely patience. "No one's getting near there with an ex... with anything. It's perfectly safe."

I continue to stare past her, seeing the platform railings hurtle into the air, pieces of metal and body parts flying outward, red streaks against the white platform. It's all I can do not to scream as I stand there shaking, gasping for breath, my face wet with tears, heart pounding, head aching...

"Stop it!" Master says. She puts her hands on my shoulders, holding them tight, her body shielding me. "The platform is perfectly normal," she says. "There are guards watching, keeping it safe. I know you've been through something awful, but you are not in danger right now. Right this minute, there is nothing to fear. Is there?"

I look around. The platform is clear, only a few people walking about. A dozen or so guards look around reassuringly at the people on the platform as they wait for the lightspeed, three women, a father with his son, an old man, a group of girls laughing together. No one out of the ordinary.

I calm down. "No," I answer Master. Nothing to fear. I'm not convinced, though, and when the lightspeed torpedoes in I have to close my eyes and cover my ears. Master does something unusual then: she pulls me against her, wraps her arms around me, and holds me tight. It's not something I'd have thought was in her repertoire, it's certainly not in mine, and I know we look weird, but I don't want her to stop. Until the lightspeed settles and nothing happens except the sides slide up. We have to run for it then, because we were standing at the very edge of the platform. A couple of the girls give me strange looks until Master gives them a Master look, which makes them turn away at once. The rest of the trip is uneventful. Okay, heart-thumpingly, head-poundingly, terrifyingly uneventful, but I get through it without any more embarrassing tears or even more embarrassing hugs.

"The desert game starts in two days," Master tells me as we walk toward the gate to the estate. "I expect to see you at training tomorrow morning."

"The desert game?" I stop walking. Is she crazy? Are they all crazy? "You're going through with it? People are setting off explosions and you're sending fifteen-year-old girls out alone into the desert?"

If I wasn't still rattled I wouldn't have said it quite like that. She's made excuses for me because of what's happened, but this is too much. I can see on her face that there will be no more hugs. She pulls herself straighter, offended to her Salarian core, and says, "We will not let them frighten us."

"They frighten me!"

"Yes. I expect you to get over it."

As though avoiding death is a weakness, not a sign of intelligence. I take a breath and draw myself up straight. "I regret to disappoint you, but I'm not participating in the desert game, Master." Agatha will just have to find another interpreter.

I watch Master walk stiffly away across the sand, before I enter the fifteens' dormitory. My room is just as I left it. I fling the satchel onto the floor and fall into bed exhausted.

I wake from another dream of being chased in the desert, scorpions, snakes, and desert people throwing explosives all mixed together in a prolonged nightmare. It's light out when I open my eyes, too early for breakfast. My heart is still pounding from the dream, but my headache's gone, as the medic promised. I dress, put in my sun lenses, and go to the main mansion.

"Matriarch Ryo is at her breakfast meeting," Ichiro tells me at the door.

"I'll wait."

He leads me through the foyer this time, to a room near the end of the hall. There's a round table and several chairs in the middle of the room, as well as arm chairs and settees around low tables against the walls. Tinted windows, probably one-way glass, face out onto the estate.

"You'll be here a while," Ichiro says. "I'll bring you something to eat."

He returns almost immediately—this must be a morning room, near the kitchens, for casual meals—with a full plate, eggs and fried cactus slices, bread and jam, juice and a steaming Lato.

"Thanks, I'm good for the whole day, now," I joke. Not entirely a joke. I'm hoping he'll leave me alone for a while.

"I'll let you know when Matriarch Ryo is available to see you. There's a restroom across the hall," he says, as if he's read my mind. I thank him again and dig into my breakfast. Now that my headache's gone, I'm starving.

I give him enough time to leave the hall before I tiptoe to the door and peek out. No one in sight. Every door along the wide hall is shut, with no windows into the rooms behind them. That works in my favor—I won't be seen creeping down the hall, checking the rooms out—but it also works against me, because I won't know if anyone's inside until I open the door, unless I hear them talking. I take a breath and walk carefully to the first closed door. Holding my empty juice glass to the door, I put my ear against it. Nothing. I take a deep breath, open the door, and peek inside the room. Empty. I let out my breath and move on to the next door.

The fourth room is as silent as the first three, but this door is palm-secured. I hesitate. It could be the room I'm looking for, or it could be where they're meeting, and just be sound-sealed. You can't enter a locked room and call it an accident. I bend down and listen through my glass again. Silence.

I look up and down the hall once more, and pull from my pocket one of the gloves I brought with me. I slip the thin plastic card hidden inside it into my palm. As I hold it, it warms to body temperature, becoming more and more flexible, until it follows the contours of my palm. I stretch it gently to cover my fingers and thumb as well. The swirl of tiny wires encased within it mimics the pattern of lines in a human hand. I rub my thumb lightly over it, adjusting the wires delicately to cover my own palm and fingertip signature, to fool the infra-red sensor beside the door.

Preparing a palm override can't be rushed. One tiny wire out of place and the sensor will recognize an error and sound the alarm.

So even though I'm sweating and every second feels like forever, I take my time before I press my hand against the sensor. The door slides open onto an empty office. I say a quick prayer of gratitude as I enter and close the door behind me.

My luck holds, the comp is running. I guess my grandmother thinks a guard at the gate, a man at the mansion's door, and a palm sensor on the room door is enough security for her office. Now I just have to hope the new device I picked up from Sodum before I left works. I take it out of my pocket and put it in my mouth, positioning my tongue and lips as he showed me. It worked in his back room when I practiced on his comp, but for all I know he'd fiddled with the voice recognition system to fool customers. The thought makes me pause. I've never wondered if he's trained any other thieves. Correction: in my case, ex-thief.

I take a breath—enough stalling—and say, through the voice distort, "mine four, personnel." Instead of the 'unauthorized voice' message and shut-down I'm braced for, a list of Salarian male names comes up, along with their positions, salary, and so on.

"Mine four, indentured servants," I try. A little note appears to tell me there's no page matching that. I try a few more words, keeping a careful count, before I blurt out in frustration, "mine four slaves!" To my surprise a list of names appears. I should have guessed, Grandmother Ryo is not one to mince words, I think as I scroll through them. There it is: Oghogho Ugiagbe. Followed by a note dated yesterday: "Moved to Number Two mine." I smile.

"Erase last six commands from memory," I say. The comp returns to the page that was showing when I entered. I put the voice override back in my pocket, and walk to the door. Opening it a crack, I check the hall. Empty. I leave, making sure I hear the door lock behind me, and head back to the morning room. All I have to do now is go to mine two, find Oghogho, free her, and get us both to Prophet's Avenue, where I will threaten to expose this whole operation and everything else I know about the O.U.B. if they don't find a way to smuggle Oghogho and me back to Seraffa.

I'm almost at the morning room when a door across the hall opens. A Salarian woman about my grandmother's age comes out. She looks up, sees me, and stops.

I bow. It's almost automatic now. "I'm looking for the restroom, Matriarch," I say.

She gestures toward the room Ichiro pointed out, on her side of the hall.

"Thank you." I head toward it. Unfortunately, she's going there, too.

"You are Idaro, the girl Ryo says is her second cousin's daughter," she says as she sweeps through the door ahead of me.

"Yes, I'm Idaro."

"You're here to join the desert game?"

"I have been considering it," I hedge politely. "It was gracious of Matriarch Ryo to let me train with the fifteens."

"Wasn't it? An unusual trait for her, graciousness."

"I am grateful for it." I bow again.

I hear her lingering at the sand scrub afterwards, but I stay in my cubicle until she leaves.

So now I know which room the meeting's in. They may only be talking about the running of the estate. But what if they're discussing the desert game, calling it off or something? They can't all be as blind to the danger as Master. They might talk about desert people in the city being rounded up, too. Did they catch Nyah, or did I warn her in time?

My grandmother's lost a mine, and she's not the forgiving sort. She's a big player on this planet. People know who she is, the customs director, the Select, everyone I talk to. If they've found out anything about who's behind these explosions, my bet is she'll know about it. I tiptoe back to the room the woman came out of, place the rim of my glass against the door and bend to listen.

"It's settled then." My grandmother's voice. Calm. She could be talking about putting another row of globe cacti in the gardens next year, or the death of every suspected member of Out of the Desert.

"What about our daughters?" A younger voice, one of the fifteens' mothers. Good.

"We're moving the location of the desert game. I'll let the other four estates know in the morning, just before they leave. We'll launch a drone overhead to watch for anything suspicious, and each estate will post a unit of guards four or five miles from the camp. Far enough not to interfere in the desert game, close enough to monitor the drone and prevent an attack, if that becomes necessary. The fifteens will be perfectly safe, except for the normal dangers, of course."

"I don't know. Wouldn't it be better to wait until after the girls get back?"

Wait? Wait for what? I press my ear harder against the glass.

"And let the savages who destroyed our mine and killed our workers and their supervisors, think they can attack us with impunity?" Grandmother's voice is fire and ice. No one else speaks for a few minutes.

I wish I'd arrived earlier. They're planning something, but that's not much to go on. I need to know what they intend to do, but judging from the silence in the room, the meeting might be ending. I'm about to leave when a cool voice, the voice of the woman I met in the hall earlier, says, "It's possible, Ryo, that the people in the desert aren't involved. That the explosions are the work of only a small militant group from among those in our city, and most of them have been detained. Only a few escaped the round-up. Do we really want to get the whole race involved?"

"They *are* all involved. Those who live in Tokosha already have their citizenship, they have nothing to complain about. You think they'd risk their status to gain what? What they've already got, the rights of a citizen? No, I believe 'Out of the Desert', as they call themselves, is for those who are still in the desert, and don't want to earn their way out honestly. They want to steal their citizenship from us with threats and explosives, just like they stole their way onto our planet. Well, I won't stand by and let them. Will you?"

"A little dramatic, as usual, Ryo." There's a brief silence, then she continues, "We all have family who died in the mine or on the light-speed platform. I won't oppose you. But wait a week. The fifteens will have left their camp then, to walk out through the desert. They won't be a sitting target if the desert people do find their drop-off camp, and if we have to get them out, at least they will have formed their triads."

There are murmurs of agreement, rustling movements. I hear Ryo agree. When I hear a chair scrape backward I slip the glass into my pocket and run, on tiptoes, across the hall. I wave the door to the morning room closed behind me just as I hear the door across the hall open.

I sit down, stunned. They're planning some kind of reprisal in the desert, against the desert people. By themselves, not the Salarian government. Just how powerful *is* my grandmother?

She doesn't think the desert people in the city are setting off the explosions. I don't think she's right, but I wish she was. Despite everything, I liked Nyah. I don't believe she was involved in the explosion that killed Norio. Then I remember: Agatha's out there in the desert, talking to the leader of the desert people. Exactly where a retaliation is most likely to take place.

What can I do? I don't even know where Agatha is, I have no way of warning her.

But I know who can. I jump up. I'll tell the Select on Prophet's Avenue what I heard.

Chapter Fifteen

I get to the door and stop.

What exactly did I hear? They blame the desert people for the explosions. We all know that. They don't want them to get away with it. Well, nobody does. Even if the Select agrees my grandmother's triad is planning something, I have no proof, no details, nothing she can act on.

Even if I had heard something definite, the Select here wouldn't do anything about it. The O.U.B.'s position is clear: It's a planetary issue. They know about the explosions set off by Out of the Desert, and they haven't even made a statement condemning them. I grit my teeth. The militants have killed off-worlders, including Lady Celeste. What do they have to do before the Interplanetary Council intervenes, kill a Select?

I sit down again, slowly. They have to kill a Select. But Out of the Desert can't bomb their own people. No one would back them then, they'd lose whatever sympathy they have among their people. So they bomb the mine of the most powerful triad on Salaria, outside the government. Where a wealthy, well-connected off-worlder happens to be working. On the day a Select is going to inspect it. The pieces fall into place horrifyingly. Agatha escaped because her train was stopped after the bomb went off early. Because someone called it in. Just like the other time. Who's calling them in? And why?

I think of Nyah, and her complicated love for her sister, Malah.

If I can figure out who the leak is, they can, but it probably doesn't matter now. They've done what they intended to do. Out of the Desert *wants* a reprisal. Their own people are the target now, as well as Agatha. She's their insurance if the Interplanetary Alliance doesn't care about the desert people who're going to die. Killing a Select or an Adept means an automatic intervention by the Alliance.

Agatha is still their target and my grandmother is their bomb.

The militants probably justify it as a 'calculated loss'. I've read about such things in history books, but I've never come face-to-face with it before. I want to throw up.

I have to do something to stop them.

What if I told Matriarch Ryo she was being used? Right. That would go down well. And I could add that I eavesdropped on her meeting, and I know Agatha's with the desert people because I'm actually working with the O.U.B., and I've been fooling her all along about the reason I'm here. She'd probably drop me into the desert strapped to the bomb.

The door to the morning room slides open. The dragon walks in.

"Hello, Grandmother Ryo," I gasp, bowing.

"Matriarch," she snaps. "There is no family bond between us. Why are you here?"

For a moment I'm speechless, then I do the only thing I can do. I bow once more and say, "I've come to tell you I'm joining the desert game."

༄

We are taken by aircar deep into the desert. Kama looks fiercely ec-static, the others chat and fall silent in varying degrees of excitement and nervousness. Kayo has the sense to look depressed. I sit by myself, holding my backpack like a kid with a security blanket. Scorpions, snakes, scorching hot sun, I'll be lucky to get out of this desert alive, let alone do what I've come for. At least I'm wearing boots like eve-ryone else, soft inside, lightweight, wrapping my feet up to mid-calf with a breathable plastic blend that's tough enough to repel any snake or scorpion that comes near me. Our tents are made of the same stuff, and soaked with the repellent that keeps the creatures away.

Through the window I see a small camp of armed guards below us. I frown down at them as we fly over. A few minutes later I notice an airborne drone in the sky, monitoring the area around our site. According to Master's last words to us before we took off, it's staying there, "until the threat posed by the desert people has been dealt with"—as chilling a phrase as I've ever heard. The other fifteens cheer when she says it, though.

The aircar sets down in the middle of a circle drawn in the sand, about sixty feet across. This area was sprayed just before dawn, in preparation for our arrival. Two other groups of girls are already there, setting up their tents. We scramble to get our supplies out of the aircar and set up our tents before the last two aircars arrive, bringing in the fifteens from two more estates. Those who set up their tents earliest will be closer to the center of the circle, and farther away from the untreated sand. Not that we get to avoid the desert sands; we'll have to forage for food and cactus milk, and eventually we'll have to walk out through it. But in the meantime the center of the circle is prime real estate.

I'm one of the last out. I thought it was hot in the city, and even hotter on the estate, but this—I've never imagined heat like this. Drawing a breath is like breathing in fire. I stand beside the aircar, swaying, imagining myself curling up right here like a singed leaf.

"Move it," the pilot shouts out at me, "unless you want to get burned by the exhaust when I lift off."

It's possible to make this air hotter? I pick up my pack and my tent and stagger off to stake my claim like the others, only I pop my tent near the edge of the circle. As soon as it opens, the thin solar panels on the top catch the sun. I duck inside and seal it, roll out my sleepsack and fall onto it, gasping. In a short while the panels start producing energy. I hear a soft hum as the air cooler kicks in. Slowly it revives me. I stretch out in my tent, glad I've got it to myself. The other girls are sleeping two to a tent, just like in the fifteens' dorm. I wonder who decided that—Matriarch Ryo, to keep me isolated, or Teacher, to give me some freedom to act?

While I'm waiting, I go through the backpack Teacher handed me as I boarded the aircar. A spare bodysuit, waterbottle, hand-light for nighttime which we're not allowed to use till we leave the circle. A flare in case I get lost, fire-lighters, a small roll of tent-seal, a spile to tap the liquid from cacti, a tightly-rolled sheet of the same flexible material the tents and my boots are made of, a plastic bottle of repellant to treat enough sand to sleep on if I get caught without my tent or the sheet, and a compass. The compass is programmed to steer us toward the nearest estate, whichever way we go, and it has a locator. I thought they'd inject a locator in our arms, in case any of us couldn't make it out, but I guess they don't want the failures back.

I reach inside for my "personal item," and pull out my disguised jewelry box—Teacher must have wondered about that. A lot of good it will do me in a desert, but I don't expect to get back to the estate to pick it up, and I can't risk it being discovered in my absence. At the bottom of the pack is my knife in its sheath. That's a surprise. Did Kama get hers back, too, or did Teacher slip mine in my pack when Master wasn't looking? I reach in to see if there's anything else, and pull out a little vial of liquid. I recognize it from the ones Norio gave me to drink after getting stung or bitten. The memory makes my throat tighten up. I swallow a couple of times. Teacher must have put it in, in case I get stung again.

I repack everything, rolling my knife in my extra bodysuit and putting it on top, in case I need it quickly. Never leave the circle without your pack, Master warned us several times. I drop it near the opening of my tent.

"Hey, stupid."

I take a deep breath. Only a little longer, I tell myself as I stand up and unseal my tent.

"You were supposed to set up closer inside the circle, like we did," Kama says. "Now the other girls have all arrived, it's too late.

You're stuck here sleeping right beside the untreated sand." She laughs.

"I guess you should have told me, since you can't go back without me."

"Oh, I'm not worried about that. Nobody said I had to bring you back alive."

That's actually a good comeback. I'd laugh if she didn't look like she meant it. She's the least of my problems, though. "So, where's the caf?" I ask, like I did the first time we met. I step out, seal my tent, and brush past her.

Looking around, I estimate there are fifty to sixty girls here for the game. At some point we'll have to start integrating, getting to know girls from the other estates so we can choose our triads, but for now each group has built its own campsite. I head for the Kicho-Ryo-Tomiko estate's site.

After we've eaten the lunch they sent with us—thick slices of cactus-dough bread with chicken and boiled eggs, stuff that won't last beyond today in the heat of the desert—Kama divides us up. One group to find and harvest Salarian cacti, another to get wood cactus in case we need a fire, a third group with bottles for collecting sweetwater cactus milk, and the fourth group to dig latrines outside the circle. Guess which group she puts me into? Two days, max, I tell myself, as I grab a shovel and head out with Kayo and another girl, Akako, who I thought was among Kama's favorites. Apparently not any more.

It's hot, hard work. Dig in; take a breath of fiery air; lift and toss aside the shovelful of sand, which, as I dig deeper, becomes a coarser, heavier dirt; drop the empty spade into the dirt and lean, gasping, against the handle; dig in again. I'm sweating like crazy, my hands slipping on the handle. The hole reaches the top of my boots, a little over twelve inches deep. Akako climbs out to get some repellant to treat the sand, while Kayo and I keep digging.

I eye the sand around the hole as our boots get lower and lower. What's taking Akako so long?

"Kayo, I can't find my repel," Akako calls. "I must've left it in my tent. Do you have yours?"

Kayo sighs and drops her shovel with relief, then glances at me guiltily. "Go ahead, get it," I smile, more like a grimace of heat exhaustion. "This is almost done, anyway."

"Where'd you leave the packs?" I hear her ask Akako as I go back to digging.

"Over there. You get the repel, I'll sort the tent." I hear Akako drag the outhouse tent to the edge of the hole. One more shovelful and I'm calling it done. It's deep enough, above my knees now—

I feel a scatter of loose sand fall from the top of the hole against my bare leg, some of it trickling down into my boot. Something pinches, scrabbling up my leg, then an unmistakable sting.

"Scorpion!" I scream, swiping at the back of my knee, sending it flying to the side of the hole as I scramble out.

"Where?" Akako says, looking into the hole. Looking from the side the dirt came falling down from. "Are you alright?"

I collapse onto the folded tent as the sting blossoms into a burning pain, spreading out along my leg.

"Did you get stung?" Akako asks, widening her eyes in horror.

Kayo comes running with the repellent, takes one look at me and races back for her pack.

"Go get help," I gasp to Akako. "Go… find someone to… help carry me back." I pant for breath, fighting the pain in my leg and the panic that rises so easily in me now. "Go…"

"Run, Akako!" Kayo cries, dropping to her knees on the tenting and emptying her pack beside me. "I've got the antidote here, and a pain block, and some sap from the D-doc cactus, and—"

"Is she gone?" My voice is nearly inaudible. Breathe, I order myself. "Kayo, she's gone?"

"Yes, she's getting help. Here, drink this." She holds her single dose of antidote up to me.

"Not that. Get my pack."

"There isn't time, Idaro. Drink it!" She pushes the tube against my lips. I turn my head aside.

"That won't help me. Get my pack, Kayo. Quick!"

She hesitates a moment, staring at me, then leaps up, dropping the tube of antidote, and runs to get my pack.

The pain is spreading, cramping my foot, locking my knee and burning up my thigh. Am I too late? Norio always made me drink it at once.

Kayo is back, opening my backpack as she kneels beside me, reaching inside. "What am I looking for?"

"Vial. Little vial, with stopper," I pant. I'm dizzy, nauseous. I hear Akako's voice, and two others, through a blur of pain. They're coming back. "Hurry, Kayo," I urge, just as she exclaims, "Got it!"

She holds it to my mouth. I gulp it down. "Hide it," I whisper, "before they come."

So dizzy. Darkness folds over me, the air swirling, round and round my head spins.

Too late, I drank it too late…

Chapter Sixteen

I dream of fire as the poison burns through me. I see Agatha surrounded by desert people, and they're all burning. They're facing away from me, standing in the center of a circle of flames crackling as loud as explosives. Agatha turns her head to look at me. Her face twists as the fire devours her, her mouth open in a silent scream—

"Ahhhh!"

Kayo shakes me awake. I open my eyes to see her peering down at me in the dark. I'm panting, half-way to sobbing, still shaken by the nightmare. Agatha! I have to warn Agatha! I nearly say it out loud. I thought I had time. I heard Ryo agree to hold off her attack for a week. But the next time I'm bitten—and now I know there will be a next time, Kama and her followers will see to that—I won't have any serum. I have to warn Agatha while I still can.

"How long have I been out?"

Kayo gives a shaky laugh. "For *hours*. It's the middle of the night."

I try to sit up, but pain and weakness, and Kayo's hands on my shoulders as she tells me, "No, lie down, you need to rest," prevent me. I close my eyes, just breathing for a minute. I'll try again in a minute. I have to get up.

I grit my teeth and sit up. Kayo squeaks a protest which is nothing compared to the protest my body makes. I'll never make it outside my tent, let alone into the desert. I can't even stand up. I glance at Kayo's anxious face.

"Do you trust me, Kayo?"

She looks at me, confused. "Yes?" she asks, as if she's unsure what the right answer is.

I feel a pang. Kayo just wants to do the right thing, to please everyone. And I'm about to lead her as far from everyone's approval as she could possibly get. I hate myself for using her. I take a breath and do it anyway.

"I have to go out into the desert and set off a flare. I need your help."

"But you're okay! You're getting better!" She leans closer, scared, her words tumbling out. "You are, aren't you? I thought you were going to die. Kama said you wouldn't, she told me not to bother staying with you, not to waste any D-doc juice on your bite. But you're awake now. You're sitting up. No one dies after they start getting better! No one!"

"I am better. Really. It's not for me." I don't want to overturn her entire faith in how the world works.

"I'm glad I used my D-doc juice." She says fiercely. "It was mine to use, I tapped the cactus so I'd have an extra one. It was my personal thing."

"Thank you Kayo. I mean it. But why do you care?"

"Because you're nice to me." Her voice is low, embarrassed. Not many people are nice to her. "And my brother said we should help you."

"Your brother?" I get a sick feeling. "Norio?"

Her shoulders droop.

"I'm sorry, Kayo. He was a good guy. He helped me a lot." I'm thinking of the serum, and taking me out in the desert, which I didn't appreciate at the time. I'm trying hard not to think of his kiss. Then I remember she doesn't know about any of that. She does know he saved my life, which is a bit more than "helping me".

"He was good." She nods to herself, then straightens. "I'll help you now. Tell me what to do."

My turn to hesitate. The drone will see the flare. Will its camera also capture who set it off? I can't let her take the blame if things turn out badly. A wave of nausea and dizziness hits me. I close my eyes and lie down again.

Kayo stands up. "Tell me what to do," she says again.

"Take my flare out of my pack." I think a minute. "And my flexsheet. Wrap it around you, cover your head, too, so the drone won't be able to identify you. Don't look up." I stop, catching my breath. When I open my eyes, Kayo is looking at me.

"Do you want the guards to come?"

"No."

"They will, if they see a flare and don't know who set it off, or why."

I'm about to say I'll tell them it was me, when she says, "Unless... Unless they see me coming out of your tent on my way back to my own, and because it's night I can't see in the dark, so I stumble and drop my knapsack, and everything falls out..." She grins. I'm grinning too, because this is all just like Kayo and I can guess where she's going with it.

"And when I pick up the flare, it just accidentally goes off, and I look straight up at it and say clearly, 'Oh no!'" Kayo giggles.

Even though I feel awful and my leg is in agony, I can't help laughing. "Kayo, that's brilliant," I tell her.

She stands up and picks up her pack just like that, without a single question.

Guilt makes me ask her, "Don't you want to know why?"

"Is there time?"

"Not really."

"Okay then." She walks to the tent door, stops. "I'm not really brilliant, no one but you has ever said that to me. But I do know this: things aren't right here, aren't fair. Norio wanted to change that, and I trust Norio. And he trusted you." She opens the tent and slips out, closing it behind her.

I'm thinking she changed her mind when I hear a *thump*, and some scrabbling around, and then a clear "Oh, no!" as the outside gets suddenly lighter.

Then there's a lot of scrabbling, and Kama's voice, saying "Kayo, what did you do now?" followed by words like *clumsy* and *idiot* and *right outside my tent!* I hear Kayo apologizing and Akako saying, "Oh, just drop it, Kama, it was an accident," and after another minute or two everything quiets down again.

There's nothing I can do now except lie in my sleepsack worrying. Will Agatha see the flare and know what it means? Will she and the desert people, if they come, notice the guards posted a mile off in the desert to protect us? What if the flare leads her right into them? What if that's what makes my nightmare come true? I toss and turn and finally fall asleep as the sky is brightening.

The next day I mostly lie in my tent putting D-doc on the sting and trying to sleep. Kayo brings me some food. Akako pushes her head through my tent flap and withdraws it quickly when I yell, "Get out!" Kama comes in later and ignores me when I order her to leave.

"The antidote only works once," she tells me. "If you get stung or bitten again, you'll probably die."

"Is that what you're hoping?" I ask. "Because I wonder what Master will say if you go back without me? Especially if one of your *friends* is nearby when I happen to get stung?"

"You're being stupid," she says. "Just give up and ask the guards to send you back. What do you care about the desert game? You're not even from here."

"Go pick cactus or something, and let me sleep."

Not that I can when my leg hurts every time I move. By nighttime it's feeling better, though, and I finally get some sleep.

When I wake up the next morning I notice three things: 1. The back of my leg is itchy from my bum to my heel. Crazy, insane, scratch-till-you-bleed itchy. 2. Nothing hurts. I stand up, scratch, jump on both legs, scratch some more, jump on what should be my bad leg, scratch it again, poke the spot where I was stung, scratch vigorously. No pain at all. 3. I don't hear anything outside my tent.

I dress quickly and open my tent to look outside. The heat burns my face and makes me squint, even with sunlenses. A few girls are sitting at their campsite, no one at ours. No one walking around the circle, chatting with friends. Then I remember: today everyone was supposed to make five groups, mixing girls from different estates, to go on a trial walk in the desert. They'll be gone all day. How could I sleep in and miss a treat like that, I wonder?

I stroll across to the nearest campsite and introduce myself to the girl sitting there. She tells me her name is Kenja. So how did you escape today's hike, I'm about to ask, but she looks dejected so I ask if she's okay instead.

"You must be one of the Kicho-Ryo-Tomiko extras."

"Extras?"

"The extra girl, after the groups were chosen." I'm looking blank, so she says, "Each estate left behind one girl to guard the campsite. Only yours left two, because one got stung yesterday. You, I guess."

I look out at the vast, flat, white desert, completely empty in all directions. "Guard it from what, exactly?"

"We've got stuff here. Stuff that could save our lives when the desert game really begins." She gives me a look. I've received that look before, usually when some rule needed breaking, so I know enough to just agree with her and suggest we go meet the other extras. No deal. She's at her post and won't be distracted from her duty. I am reminded why I've never gotten along all that well with my peers, but I go check out the others, anyway.

Kayo's sitting with them. She jumps up, grinning, when she sees me, and introduces me to the three girls sitting with her: Chowa, Erity and Lien. I tell them Kenja won't be joining us. Erity laughs, but the others look guilty. We eat a lunch of dried cactus and eggs.

They left a pan in the sun an hour ago, and when they drop the eggs in it, the things sizzle and fry in one second flat. On Seraffa we say, 'hot enough to fry an egg,' but this is the first place I've actually seen it done. I'm going to end up like the eggs if I stay outside much longer, so after lunch I return to my tent to cool off, ignoring Kenja's meaningful frown as I pass her.

"Hey, everyone!" Kenja's voice wakes me from a semi-stupor. By the time I get my sunlenses in and stumble outside, Chowa, Erity, Lien, and Kayo are all standing around her, staring out into the empty desert to the north. I shade my eyes—it's late afternoon and the sun has fallen, but it's still blindingly bright out here—and look where Kenja points. Nothing. I'd go back to my tent except that the other three are obviously watching something out there.

I look again. Is that a tiny white speck bobbing on the white sand? It could be a reflection of the sun or a gust of wind stirring the sand, but something makes me keep looking. Is it getting bigger? The bobbing is steady, rhythmic, like… like someone walking.

"How many, you think?" Chowa asks, her voice hushed.

"Only one," Kenja says at the same time as Lien says, "One."

I feel them relax beside me, but I'm thinking, carrying what? It only takes one person to lob an explosive. What was it that other matriarch in the meeting I overheard called us? A 'sitting target'.

I stare at the speck, which has now become a small blob approaching us. We should get out of here. We should run, now! I feel panic rising through me, my heart speeding, my throat constricting. Red streaks on the white sand! A mirage? A premonition?

The figure is getting closer. I stare, frozen in place like I'm trapped in a nightmare, at the approaching figure. Only I'm awake. It's going to happen again! I open my mouth to shout a warning—

Blue. Is that a tiny swatch of blue? Blue and white? Walking toward me out of the desert as cool as if she was coming to tea?

"It's okay," I stammer. "I think I know who it is. You wait here while I go talk to her."

Erity makes a move to come with me, so I add, "If I'm wrong, and she kills me, you'll have to find the others and warn them."

The truth is, right at this moment I'm more likely to kill her for going off and leaving me on my own, but at least she saw the flare, and came in time for me to warn her about Matriarch Ryo's plans. I don't want these girls to overhear that, though. I head out toward Agatha, walking fast so I can reach her before they recognize the habit she's wearing.

"What are you doing out here alone?" I shout as soon as I'm far enough from the circle of tents not to be heard, and close enough that Agatha will. Her head is bent, she's exhausted, imagine walking in this heat in a Select's gown! I'm not sympathetic, though, I'm furious. "Why did you go off like that? I had no idea where you were, you could have been dead!"

We're only a couple of feet apart by now. Her head comes up—and I'm staring into a pair of green eyes that are definitely not Agatha's. I stop dead, my mouth falling open.

"I didn't know you cared so much," Nyah says, grinning.

Chapter
Seventeen

"What have you done with the Select?" I grab the shoulders of the robe as though I'm going to tear it off her. She's taller than Agatha; I should have noticed that earlier and not been fooled. "Where is she? Is she hurt?"

Nyah pulls away from me. "Stop that! The guards may be watching. As far as I know, the Select is still alive and unharmed. She loaned me her robe so I could get past the drone guarding your camp. It's not like she'd be able to walk through the desert to warn you."

"As far as you know?" My voice rises a little.

"Don't shout at me! Your people attacked mine."

"My people?" Seraffa's a trading planet, we don't attack anyone. Then I remember I'm Salarian here. My people. My Grandmother Ryo. "Didn't you see the flare?"

"We saw it." She takes a breath, calming herself. "We saw it, Idaro. The Select told us it was a message from you. It told us the desert game had been moved secretly, at the last moment. And that told us your people were afraid we would attack their children. There's only one reason for them to think we'd do that. We got our people into the lower tunnels and farther out, just in time. You saved thousands of lives."

"But it's not for a week! They weren't going to attack for a week, till we started walking out. I heard them plan it."

"They didn't want to wait a week to kill us. Or else they were afraid your flare would alert us, as it did. "

"So everyone's safe? The people in your..." City? No, settlement, they call their underground communities settlements. "...

in the settlement where your leaders and the Select were? They're all safe?" I try not to emphasize the Select, like she's the only one I care about, but I have to be sure.

"They're safe. A few people... didn't make it. But Sven and the other leaders, and the Select, they all got away in time. We went out through underground tunnels, so it would look like the attack was successful. So they wouldn't think there'll be any reprisal."

"You're telling me there will be?"

"I came to warn you, because you warned us. Out of the Desert, some of them were there. A few got out of the city in time, thanks to the warning you gave me, and they'd been talking to Sven and the other leaders, and the people in the settlement. Telling them it's time we were all citizens, we've waited long enough. And then the attack came—the explosion destroyed our homes, everything we had, it killed people, the old and the sick who couldn't move fast enough..."

"I'm sorry."

She lowers her head a moment, then raises it again. "They're coming for the girls. We have to get the girls away from here."

"They're coming..." I look back the way she came. "They mean to kill us?"

"I don't think they'll hurt you. I can't believe they would, but they've lost a lot."

"But the guards, they'll protect us."

"Against desert people?" She laughs briefly.

"How did you even get past them?"

"They signaled the drone to check me for weapons and when I came up clean, they let me pass. Everyone knows by now there's a Select on Salaria who looks like the desert people. Those guards," she shakes her head, "Salarians don't give their men enough initiative. They spend their whole lives obeying females, what can you expect? They'd never have let me through if I was a male, but a female, in a robe which establishes me in a position of high authority? If I'd ordered them to give me all their weapons, half of them would have done it and the other half would have had a melt-down trying to refuse a command from a female in authority. Anyway, they weren't concerned, they were all still laughing about some girl who accidentally set off a flare two nights ago." She grins.

"Why didn't you tell the guards they were coming?"

She draws back a little. "So they could kill more of my people?" she says coolly. "I owe you a warning. I don't owe your people anything."

"Okay, you've warned me."

"Look, I don't want a bunch of frightened girls being hurt by accident. I'll help you get them away from here." She starts walking toward the circle in the sand.

Everyone's out on their stupid practice hike. What if they don't come back in time? I look around at the empty desert, but don't see any of them returning yet. The sun casts a shimmer in the air, and they're all wearing white. They could be anywhere.

Then I wonder *where does she want to take us?* I squint in the direction she came, shielding my eyes, but I don't see anyone else coming.

I look at Nyah, striding through the sand toward our little tents. I don't think she'd harm me, or any of them. But what do I know about her, really? She's wearing Agatha's habit, but was it given to her willingly? *A few who got out of the city in time,* she said. She's one of the ones who got out.

They've lost a lot. They're coming for the girls.

What has Out of the Desert lost? If I guessed right about them, and if Agatha and Sven and the desert people in their underground settlement are all still alive, what they've lost are martyrs. What they've lost is a reason for the Interplanetary Council to get involved in their struggle for citizenship.

I run to catch up with her. "I'm glad I warned you in time to leave Tokosha," I say. "Did Malah get out, too?"

"No." Her face is hidden by the hood of the O.U.B. habit. I have only her voice, tight and curt, to go on, and maybe one minute to decide whether she's here to save the girls or betray them.

Nyah and Malah. Sisters. What would I do for my sister?

"Let me talk to the girls first. You'll frighten them, even in that habit. They trust me. I can convince them to trust you."

She stops and looks at me, considering.

"I saved your life twice, let me help you save theirs."

"Their lives aren't at risk," she says, but she's already nodding. I run ahead before she changes her mind.

Chowa, Erity, Lien, and Kayo come to meet me at the edge of the circle. Kenja, of course, sticks to her post, so I have to lead them quickly over to her.

"She says Out of the Desert is coming for us, and I believe her."

Lien turns white. Chowa's mouth trembles like she's about to cry, but I don't have time to reassure them. I don't have anything reassuring to say. "The guards will try to protect us, but she doesn't think they'll be able to. We've got to find the rest of the girls." I take a breath, letting that sink in. "Get your backpacks and whatever stuff from your campsite you think you'll need, as much as you can carry, and fast. The desert game starts now."

Kenja frowns. "Who put you in charge?"

"How did they find us?" Erity asks. Then she looks at Kayo.

Kayo looks sick. I can't tell her why I asked her to send up the flare, or that it saved thousands of lives. I have to leave her thinking she put everyone here in danger, and maybe wondering whether she can trust me, what game I might be playing.

"It's not your fault, Kayo. It was an accident," Erity says.

"I'm not in charge, Kenja," I say. "This is just what we have to do if we don't want everyone coming back here to find armed Out of the Desert militants waiting for them."

Even Kenja looks shaken at that. I continue, not giving them time to think. "Each of you find one group. Don't bring them back here. But don't all go the same direction. Chowa, you lead one group west; Lien, you go east; Kenja, go southeast; Erity, southwest; Kayo, just pick east or west, and try not to meet up with another group. You'll be harder to find in small groups, all spread out. Try to cover your tracks as you go." I think of telling them to walk at night and hide when they need to sleep, but where is there to hide in this desert? Stupid advice, but it's all I can think of. They'll have to improvise. They know more about surviving out here than I do, anyway. "Just keep going till you reach one of the estates."

"We should tell the guards," Kenja says.

"If you do, they'll make us stay with them," Erity says. "We won't be allowed to go find the others. And if the desert people are better fighters, like Idaro says, they'll take out the guards and capture us and wait for everyone else to come back here."

"They'll alert our families." Kenja isn't giving up. "They'll send help."

"Which will arrive too late," Lien says. "It's the *desert game,* Kenja. We're supposed to handle whatever happens ourselves. The guards aren't supposed to interfere. You want to run crying for help just because you're afraid? That's not how the game is played!"

Unbelievably, everyone nods. This is the dumbest reason I've heard and it convinces them all.

"Hey! It's a Select," Chowa calls. "You didn't tell us it was a Select." The other girls look out into the desert. Nyah is getting close, even going slowly to give me time to convince them. Her habit is clearly visible now.

"That's how you know you can trust her," I say.

"The habit might not be hers." Kenja faces me. "Even if it is, she's not Salarian and neither are you. How do we know we can trust either of you?"

"You can trust her," Kayo says quietly, stepping up beside me. She still won't meet my eyes. "She's part of my estate. I know her."

"Kayo also knows I came here with a Select. That's her. I recognize her."

"That's good enough for me," Erity says. "You can stand here debating if you want, Kenja. I'm going to grab what I can and warn my friends."

"What are you going to do?" Kayo asks me quietly when the others are out of hearing.

"I'll go north with the Select, back the way she came. We'll drag stuff with us, leave a trail leading them away from the rest of you. Don't worry, I'll be okay. You have to get away now, Kayo."

"I'll stay with you."

"You can't. There are five groups out there. You have to warn one of them, same as the others."

"Why don't you trust her?" Kayo asks.

How did she guess? I open my mouth to lie, but then I can't. Not after she stood by me. For a moment I can't stop the fear I'm feeling from showing in my face.

"Is she one of them? Out of the Desert?"

"I don't know. I hope not. I might be making a mistake here, Kayo, I just can't tell."

"But you think it's more of a risk for us to trust her, than not to."

"It's a risk either way. But I think more of you will get out this way. Maybe everyone."

"How will you keep her from following us?"

"I'll tell her we've agreed that you'll find the groups and bring them to meet up with us. I'll say I told you to set your compass for thirty miles due north of here. I can keep her waiting there two days, maybe three."

"And then? How do you plan to get away from her? From them, if you're walking into a trap?"

"That part hasn't come to me yet." I grin. Kayo's not buying it. "She won't hurt me, Kayo. Look, you really have to go now."

She hesitates.

"What?"

"The guards…"

"I know," I say. "I'm going to stop by one of the units on my way out, after you've all gone, and tell them we've started the game, we won't be back here, so they can go home. I won't leave them waiting here to be attacked without warning, if that part is true."

"Okay," she says. "I'll go. But the game isn't over yet."

Chapter Eighteen

"They should be here now." Nyah enters my tent and frowns at me.

"Watching the horizon won't make them come any sooner. It's too dark to see anything out there anyway."

The frown continues, only now it looks more suspicious than annoyed.

"You're a desert girl," I tell her. "You half-killed me, making me race to get here. Do you even know how hot it is out there?"

"I know exactly how hot it is in my desert."

"Right. But do you really think they can travel as fast as we did, a whole group of them, everyone needing to stop at different times, some of them not as strong as others? And they had already been hiking in the heat most of the day, they were exhausted to start with. On top of that, the girls at the camp had to find them first."

"Even with all that, they should have beat us here. You made us take down half the tents and pack them up and drag them with us. And stop and talk to the guards."

"The tents are lightweight, you hardly noticed." This isn't just flattery, her wiry strength is daunting. I hope I never have to test my measly self-defense lessons on her. "We'll need the tents. Estate girls aren't used to sleeping on the sand, any more than I am. You do know we're allergic to snake and scorpion poison, right?"

"They've been sleeping on the sand for two nights now." She's still frowning. The fact that she's just frowning, that she let me bring the tents and isn't frantic about the delay, tells me I guessed at least partially right: Out of the Desert probably wasn't coming for us. Either Nyah's playing her own game here, or they're waiting somewhere for her to lead us to them.

"Look, I'm worried, too." What can she say to that? That she's
not worried, she's ticked? That she's beginning to fear she's lost the
captives she was so sure of? "I don't want anything to happen to
them any more than you do. I keep imagining Out of the Desert
has found them. You don't think they have, do you?" I let my lower
lip tremble a little. Not too much. Then I wonder if it was enough.
I'm used to the Select, where even a little is too much to fool them.
Did she notice? Should I make it tremble again?

"I'm sorry. I don't mean to frighten you, Idaro."

I see two little muscles, one at each side of her mouth, tighten.
She's a tough desert girl, and I'm just a little city girl. She's right.
Except that I'm a smart little city girl.

"It's just that I have to go back and tell the Select—" She says
"the Select" like it just came to her. I know what it sounds like
when someone's improvising as they speak, I've done it myself often enough. "—that I found you in time, that you're okay." She
stops talking and looks away. Honestly, she's an awful liar.

I wait, but she doesn't say anything more, just turns back to the
front flap of my tent like she lost her train of thought. She stands with
her back to me, not moving to open the tent, just standing there.

Then, so quiet I almost don't hear her, she says, "If anything happens to them, it will be my fault."

She unseals the tent flap and leaves.

I stare after her. No way that was anything but a guilt-stricken
confession. What game is she playing? Not the one I thought.
Unless she's changing tables mid-game?

I shake my head. I've been here too long, I'm beginning to think
like the Salarians, in gaming images. Nothing about this is a game.
I crawl into my sleepsack and close my eyes.

Sometime in the middle of the night I'm suddenly awake. There's
something moving just outside my tent, very quietly. I lie rigid
and sweating, listening intently. The sand shifts as whatever-it-is

moves silently around me, with only a thin layer of flexsheet tenting between us. It stops at the opening flap. I should get my knife, or scream for Nyah, but I'm frozen with fear, unable to move a muscle or utter a sound. Slowly, excruciatingly slowly, the front of the tent begins to unseal.

If it's some militant from Out of the Desert, I'm dead. It's only a matter of time till they realize the girls aren't coming. I might talk Nyah into sparing me—I warned her of the city round-up—but anyone else in that group will only wait long enough to decide the best way to use my death.

If it's someone from Out of the Desert, being this quiet, being this careful not to wake Nyah, then Nyah isn't one of them. I watch in terror as the flap slowly folds away from the front of the tent. In the darkness beyond I begin to make out a shape. I struggle to open my mouth, to scream for Nyah!

A head pops in and peers around. In one quick step the rest of the body follows, and kneels beside my bed, knife outstretched a little shakily.

"Who's here?" she whispers, her voice as shaky as her hand.

"It's me, Kia—Idaro," I cover my slip quickly. "What are you doing here, Kayo?"

Before she can answer the flap is yanked open and Nyah appears. Kayo stands up so fast she almost trips, her hand again holding the knife out semi-threateningly. "Stand back," she squeaks. "Idaro's coming with me!"

"Where, exactly, do you intend to take her?"

Kayo doesn't answer. The knife wobbles a little, but remains resolutely pointed at Nyah.

"Don't hurt her," I say.

"I won't if she lets us go without a struggle," Kayo says.

I bite my lip. I was talking to Nyah. "I'm going to get up now," I say. "Don't either of you move."

Nyah gives a little cough which almost sets me off. I get up and stand beside Kayo. "Give me the knife," I say, touching her arm.

She pushes it into my hands, expelling a noisy breath of relief. I'm relieved, too, as I lower my arm, pointing the knife safely at the ground.

"Is anyone else with you?" Nyah asks.

"Yes! A whole division of armed guards!" Kayo says. "So you better just stand aside!" She looks at me and moves her arm, a little cue for me to brandish the knife threateningly. If we both had knives—which we do, except that I was too frozen to get mine out—Nyah could still disarm us in two seconds flat.

"In that case, I think I'll go back to bed," Nyah says. "You two should get some sleep."

Kayo stares wide-eyed as the flap falls shut and reseals behind Nyah. "Well, that was easy," she says.

I hand her back her knife. "What were you thinking, coming here?"

"I'm rescuing you." She looks at me, like, isn't it obvious? "So get dressed and let's go."

I want to think of a way to say it that won't completely deflate her, but there isn't one, so I just tell her flat out, "The nearest estate is close to a hundred miles from here. She'll get up in the morning and track us down before we've gone five."

"You're giving up?"

"No, I'm going to outsmart her."

"How's that working out for you?" She glares at me. I'm obviously still here.

"Better than the knife." I sigh, trying not to let it show. "We can't out-run her in the desert, Kayo."

She looks a little deflated, which makes me feel bad. "Are you hungry?"

"Starving!" she says.

I get her some cold fried cactus and strips of dried snake flavored with something Nyah called desert salt.

"What is it?" Kayo asks, chewing on a piece. "It's not bad."

"I'll tell you when you're done. Tell me about the others. You found your group?"

"Yeah, Kama's leading them," she mumbles around a mouthful. "I gave them the message and then came after you. What'd you do, run all the way here without stopping?"

"Something like that. Do you know if the girls from our camp found the other four groups? They're headed away from here, right?"

"I saw Erity before I left. She asked me where you were going to lead—it's Nyah, isn't it? The desert girl?" I nod. "I told her, *straight north,* so she won't lead them this way when she finds her group. And after I left my group I passed Kenja. Her group was arguing, it looked pretty intense. She asked where I was going so I told her. They were still arguing when I left. Probably trying to decide which estate was closest." She swallows the last of the food and licks her fingers. "So what was it?"

"Desert chicken."

❧

"They're not coming, are they?" Nyah asks in the morning while we're eating breakfast. She looks like she hasn't slept since Kayo woke us.

Kayo opens her mouth to give her impression of a convincing lie. I save us all time: "Nope."

"I'm not the enemy," Nyah says.

"I believe you." I realize as I say it that I do. "But you're not a friend, either. There's too much at stake for you."

She doesn't deny it.

"What did you want with us?" Kayo asks.

"I wanted to protect you."

"But not get us home," I say.

"No."

"You were playing a double game. Hiding us from Out of the Desert, but hiding us from our estates, too. Were you going to use us as hostages, to get your sister freed?"

"Time to go." She stands up. "Grab your packs. You can leave the knives here."

"Where are we going?" I don't stand up. Kayo, half-risen, sits down again.

"To the settlement. The Select is waiting for you." I watch her carefully as she says this. No sign she's lying. I'm not as sure of that as I'd like to be, as Agatha would be, but I'm sure enough.

"How far is that?"

"Two..." she looks at Kayo. "Three days walk."

"We'll need a tent. I'll take mine down."

"We don't have time. If they find you before I get you to Sven..."

"We're not any safer with Sven. Don't play dumb. What the militants need are bodies, not hostages. And Sven and the Select will do just as well as a game of fifteen-year-olds."

"What are you talking about? What bodies?" Kayo's voice cracks.

"What we needed were hostages!"

"Is that what they told you? And you believed them?" I don't try to hide my disgust.

"*They* didn't bomb our leaders' settlement."

"No. What they did was infuriate the powerful Kicho-Ryo-Tomiko triad, and kill a lot of helpless slaves. But you don't care about that, do you? Well, I wonder how Matriarch Ryo got the coordinates for the settlement where your leaders just happened to be? The ones who don't share Out of the Desert's philosophy."

"Matriarch Ryo? Our family bombed the desert people?" Kayo looks from me to Nyah.

"They were warned in time, Kayo. You warned them with the flare you set off. You saved their lives." I don't mention the ones who didn't make it. Kayo couldn't bear it. But I notice the way Nyah's looking at Kayo now. Good. She owes us both.

"Okay, let's get moving." Nyah starts walking toward the tent she's been sleeping in to collect her stuff.

"Where?" I still don't budge.

"Where you'll be safe. Let's move it!"

I refuse to leave my tent. She can sleep outside with snakes and scorpions if she likes, but Kayo and I aren't going to. I don't ask, I just start taking it down, and Kayo helps me. We leave the rest of the tents up. If Out of the Desert finds them, they'll think we were all here, and be looking for a large group.

If anyone else finds them, they'll think it's Christmas.

Chapter Nineteen

"Get down!" Nyah drops to the sand. "Down!" she hisses again as Kayo and I hesitate.

I fall to my knees, and then my chest. *No snakes, no scorpions,* I'm thinking desperately, scrunching my arms and legs in close. "What is it?" I squint behind us, where she's looking.

"Eighteen-twenty people, following us."

I wait but she doesn't elaborate. All I can see is burning sand and heat rippling in the air above it.

"Come on, but stay down. There's a dip in the sand ahead. We can get up after we reach it."

I look ahead. White on white as far as I can see. How does she know these things?

She starts crawling through the sand. "Hurry!"

"You okay, Kayo?" I ask over my shoulder.

No answer. Then, "yes," so quiet I barely hear it. I look back. Her face is nearly as white as the sand, but she nods at me.

"Okay, let's go." I start crawling. Behind me I hear the movement of sand as she follows. *No snakes, no scorpions,* I think, glaring at the sand around me. I don't see any nest holes. Snakes are attracted to movement, Norio said, but you can outrun them. I crawl faster. Where is that *flickis* dip?

I look up, sweating, from my anxious inspection of the sand for scorpion nests, in time to see Nyah sink down into the sand ahead of me. Quicksand! For a moment I'm back on Malem. "Nyah!" I cry. Her head pops up.

It's the dip. Everything still looks white on white to me, but she is unmistakably lower than us. "It's just ahead," I call back to Kayo. "We're almost there."

She doesn't answer.

"Kayo?" I look behind. She's lying on the sand, gripping her forearm just below the elbow.

"Kayo!" I scramble back to her. "What is it?"

"Snake," she says through gritted teeth, trying not to cry.

"Nyah, Kayo's been bitten!" I grab Kayo's pack. "Where's your antidote?"

"D…don't have any."

"What do you mean, you don't have any? Everyone got some." I'm pawing desperately through her pack when I remember. I got stung. She wanted me to drink her antidote, she opened it and put it to my lips, and when I told her to get my vial, she just dropped it and ran.

"'Sokay, Idaro. Knew I'd die here," Kayo stammers.

"You're not going to die here!" There has to be something in her pack. She's like a walking med clinic.

"D…don't stay. G…go before they get here." Her voice is getting weaker.

"Here's something!" I pull out a bottle. "What's this?"

"D…D-doc…" It's just a pain block. It won't stop the poison. "L… leave it…" She reaches a shaking arm out for it.

One swallow is enough to stop your heart, Teacher said. I blink hard, but my face is damp when Nyah slides in next to me.

She pushes me aside. There's a knife in her hand. "Don't!" I scream.

"Be quiet! The desert carries sound! Get out of my way." She shoves me again.

I'm about to grab her but she's not killing Kayo, she's cutting away her sleeve. Then I notice what's in her other hand: a limp white snake, minus its head and poison sack. She holds it just above the bite on Kayo's arm, and squeezes. A squirt of pinky-white liquid falls into the wound.

"The snake's own blood contains an antidote," she says, squeezing a few more drops out before tossing it aside. "Give me the D-doc juice." I hand it over to her.

"Kayo," Nyah leans closer, right over Kayo's face. "Can you hear me Kayo?"

Kayo blinks. Her mouth parts, like she's trying to say yes.

"That's good, Kayo. I'm going to give you two drops of D-doc juice. It won't hurt you." She motions me back, stopping my protest. "I need to slow down your heart, slow the dissemination of the poison, until the antidote can work. Can you open your mouth wider?" Carefully, she pours two drops into Kayo's half-open mouth. "Swallow," she says when Kayo doesn't.

The fear in Kayo's eyes nearly undoes me. She closes her eyes and swallows.

"You can sleep now," Nyah tells her.

I spread out the flexsheet I pulled out of Kayo's pack when I was looking for her antidote. Nyah and I lift Kayo onto it and drag her on our knees over to the gully and down into it.

Her face has a waxy sheen to it. I put my ear to her mouth. "She's barely breathing."

"That's okay. That's normal."

Like any of this is normal. What kind of game is this? What kind of people would risk their own daughters? For what? For the right to keep slaves? For the right to gamble with the lives of people who *aren't* their kin? I want to throw back my head and scream! I want to bomb them all into oblivion!

I gasp. That's not me. I don't want more bodies, more red streaks across this harsh white planet. I don't want anyone else to die. This is how it happens. You hurt me and I hurt you back and you hurt me back... That's how it starts. How does it stop?

If that's what I'm here for, the Adept on Seraffa picked the wrong person. Whoever had that vision really messed up. Because I have not the tiniest idea how to undo a centuries-old bitterness.

"We'll have to wait for them here. Ambush them." Nyah's voice startles me.

I squint out at the distant figures following us. "Won't they see the dip? You did."

"They will too. But it curves there," she points to the right. Now that I'm in the gully I can see the curve of its sides. "You two hide around the curve. Can you drag her there? I'll wipe away your trail and make fresh tracks that way." She points ahead, in the direction we were going. After a hundred yards or so the sand rises again. "Then I'll backtrack and wait for them there." She points to the left where the side of the gully protrudes a little.

"Eighteen to twenty people?" Even she's not that good, especially up against desert people like her. "What are you going to do when they get here?"

"I'll think of something then."

In other circumstances I'd laugh. I'm the one who usually says something like that. "That's your plan? You'll think of something?"

"That's it."

"I can't even protect Kayo. You made us leave our knives behind."

"You're safer without one. If whoever comes over that rise looks dangerous, don't antagonize them."

I drag Kayo around behind the curve in the gully and sit beside her on a corner of the flexsheet, waiting for whoever's coming after us. I can't fight them, and I can't run—not and leave Kayo here unconscious. That leaves surrender. And prayer, Agatha would add, if she were here. "A rescue team would be helpful anytime soon," I mutter, just in case Agatha's right about that.

I look up at the sky. One of the groups must have reached an estate by now. You'd think they'd send an aircar out at least, when they heard their story. Unless they did, and they've been busy finding the other girls and taking them home. They could have done that by now, so why aren't they here? Kayo told both Erity and Kenja where I was going.

Okay, fine, I'm not one of theirs, but what about Kayo? I get mad again as I look at her, barely breathing beside me, fighting for her life against this desert's poison.

I stand up carefully and peek over the side of the gully. I can see them now. They're not close enough for me to make out their faces, or even their clothes, just white shapes coming nearer through shifting sheets of heat and sunlight. I duck down again. Nyah's right: resistance is useless. I hope she won't try anyway, and get herself killed.

And then there's only waiting. Watching Kayo breathe, listening for the sound of footsteps muffled by sand, trying to ignore the pounding of my heart, wondering what Nyah's thinking, what she'll do, what they'll do...

They're close enough I can hear their voices now. I strain to make out the words. They're probably speaking the language of the desert people, though, a variation of an Old Earth language I don't know.

"Are you sure you saw something?"

"I said so, didn't I?"

No, they're speaking Salarian. And they're quarreling. I could work with that...

They don't say anything more. All I hear is the sound of the sand sifting under their feet as they get closer and closer.

"Hey, there's a dip here in the sand!"

She's almost on top of it. They can't see any better than I can in this white desert. Not desert people, then?

"The tracks go down into it and across to the other side."

I know that voice! And Nyah's waiting to...

"Stop!" I yell, jumping up. I startle Kama so much she slips, and slides down the side of the gully.

I look from her, flat on her ass in the sand, up to the others, every fifteen from the Kicho-Ryo-Tomiko estate and half-a-dozen others.

"What are you doing here?" I shout at them. I vaguely remember that that was the first thing I said to Kayo, too, when she showed up. So it's not entirely a surprise when Kama stands up, brushes the sand off her butt, and says, "We're here to rescue you!" She glares at Nyah.

I take a second to send a silent message skyward: *I was thinking of an aircar!*

To Kama I say, "You tried to poison me and now you've come to rescue me?"

She looks embarrassed, steps closer and lowers her voice. "Don't make a big deal of that. The first sting isn't fatal. I knew you had the antidote. I just wanted you sent home so I wouldn't have to worry about keeping you alive. It's turning out to be a real pain in the butt."

Erity jumps down into the gully. "Where's Kayo? Didn't she find you?"

"She got bitten by a snake." I decide not to go into the rest of it. "Nyah's taking us somewhere safe while she recovers, where Out of the Desert won't find us."

They're all in the gully by now. Kenja pushes to the front. "Where's the Select?" She eyes Nyah suspiciously.

Now it's my turn to look embarrassed. "It was Nyah, in the Select's robe."

"You lied to us? What's going on?"

"You wouldn't have listened if I told you it was a desert girl," I say. They frown, mostly at Nyah but also at me, now, which proves I'm right. "And the rest of it is true. Members of Out of the Desert are looking for us. We were afraid that's who you were. Why didn't you go to an estate where you'd be safe?"

"Because none of us can go home without you and Kayo!" Kama shouts. "You know that! Believe me, I'd like nothing better than to leave you in the desert!"

"You should have! I don't need any back-up!"

"You are the most ungrateful rescued person I know," Erity says, stepping between us. "And you are the most bad-mannered hero," she says to Kama. "I'm going to go see Kayo and hope for a better response."

"It isn't true, you know," Akako tells me as the others go to see Kayo. "Not everyone wanted to come, but Kama argued, shamed and bullied them into it. Even six girls who aren't from our estate decided to come by the time she was through. She said no one who would let a team-mate in the desert game die without even trying to save her was worthy of being in a triad." She looks down. "I wouldn't have let you die, you know. From the sting."

"I didn't know."

"I guess you do now."

I laugh despite myself. "What did you think you were going to do against a group of armed militants?"

She shrugs. "The best we could. We would have had surprise on our side."

"No doubt about that."

When we get to Kayo, her eyes are open and she's smiling.

Not one of them understands the danger they're in. This isn't a game, I want to shout at them, but they wouldn't understand me. They've been taught that everything's a game, death is just one of the pieces. I go back to where Nyah's standing, looking north over the desert.

"They're just a bunch of kids, you know," I say to her.

"Yeah, well, that's what the desert game is all about, isn't it? They're not supposed to come out of it still kids. Not your fault or mine."

"I'll settle for them coming out of it. Do you have a safe place for us?"

"Them, yes. If they'll agree to go there with me. You, I have to get to the Select. Did they know when they sent her that she can't speak a word of any language spoken here?"

Chapter Twenty

We arrive at night. Nyah puts her finger to her lips and leads us through a pathway in the sand visible only to her. I notice small tubes sticking out of the ground and a series of three-foot-square indentations in the sand, each one surrounded by a low wood barrier, about forty feet apart. When I look closer at one, it's a slat made of wood cactus, with the desert sand cleared away. Nyah stops in front of one.

She reaches down, fiddles with something on top of it, and slowly raises it. Inside I see a wide square hole, lined with wood, a ladder on one side. She motions us down inside. No one moves. It took a lot of convincing just to get them to follow a desert girl; they aren't going down into the ground on her say-so.

"What is this place?" I whisper, because she's urged us to silence since we got here.

"My parents' old house."

"Old house?"

"My father is now one of the leaders of our people. They moved to Sven's settlement. So technically this house is mine and my sister's, when we come back."

I look down into the hole. "It won't cave in?"

"It's cut out of siltstone, a sedimentary rock composed of sand and clay. In certain places, like here, it lies eight to ten feet below the desert sands. We dig our houses out of it. So no, it won't cave in."

I nod at the girls to start climbing down the ladder. "Your neighbors won't give us away?"

"I grew up here. I don't think they would, but I don't intend to tell them the girls are here, either. It's better if nobody knows."

Erity's the last to go. I wait till she disappears down the hole. They're all waiting below, in the dugout, because I told them it was okay. When did they decide to trust me so completely? They're only a year younger than me, but it seems a decade since I was that confident nothing really bad could happen to me.

"I hope we understand each other," I tell Nyah.

She waits for me to continue.

"They aren't hostages. They're your guests."

"The Ruling Triad in Tokosha doesn't need to know that." Nyah grins.

I don't return the smile. "But you need to know it," I say. "You need to remember it every minute they're here. You need to worry about it, because if you don't keep them safe, I swear I'll kill you."

Totally impossible. Never in a hundred years will I be able to kill her. But I'm willing to die trying.

"I'll keep them safe," she says.

I lean closer. "I get it about your sister. I have a sister, too. She was a slave in the mine your sister blew up." I let that sink in. "And after that I saved your life. So I don't care what you have to do. I don't care what choices you're given. This isn't a choice. You keep these girls safely hidden."

She doesn't repeat her promise. I respect that. She's given her word; if once isn't enough, twice won't make it so. But she meets my look and holds it, and I believe the girls will be safe with her.

I climb down to them. A short tunnel sloping downwards takes us to the living quarters. A kind of lounge area, furnished with chairs and benches, a kitchen with a primitive cook stove cut into one wall and chunks of wood cactus piled beside it, and three bedrooms—not nearly enough beds for all of us, but Nyah pulls some blankets onto the floor and we'll manage.

The next day passes slowly even though we all sleep late in our dark, underground bedrooms. Each room has a chimney—the tubes I saw sticking out of the ground—which lets in fresh air and a small amount of light, but it's way darker than the tents. I think we were all becoming sleep deprived, but maybe that's part of the game. When I finally wander into the kitchen, Nyah has lit lamps to brighten the place and is setting out eggs and cactus milk while Erity slices up flat, round things she calls cactus bread. It's wonderful for breakfast, okay for lunch, a little tiresome for supper, but no one complains. I figure that'll change if they have to stay cooped up in here for too long.

Late the next night Nyah returns from checking outside to give me the all-clear. "Head straight north," she tells me.

"Give me the co-ordinates." I reach for my compass, which I've clipped to my belt.

"When you get close enough, they'll find you, if they want to."

"That's it?"

"That's it. They've already been bombed once."

"You don't trust me?"

"I do, but you might run into the wrong person."

No use wasting my breath. I go into the lounge area to get my pack. It's lighter now; I took out everything unnecessary, even my jewelry box. I wrapped my tools, which aren't that bulky, in a cloth and stuck them inside my shirt. I sling the half-empty pack over my shoulder.

"What are you going to do?" Kama asks.

"I'm not sure. But the Select I came with, she's with the leaders of the desert people, trying to resolve this conflict. And she can't speak a word of Salarian." I give them an ironic grin, which makes several of them laugh. They probably think I'm joking.

Kama doesn't laugh. "I was wrong about you," she says.

"I was wrong about you, too."

She nods once, as if that's done. No need to belabor the point. My kind of apology entirely.

I look around at them. The only reason they're here, and not safe at home, is because they wouldn't leave me behind in the desert. I'm suddenly so choked I don't know what to say.

"Don't get all blubbery," Kama says. "Mucks up the sunlenses."

"It's night time, I'm not wearing them."

"Yeah, well, no need to embarrass yourself, anyway. Just go."

"Be careful out there," Akako adds.

I nod. "Thank you," I say to all of them. I glance at Nyah, who's come in behind me. "You can trust Nyah," I tell them. "And Kama's second in command. When they agree, do it."

I don't grin till I get to the tunnel, out of their sight. No one else appreciated the humor in that, but I'd give a lot to have a little cam somewhere, so I could watch Nyah and Kama working things out.

At the end of the tunnel, right below the hatch, Kayo is waiting. She has her pack slung over her left shoulder. Her right forearm is still wrapped in bandaging and her face looks pale and weary but determined.

"You're not coming," I say.

"Yes, I am. You won't survive in the desert, you missed most of the training."

"You won't survive another sting."

"Kenja gave me her tube of antidote."

How have I deserved this loyalty? She knows what she's offering. I can't accept it, though. "I'm not Nyah. I can't keep you safe out there, Kayo."

"I know. I'm going to keep you safe."

"I can't carry a tent to sleep in, I have to travel fast, and a tent might be seen."

She gestures to her pack. "Extra flexsheet, three containers of re-pellant, two full bottles of D-doc juice." She smiles proudly. When I don't smile back, she adds, "I'll just follow you, you know."

She will, too. "Don't slow me down," I say, reaching for the hatch. Then I stop, and look at her standing there. "Kayo, you'd be the first person I'd pick for my triad."

"Me, too." Erity enters the tunnel behind us. She's carrying her pack.

"Erity, no. You're safer here."

"Oh, what's the fun in that?" she says.

I'm lining up my arguments when Kama joins us. Carrying her

pack! She holds up her hand. "Don't waste your breath. I left Kenja in charge. She'll drive that desert girl even crazier than I would have." She doesn't actually grin but the look in her eyes tells me she was on to that.

I'm not in a laughing mood, now. "You realize we're going to get ourselves killed out there, don't you?"

"It's all part of the game," Erity says.

"What game? This isn't a game! Death isn't a game! It's the end. It's never seeing someone again. Ever!" I sound a little hysterical. I make myself stop and take a breath. No one moves.

"We know that." Kama breaks the silence. "We drew lots. I lost. Now open the bloody hatch."

"You can *so* go back without me!" I shout.

"Well, I'm not going to." Kama shoves past me and opens the hatch herself.

&

Even with Salaria's double moons I wouldn't be able to make out the path between the houses if Nyah hadn't marked it with her footprints just before coming back down to us. We follow it carefully, in single file, so Nyah won't be faced with questions she can't answer tomorrow because her neighbors heard people walking over their roofs in the night

We walk all night. My compass, automatically set at the start of the game to guide me to the nearest estate as soon as I left the circle, keeps trying to get me to turn back, or veer off east or west. I turn off the speaker and the locator and use it as our ancestors did, for direction only, heading straight north as Nyah said.

At dawn we stop for a meal of dried cactus and strips of snake seasoned with desert salt, sitting on a flexsheet. Kayo still thinks it's desert chicken and eats it willingly. Kama frowns—she's not the kind to baby anyone—but I casually reminisce about the time Kayo saved my life when I was stung by a scorpion back at camp. Kama snaps her mouth shut and eats her "desert chicken" in silence.

As soon as I've eaten I get up and start walking. We can be seen for miles in the desert and there's nothing we can do about it, so the sooner we reach the settlement, the better. Unfortunately, Nyah told me it's nearly a hundred miles away. Three days hard walking in the desert sun before we're safe. I glance behind me. Kama should make it. Erity might.

I stop. "Kayo, give me your pack."

"No. I'm fine," she pants.

"Give it." I grab it off her shoulder. "Your job is to look out for…" I'm about to say desert people, but I don't want to scare her. "…sweetwater cacti. We need to keep replenishing our liquids."

When the sun reaches its zenith I finally stop. Kayo has found a sweetwater cactus. She stabs her spile into its globe-shaped belly and we take turns refilling our bottles. Then we spread out two flexsheets to lie on.

"Kayo in the middle," I say. They don't argue. She's been bitten once; all the antidote on the planet won't save her if it happens again. We lie down and pull a third flexsheet over us, its rough side up to diffuse and deflect the sunlight, so we won't cook alive in our sleep underneath it. It's white, like everything else on this planet; with luck, we'll just look like another mound of sand.

We're walking again three hours later, barely refreshed from a too-short sleep in the relentless heat. The hottest part of the day is over, which means it's still hotter than any other habitable planet in the human universe. I think I would let myself be captured by Out of the Desert if they promised to let me sleep in an air-cooled tent before they killed me.

It's too hot to talk. It's too hot to think. We just keep moving, one foot in front of the other, northward. We suck in the heat with every breath and sweat it out again. The desert stretches away from us, horizon to horizon, empty and silent. I have never known such silence. It's as heavy as the heat, an invisible entity pressing in on us until the sound of our own heartbeats, our breathing, seems alien and unwelcome in this hot, silent world. We have brought noise here: aircars and construction, voices and technology; city noises springing up and mining noises burrowing down and now, explosives. We have disturbed the vast silence of this world and only our death will restore it...

"Movement!" Erity cries. "Get down!"

For a second, stupid with the heat and the silence, I don't understand. Then I drop to the ground like the others. I squint into the east where she's pointing. "Where?" I whisper, still caught in the spell of the silent desert.

"I see it," Kama murmurs.

"I don't." Kayo shades her eyes. "Oh. The wind?"

"I don't think so. It's too steady."

I'm still desperately trying to pick out anything anywhere in this vast emptiness. Erity aligns her head with mine and points. I stare, willing myself to see it, whatever it is. "Is it coming this way?"

Erity sighs and stops pointing.

"It's too far to tell," Kama says.

"If it is desert people and we've seen them, then they've already seen us," I say. "There's nowhere to hide, and we're losing our head start." I remember the pace Nyah set for us when we left the camp circle, and I know I slowed her down. We'll never outrun them, but we have no other choice than to try. If it is desert people. If it's not just the wind stirring the sand, or a sunlit mirage.

"Let's go before someone gets stung." I stand up. It feels like making a target of myself, like shouting to the distant whatever, come and get me! I think I see a streak of red on the white sand and my heart stammers, but I push it aside. There's no time for imagining things, no time for fear. I check my compass and start walking north. Fast.

Chapter Twenty-One

Something is following us. We've increased our pace, but still they're gaining on us. I can see them now, not individual shapes yet, just something bobbing on the eastern horizon.

The sun is falling. It'll be dark soon. They won't be able to see us, but we won't be able to see them either, or tell how fast they're coming. And they don't need to see us; they've already had time to note our direction. We can't turn aside. I have to get to Agatha, and anyway, there's nowhere else to go.

Maybe it's not Out of the Desert militants. Maybe it'll be friendly desert people, who'll help us get to the settlement. Maybe it'll even be a party of Salarians trying to find us. Real rescuers. I don't mention that hope out loud. We all know nobody comes for the girls who disappear in the desert game. I wouldn't be surprised if they're laying bets on everyone who hasn't turned up yet.

I glance behind to make sure Kayo's keeping up, and notice clouds in the sky. Dark, heavy clouds lying low across the southern horizon. We've been looking east and didn't see them forming. Rain, I think. Water. I imagine being wet, wet all over, and even the thought revives me, despite the danger from the east. "Rain!" I call, excited.

Kama looks behind. "Run!" she screams.

I'm thinking she means into it, but she veers off, northwest, as though she's trying to run out of its path, and the others take to their heels, too. I look again and race after them. Tornado? I think. Hurricane? I've never been anywhere either could occur, but I've seen them in actionvids, with human bodies being hurled into the sky and houses torn apart by one or the other of them. I run faster.

I hear a low growl behind me, which quickly becomes louder, as if some ravaging beast has caught our scent. I risk another look back. The whole desert is being swallowed by the roaring wind at our backs. It's reaching for us now; it whips around me, tearing at my clothes, a biting, stinging wind, laced with millions of grains of sand. We run flat out, run for our lives, and we're losing.

"We can't outrun it!" Kayo screams. "Get under your flexsheets!" Her words are torn from her mouth by the wind.

Nobody stops running, but Kama, beside me, slides her pack off her shoulder. The wind tears it from her hands and flings it behind us before she can reach inside. It disappears into the storm.

The wind is upon us now, buffeting us in every direction, its howl deafening me. The air is so thick with sand I can't see. I'm breathing in sand, choking on it...

"Get down!" someone screams. Kama grabs my arm and pulls me down, and Erity falls beside her. We press together, protecting each other, our faces buried in our arms. We're going to be buried alive! Kayo! Where's Kayo?

She falls on top of us, arms and legs outstretched, cutting off the wind and sand. "Grab a corner," she pants. "Help me hold it!"

I reach up blindly and grab the flexsheet Kayo's trying to spread over us. Together we pull it over our heads and hold it against the ground. The relief is immediate. We can breathe again without inhaling sand. I wipe my face on my sleeve to clear away the grit and sand, and open my eyes. Squeezing aside, I make room for Kayo between me and Kama. The wind pounds against the sheet. It flaps it wildly around our legs until we manage to pin it down with our feet. And then we are as snug as if we were in a tent. A flimsy tent, barely able to shelter us from the wild fury of the sandstorm. Erity gives a shaky laugh.

"How long do these things last?" I ask, thinking, don't say days, don't say weeks. Some planets have storms that last for half their solar orbit.

"It could be hours," Kayo says gloomily. It's my turn to give a shaky laugh.

"I lost my pack," Erity says.

I realize mine is gone, too. "Anyone still got their pack?" I ask.

"I do," Kayo says. "I pulled it round in front of me."

The rest of us lie there awhile wondering why we didn't think of that.

"At least we don't have to worry about getting bitten or stung," Erity says. "Scorpions and snakes burrow down deep when there's a sandstorm."

We take turns sleeping, two of us holding onto the sheet while the other two sleep. No one's going to be tracking us through this.

It happens after Kayo wakes me up, when she's transferring her hold on the sheet to me, so she can rest. The wind grabs the corner of the flexsheet and tears it out of my hand, and with that advantage it's impossible for the others to hold onto it. It whips into the air and away, and we can only lie with our heads pressed into the ground, trying to suck some oxygen out of the sand.

Fortunately, the worst of the storm has already blown over us. In another half hour it dies down altogether.

We've lost hours. And somewhere back there, if they survived, and they probably have if they're desert people, whoever is behind us will still be coming for us.

"Do you see them?" I croak. As if we could see anything with all the grit in our eyes.

Kayo, practical Kayo, digs in her pack and hands round a bottle of solution to clean our sunlenses with, followed by her marvelous eye drops.

"I'll never laugh at you for sleeping in your lenses again," Kama says, applying the drops. Erity looks at Kama. "I'll never laugh at you again," Kama amends.

"A lot of stuff blew away when I got out my flexsheet," Kayo says apologetically, looking through her half-empty pack.

"Whether we see them or not, they're out there." I stand up. "Let's get going."

We walk all night. Even with Kama carrying her pack, the only one we have now, Kayo is staggering long before dawn. I have to slow our pace and stop to rest more often than I want. I can almost feel our pursuers coming, silent shadows moving through the folds of night, closer and closer. I keep looking east, expecting to see their eyes in the darkness.

Two days, I tell myself in the gray light just before dawn. Two days till we reach safety.

Kayo stumbles, catches herself, and stops. We all wait once more, while she catches her breath.

"I'm going west," she pants. "I'll draw them away from you, at least some of them, for as long as I can keep going."

"We're not splitting up." I glare at Kama and Erity in case they were about to agree with Kayo.

"I'm just slowing you down, staying with you. I'm putting all of you in more danger. I'm sorry."

"You saved our lives, Kayo, with your flexsheet. You never have to apologize to us," I tell her.

"Then make it count for something. Go help the Select make peace before anyone else dies."

Norio, we're both thinking. But I can't let his sister die for me, too. She'll never survive alone out here, and she knows it. "It won't work, Kayo. They have to know already where we're headed, and there's nothing to the west. They'll know it's a ploy to draw them away."

"Actually," Kama says, fiddling with her compass, "there's an estate west of us. They might think we changed our minds and ran for home."

Chapter Twenty-One

"I'm going with Kayo," Erity says.

"Don't, Erity. You're fast. You can keep up. Idaro might need you."

"No, it's a good plan," Kama says. "If there are two sets of foot-prints, they'll have to split up and follow both."

"And it has to be me," Erity grins at Kama, "because I'm allowed to go home without Idaro." She turns back to Kayo. "Besides, you're going to be in my triad when the game's over, we might as well start relying on each other now."

"I'm... what?" Kayo stammers.

"We agreed back in the tunnel at Nyah's house before we left. I said you were the first I'd ask. You didn't say no. Don't think you can back out now."

"I've been walking in your footsteps since we spotted them," Kama tells me, ignoring Erity's earlier dig. "They'll think only one of us is still going north. They might decide two hostages are better than one." She pauses, glancing at Kayo and Erity. "I'll join your tri-ad when we get back, if you'll have me. Unless...?" she looks at me.

We're all going to die out here, probably soon, if not by the desert then at the hands of militants. And they're picking out triad-mates? I can't believe these people.

"Let's focus on getting back, first," I say. I hand Kayo her pack.

Instead of slinging it over her shoulder, she opens it. "Okay, let's divvy this up. Knife or spile?"

"Knife," Kama says, looking eastward. "I have to get Idaro to the Select. If they catch up to you two, don't resist, let them take you."

"Lens cleaner." She hands us a small container and sets aside the spare one for her and Erity.

"Lucky it was Kayo's pack that survived," Kama mutters.

"We have to hurry, Kayo." I say.

"A spare flexsheet and firestarters." Kayo looks up at me.

"You keep the flexsheet. It's your pack," I tell her.

"We'll take half the firestarters," Kama says. "Any repellant?"

Kayo shakes her head.

"Drinking bottles?" Erity asks.

"I'm sorry." Kayo pulls out a small container of D-doc juice. "That's all that's left." She looks near to tears.

"Kayo, this is good. You did great." I have no idea how we'll survive two days out here with one knife, lens cleaner, and firestarters.

"Compasses?" Kama asks.

Kayo and Erity shake their heads. I clipped mine to my belt when we left, to keep us heading north. I check to make sure it's working. No problem; these things are made for the desert. I nod to Kama.

"Okay," she says, unclipping hers and handing it to Erity. "See you two after the game."

"Wait," Kayo says. "Take the D-doc juice." She holds it out to me. "You get hurt a lot."

"I thought she was just dodging training," Kama says. She looks like she still thinks so.

Chapter Twenty-Two

The sun is past its zenith by the time we stumble to a stop near a wood cactus.

"Have to rest," Kama mumbles.

I nod, too tired to speak. The sun's too high for the cactus to offer much shade. How can we sit down, anyway, let alone grab some sleep, without any repellant to treat the sand? Neither of us has anything to fight the poison if we're stung or bitten.

Kama begins hacking the thorns off a couple of dead branches lying at the base of the wood cactus. "Snap these in half and pile them together," she says, dropping the de-thorned branches my way and moving around the tree for more.

"What for?"

"Fire." I get the feeling she'd add something sarcastic if she wasn't so tired.

Fire? I snap the first branch in half. Isn't it hot enough for her? I snap the others and pile them together. Something pricks me. "Left a thorn," I mumble, sucking the blood off the back of my hand.

"Pull it off. Can't be any thorns."

"Why not?" I hunt through the sticks for the one with the thorn.

"Smoke." She stumbles back with another handful of branches and drops them on my pile. A scorpion scuttles out and digs into the sand. Kama looks at me. I look at my hand.

There's a small red mark on the back of my left hand between my thumb and first finger. It increases in diameter and begins to swell as I watch. I feel a familiar burning sensation spreading out across my hand. That's it, then. After all this, I'm going to die here.

"Go west, to the nearest estate," I tell Kama. My voice already sounds funny, my words slurred.

"Here, put this on it." She hands me the D-doc juice. I look at her. The stinging pain is already moving up my arm.

"It's all we've got. Just do it." She blinks a couple times and bends down with the fire starter to light the dry branches, wiping her face on her sleeve when her back's to me. The branches catch. A terrible smell, worse than burning rubber, comes from them. There's a slight movement in the sand around the fire, like something's moving under it.

"They don't like the smell," she says. "Okay, lie down now, it's safe."

Safe. I laugh; it comes out more like a wheeze. I try to bend, but I'm dizzy, and I stumble. Kama catches me. She lies me down next the fire. The last thing I feel is a light coolness on the back of my hand as she pours a little more D-doc on my wound. Then the sun fades out and I slide into darkness.

When I wake up the fire's out, but the stink lingers. My left arm is insanely itchy. I reach to scratch it, opening my eyes. The sun is back. Kama's sitting beside me.

"What are you looking at?" My voice sounds strange, weak and scratchy.

"A miracle," she says. "Why aren't you dead?"

"A miracle would be if my arm stopped itching." I sit up without breaking my desperate scratching. "How long was I out?"

"A couple hours, maybe three. You want to tell me why you're alive?"

Norio. He was right about the serum. "I'm only half Salarian," I tell Kama. "Maybe the other half isn't allergic." I scratch vigorously at the half that is. "Did you sleep? Because if I'm not going to die, we have to keep going."

"I slept. And gathered some branches for our next stop." She helps me up. "Stop scratching already. Put some D-doc on it." She hands me the small container. "And be quick. They're back."

I almost spill the juice. "Where?" I look to the east.

"No, southeast now."

I see them on the horizon, still miles away. We must have passed whatever intersection point they were aiming for. I shade my eyes and count. "Three?"

She nods. "It worked. They split up." She doesn't mention that they still outnumber us.

They're desert people. One would outnumber us. I don't say it, though. No good comes from insulting a Salarian. Might as well let her enjoy the thought that she tricked them.

"We're still well ahead of them. They must have stopped to argue about what to do."

Kama smiles. "Let's keep it that way. Can you walk?"

I close the D-doc container and put it in my pocket. "I think we should jog."

"Good way to die of sunstroke." She picks up the branches she's collected and heads north at a brisk walk.

Sunstroke. Is there no end of ways this bloody desert can kill you?

We walk all day and most of the night. When our legs are wobbling so badly they barely hold us we light the branches and collapse beside their stinking fire. We don't sleep long. The sun is shining when we open our eyes again. A quick look behind us shows that our pursuers are gaining.

One day, I think. A day and a half at most. Is it possible to get so close and not make it?

We head out, moving fast. Kama even consents to jogging—twenty paces at a jog, twenty at a quick walk. Something we can keep up all day, she says.

If it wasn't the middle of a desert, if the sun wasn't nearly hot enough to boil us alive, if we weren't already exhausted, famished and dehydrated, maybe we could. We found a sweetwater cactus and Kama cut into it with the knife, but we had nothing to carry the milk in. We caught it in our cupped hands and drank as much as we could, the most delicious thing I've ever tasted. That was sometime last night.

By late afternoon we've slowed to a walk, and are barely keeping that up.

I drop into a waking sleep, jerk myself back to consciousness before I fall, and stagger on, repeatedly. *Keep going, keep going, keep going,* I tell myself, until it no longer means anything, it's just a slow, monotonous refrain at the edge of my consciousness. *Keepgoingkeepgoingkeep…*We can't be more than half a day away. But our pursuers can't be more than three or four hours behind us.

Kama stops beside a tall wood cactus and starts hacking at the living branches with the knife.

"We can't stop," I say, though everything in me longs to.

"We're not stopping." Hack, hack. "We're sending a message." Hack, hack, hack. "Collect some dry branches from the ground. Leave the thorns on." She tears the branch free, ignoring the thorns that pierce her hands and arms, and starts cutting another. When we have a pile of dead and living branches thick with thorns, she lights the dead ones, letting them light the others.

I thought the smell of the dead wood burning was bad. Not only is the smell of live wood cactus way worse, but billows of smoke rise up from the burning thorns. I hold my nose and cough, retching, as I back away.

Kama ignores the reek and starts hacking off another limb, ordering me to collect more dead branches. I'm about to toss them onto the fire when she stops me. "Bring them."

She starts walking again.

The stench must have revived us—or else we're just eager to get away from it—because we walk faster for an hour or so. The sun is falling, but not fast enough to hide us. I'm drifting in and out of brief hallucinations. I think I call Kama "Norio" once. I'm saved from spilling all my secrets only because my throat is too dry to talk.

When I fall and can't get up, Kama drops to her knees beside me, arranges the thorn-covered branches, and lights them. That gets us back up and moving again.

The smoke is more visible in the low light of evening. We leave it burning as we did the last one, and keep heading north. I glance behind but don't see our pursuers. Maybe I have smoke in my eyes, or I'm too tired to focus, I wonder groggily, looking ahead again.

I think I'm hallucinating when I see a dozen white shapes coming toward us. Kama stops walking. I cup my hands around my eyes and focus on them. Then I start running.

Toward them.

Running for all I'm worth.

One of the figures breaks away and runs toward me.

I fall into her arms. Literally. She has to hold me up. I feel her kiss my forehead and stroke my filthy hair, even though I smell like burnt wood cactus thorns.

The others reach us then. One of them lifts up Kama, who has fallen onto the sand.

"You took your time getting here," Agatha says, slipping her arm under mine to keep me upright. "What were you doing?"

"Playing the desert game," I tell her.

"I hope you had fun," she says.

Chapter
Twenty-Three

The woman whose house I'll be staying at takes one look—or
sniff—and orders me to strip. She gives me a thorough sand
scrub, including my hair, and rinses the sand off with some thin,
clear cactus sap I don't recognize. It feels like going through a second sand storm, but I emerge feeling clean again, even if I am
semi-comatose for want of sleep. At least she gave me sweetwater
milk to drink and fried cactus to eat while she was scrubbing away
the sweat, dirt, and stinking smoke. Finally she lets me crawl into
one of her clean beds and sleep.

Agatha joins me the next morning while I'm finishing breakfast.
She's wearing the white blouse and loose pants of the desert people.
I've never seen her in anything but her habit, until last night. She
looks like she's gone completely native. I don't like it, and neither
will the Salarians, but I bet the desert people are eating it up. I
hope she brought a spare robe, because I lost the one Nyah bor-
rowed in the storm.

"Sven and the other leaders want to meet you," she tells me.

"Idaro?"

"Yes, you, Idaro." She looks at me like maybe I'm still not entirely recovered. "Would you like a mirror, perhaps?"

"No, I'm good. Alone?"

"They've already met me. We haven't spoken though. They
don't understand a word of Central Ang." She looks at me accus-
ingly. "Just some Old Earth language, Dan-iss or something like
that, and Salarian. Luckily I learned a smattering of Salarian by
myself."

Oh no, I'm thinking as I finish my sweetwater milk. I'm about to insist she tell me every single thing she's said to them so I can assess the damage, when the hatch to the dugout opens. Here? My compass was missing this morning, and now they don't want me walking outside? Am I a prisoner here? I take a deep breath and go into the lounge area to be examined.

Everything comes down to words. It always does. I have a feeling if I don't get the words right here, a lot of people could die, including me.

Four men and three women file into my hostess's lounge and sit down. I stand as she proudly introduces me to her esteemed guests: Sven, who is clearly in charge, with his advisors Charlot, Marte and Hilde, and Mikal, Torin and Kay. Three women and three men. Sven invites me to sit down. When I do, his people question Idaro's past even more thoroughly than Matriarch Ryo did.

"So, you are here to interpret for the Select?" Sven asks when they're satisfied with my background, or at least have no more questions.

"About that," I say. "Has she… offended anyone? Because it's not intentional, you know, if she has. She's just not very good with languages."

"Isn't she?" Sven smiles for the first time. "What a revelation. People here practically line up to hear her speak. The way she mangles Salarian amuses us no end. I wish the Salarians could hear it."

I nod politely. I intend to do everything in my power to make sure they don't.

"As for offending my people, on the contrary, they adore her. I suspected a trap when we saw the fires, but your Select insisted on rushing straight out, and a dozen of my best fighters sprang forward to protect her. I would have faced a mutiny if I'd tried to stop them." He's still smiling, like he's joking, but underneath I sense he's serious now.

"Fortunately she was right, it was only two lost girls," Torin says.

He's not smiling. I'm guessing he doesn't like his leader's opinion overruled, much less proved wrong.

"I'm sorry," I say. "We didn't mean to cause any trouble. We lit the fires because we were being followed and needed help. We would have been caught if your people hadn't come."

Suddenly they're all serious. I realize immediately what I've said. Why did whoever was after us follow for so long, and not catch up with us? Young girls alone in the desert for the first time? Do I really think we outran them? I feel like a fool. I answer their questions, tell them everything I know about our pursuers, which is practically nothing.

"They were desert people, not Salarians," I say for the third or fourth time. "But ask Kama. Her eyes are better than mine here. She'll know."

"She is being questioned. We will look into this." Sven motions to Hilde. She nods and leaves.

"Now, tell us about the flare," Torin says.

"I set it off the second night we were in camp. I wanted to warn you."

"Warn us of what? How did you know there was going to be an attack on us?" Marte asks, crisp and cool.

"I overheard something. I wasn't sure what it meant, but I was alarmed."

"Who did you overhear? What did you hear? Where did you hear it?" Marte shoots her questions rapidly, giving me no time to think.

And I have to think. This is very dangerous territory. *I will not bring shame on you,* I swore to my grandmother. If I incriminate her now, throw sand on my own estate, even if I'm right I'll be condemned by every Salarian on the planet, and likely Agatha will be too, by association. The dragon will want me dead, and I have a feeling Grandmother Ryo gets what she wants.

Aside from that strictly personal concern, my grandmother is a very powerful woman. If it becomes known that she has committed an act of war on the desert people, she'll have to commit herself, without reservation, to making that war happen. Either she must lead her people into war, or lose face publicly for a petty, and failed, act of revenge. The dragon will never consider the second alternative.

Lies and truth, I tell myself. You can't tell one without the other. I look Marte straight in the eyes. "I was wounded in the explosion set off at the lightspeed platform in Tokosha, and taken to hospital with the other victims. I overheard some Salarians talking in the room beside mine, about retaliating, killing the leaders. I took that to mean bombing the desert people. Someone said *wait till after the fifteens finish their desert game* and someone else said *no, don't let the murderers think they can get away with it.*"

Details are good. The truth is always detailed, whereas lies are vague.

"Then the nurse walked down the hall and the voices stopped. I didn't see who it was, or recognize the voices."

And back to the truth: "I didn't tell anyone because I didn't hear anything definite. I can't prove anything. But I set off the flare when the game started, hoping the Select would find me so I could warn you."

"Why would a Salarian betray her own people for desert people?" Torin asks.

"They're not my people. My mother left because she opposed slavery. So do I. I don't like the way they treat you, either." Torin and Mikal look scornful, and Marte raises a skeptical eyebrow. Nobody really likes interfering heroes. And I'm not one, don't even want the job. Only the truth will convince them, and the truth, whether they like it or not, is that I didn't do it to save them at all.

"I'm only half Salarian. I wasn't raised here. This isn't my struggle, and I don't really care how it ends. But the Select who's here with you is my friend, and she was stupid enough to be sitting right where the explosion was supposed to go off."

I leave it at that. No sense telling them my opinion on what game their militant members are playing. If they haven't figured it out, they won't appreciate hearing it from me. And if they have, for all I know they approve. One of them, Kay, has eyes as green as Nyah's. I suspect sides shift as easily here as desert sand.

"So you set off the flare, and then what? How did you get here?"

I tell them everything. They probably know half of it anyway, Nyah must have come from here if she had Agatha's robe. They don't let on and I don't ask, but I'm careful to tell the whole truth in case she's in touch with them. Catch me in one lie and they won't believe anything. Agatha's won their trust without any coherent words; I better not lose it with one false one. That they could *prove* false, that is.

Only, when they ask where the girls are now, I just say, "somewhere in the desert. It was dark and we were exhausted." Kay probably knows, if he is who I think he is, but if he is, he'll want to protect Nyah, too.

I wonder what Kama's telling whoever is questioning her. We didn't get a chance to talk about what we should or shouldn't say. She's smart, and the four of us agreed not to let anyone know where the girls are hiding before we split up; I'll have to hope for the best.

"Alright," Sven says. "Thank you, Idaro. I can see you are still tired. After you rest, it's time we learned what the Select has come to say to us, if you will translate for her."

I don't usually sleep in the afternoon, but five minutes into my rest, I'm out cold. (Not literally cold; that's a Malemese expression that has no meaning here.) Agatha wakes me an hour later. She's wearing a blue and white Select's robe.

"I want to prepare you," she says.

I sit up slowly. *Oghogho's dead. Salaria's at war. The fifteens all died in the desert. Kama and I are going to be beheaded for leading the militants here.*

"I believe the Adept will have landed by now." She waits for my reaction.

"Okay," I say. It takes a minute for me to change direction. "That's good...?"

"I know you've been through a lot. A lot," she repeats for emphasis. In a Select, that's like shouting. "But I need you to be sharp, now. This is our part, the thing we came to do."

"The thing everyone died for?" *Norio, Lady Celeste, all the victims of the explosions...*

"Not everyone," she says. "Not everyone, yet."

"Okay," I take a deep breath. "I'm here. I showed up. I'll do my best."

She takes my chin in her hand, gently, and raises my head to face her. I'm looking into the intense, focused eyes of a Select. "Do better than your best," she says.

"I just woke up," I point out, with difficulty, because it's hard to talk around that look.

She eases back on it.

"You sent for an Adept." I work out what that means: This is interplanetary now. Which is what I think the militants want. But does Sven want it?

"Yes, I did. Before I came into the desert."

"Right after Lady Celeste died." I'm guessing, but I know I'm right. Lady Celeste was their prompt to "weigh in", and now she's their justification for coming in. A thought hits me: "Not the male Adept on Seraffa?"

"I know the Salarians well enough for that, whether I speak their language or not. No, I have sent for the Adept who came to Malem. The Salarians will be dealing with her now."

I feel a little sorry for the Salarians. Agatha's face is calm and expressionless. This is the other side of Agatha, the Select side. That's what she wanted me prepared for, I realize.

I stand up. "Let me scrub up and I'll be ready, Select."

She permits a brief smile.

This time we go to them. Sven and his advisors are waiting in a large room. Decor is not their strong suit, but the furniture is elegant, functional and comfortable, chairs and couches, side tables and one large working table in the center. A planning room for strategy meetings, everything about it screams: important decisions made here.

Agatha marches in and takes control with a single look. It's not a performance. Sven and his council are definitely not prepared for this.

Neither am I. I am terrified. What am I doing, the sole interpreter in the middle of an interplanetary crisis? I've only interpreted at social events, I'm not even certified yet! Just show up, Agatha said, back in the spaceship. Just show up for what, I should have asked.

At least I'm not wearing my student interpreter's uniform. If—no, when—I mess up, it'll be blamed on a girl who doesn't exist. I won't shame the entire community of professional interpreters when I'm the cause of an interplanetary war. *Oh my god, what am I doing here?*

I take a deep breath. I am the best interpreter at the University of Translators and Interpreters. "A rare talent," the Dean called me. If anyone can do this, I can.

Agatha glances at me. Ready or not…

"Leader Sven," Agatha greets him, holding his gaze. His initial expression of confidence slowly changes to surprise. She turns her piercing gaze on the others. "Leaders and Advisors," she says, reducing them, also, to a state of indecision in their own decision room.

"We are here to discuss your part in the rebellion."

I wasn't prepared enough. For a heartbeat I think, I'm supposed to interpret that? And then what? Run?

I catch myself, pull on the calm, professional air of an interplanetary interpreter, and turn her Edoan words into Salarian.

Sven stares at us: this woman who's been amusing and charming his people for a week and a half and a half-breed child who looks like his enemy, standing here asking the leader of the desert people to account for his actions, as though they know his secrets, and somehow making him feel compelled to answer. The mixture of emotions across his face is almost comical.

"We are alone here. It is time for honesty."

My face and voice mimic hers as I turn Agatha's crisp demand into Salarian. I am no more than her words. I concentrate on everything I've learned about becoming someone else's voice, about disappearing in a conversation, because they must not see me. I must not draw their eyes from her, from the power of her Select's gaze. Given what she's saying, our lives depend upon it.

"It is the militant group, Out of the Desert... The uprising is not of my making," Sven stammers.

"It was your making, though. Until you lost control. Come, there is no more time for secrets. We must prepare for what is coming. Tell me what happened." Agatha stares into his eyes.

"I trained them," he answers slowly, like a drugged man. "I taught them how to survive the games that would grant them citizenship and put them in place among the Salarians. I promised them that lives given to liberate their people from poverty would never be forgotten."

Mikal and Kay look alarmed. Marte opens her mouth—to object? To deny her involvement? Agatha silences them with a wave of her hand, never taking her eyes from Sven.

"They were instructed to create an interplanetary incident,

239

a minimum of lives lost, just enough to require an investigation by the Interplanetary Council. But that wasn't enough for them. Many of their friends died in the attempt to gain citizenship, and they wanted revenge for those deaths. I tried to rein them in, ordered them to wait. They turned on us, attempted to overthrow our leadership! They've lost the purity of the desert, they've been poisoned by the city, by living among the treacherous Salarians."

It's all I can do to keep my voice steady and calm, a low murmur of Edoan words flowing parallel to his Salarian words. How can they let us leave here with this knowledge?

"And so you betrayed them also, gave their names to the Salarians," Agatha says.

"Only those who were out of control, who had become ungovernable. They had to be sacrificed. Do I seem mad? Only a madman would want a war between my people and the Salarians. The day we give them an excuse to kill us, we will be destroyed, every one of us. It will be over before the Interplanetary Council is even aware it is happening."

The room is silent. Agatha waits.

"One final secret, I think," Agatha says. "Tell me."

I can see him struggling, trying to break free.

We can't force anyone to confess something if they truly don't want to, an Adept once told me. Most people want to reveal their secrets, for any number of reasons. We simply allow them to do so.

"I cannot help you unless you are honest with me," Agatha persists. "You must say it. Why did they rebel against you, these young people you trained?"

I interpret her words and hold my breath, praying Sven wants to tell his secret. If he doesn't, if he wants to keep it strongly enough to resist a Select's persuasive powers, we won't leave here alive.

His face twists with effort. His advisors look equally strained.

Chapter Twenty-Three

Say it, I will him silently.

"We found a mine! We found a crystal vein. We decided to set up a secret market, and we couldn't afford any scrutiny. The Salarians would destroy it if they knew about it, rather than share their monopoly over the crystals with us. So we told our young militants it was off, our plans had changed. If they had listened to us, had trusted us, none of this would have happened!"

"Thank you," Agatha says.

She's done? That's it? Sven and his advisors look dazed. They gape at one another, trying to understand what's happened, what should be done now, in their decision room. She can't leave them like this.

"Now it is time to prepare for your meeting with the Salarian Ruling Triad," Agatha says. "They will be arriving soon, with an Adept, I believe."

Chapter Twenty-Four

"They're going to kill us."

"I think they're going to feed us," Agatha says as we walk back to the dugout where we've been staying.

"They're talking about it right now," I tell her.

"What would they tell the Adept if we weren't here when she arrives with the Salarian Ruling Triad? They are well aware of that; they won't harm us."

"They're wondering what we'll say when the Adept gets here, not what they'll say."

"We are perfectly safe here." Agatha nods at several people who greet her as she passes. "That's why we were chosen. I am immune to this planet's poisons, like all desert people, and you are immune thanks to our friends at Idaro's grandmother's estate."

"You arranged that?"

"The Select here did, but I knew about it."

"It would have helped if you'd told me."

"I didn't know beforehand. I assume the Adept on Seraffa didn't think it was the kind of thing you'd be likely to go along with in advance."

"He was right!" Thinking about the Adept on Seraffa reminds me of Agatha's initial reaction. "You didn't want to come here, did you?"

She doesn't answer. I'm figuring I'll never know the reason for that look that crossed her face when she says, as though she's confessing to a crime, "I was afraid to come here."

"I thought you didn't know your parents were desert people until you saw the pictures on the comp just before we landed."

"I didn't. I was afraid because my parents died here. I've never been told what their mission was. I realize now they must have been chosen for it because of their origins. But for us, the O.U.B. is our only affiliation, so I was never told that, either. My father was an Adept, and my mother was his assistant. They left me on Seraffa where they lived, thinking they'd only be gone a short while. Their ship exploded leaving orbit to return home. A mechanical malfunction. I was five years old."

"Oh," I say. "Um, did you... did coming here help?"

"Yes." She smiles. "Coming here, being among these people, felt a little like coming home. Like being a child again. Then, this morning I put my robe back on, and I knew where my real home is."

I nod as though I understand, but I'm wondering, where is my real home?

After supper, I hang out with Kama a bit. The family she's billeted with is teaching her their language. I raise my eyebrows at that.

"They're okay, you know, even if they are desert people." She shrugs and continues her story. There are two little girls, about eight and nine, who think it's a great game, and naturally a Salarian is always up for a game. Kama tells me she bet them the necklace and bracelet she always wears that she could learn and remember twenty new words a day, every day she's here.

"How are you doing?" I ask.

"Nineteen words a day," she says.

I look at her.

She shrugs. "They giggle so hard they fall on the floor, and then they apologize and tell me I'm sure to remember twenty words the next day. But I guess nineteen is all I can focus on."

An aircar hums overhead before the sun sets. I wonder how the Adept and the Ruling Triad found us so easily, then realize Agatha's locator must be working again. How lucky is that?

The Adept emerges first. I recognize her from Malem. She glances over the crowd of desert people—I know from experience each one of them will believe she looked directly into his or her eyes, and maybe it's true—then nods to Agatha, raises an eyebrow when she sees me, and descends onto the sand. Four male Salarians come out next, probably armed though their weapons aren't in sight. Then three women, the Ruling Triad, I assume. They stand stiffly beside the aircar, looking at the desert people in distaste.

An entire dugout has been cleared for their accommodation. When they're led over to it they balk. I'm betting they'll get back on the aircar and return to Tokosha before they'll climb down into their underground quarters. The Adept says something to them, very quietly, and they start climbing down behind their guards.

"First things first," one of the Ruling Triad says when we're all assembled in the decision room the next morning, and the correct bows have been exchanged. "A number of the fifteens have not returned from their desert walk."

I feel sick. How many did I put in danger? Correction: I put them all in danger, how many didn't survive it?

"How many are missing?" Torin asks.

I close my eyes, as though that will somehow distance me from the answer.

"All of the girls from the Kicho-Ryo-Tomiko estate. We believe they were targeted for some reason. Six others from several different estates. Those may have died in the desert."

"They are safe," Sven answers. "One of our people is protecting them. No harm has come to them, nor will it."

"I will need more than your word on that," the Salarian woman replies. "I want—"

All of the girls? "Where's Kayo?" I cry. "Has Kayo been found? And Erity?" It's a terrible breach of conduct, interrupting a member of the Ruling Triad. I'm an interpreter here, a voice for other people. Right now, I don't care. "They were trying to reach an estate west of here!"

The Salarian I interrupted stares at me, affronted. She is of the Ruling Triad.

244

"There was a desert storm," One of her triad-mates says.

"It passed us! We separated after it was over."

"Idaro," Agatha says. No one else will look at me. They don't go looking for individual girls lost in the desert game.

"I'm going to find her!" I turn to the door. They can have their meeting without me. Kama will come with me. All I'll have to say is, "they're missing."

"Idaro." Agatha's voice stops me. "You are needed here. Please tell Sven I would like him to send four of his people, the ones who went into the desert with me, to look for them."

I interpret her request from Edoan into Salarian. "And ask him to have Kama brought here," she adds.

Kama arrives and drops into a startled bow, low enough to touch the floor, when she sees her Ruling Triad. I've regained my composure somewhat, and manage not to interrupt when Sven instructs her to tell the Ruling Triad what she knows about the girls from her estate. She glances at me once and tells the story as I did, claiming not to know exactly where the girls are but confident that they're safe with Nyah.

"Nyah?" one of the Salarians says. "Nyah the desert girl who won her citizenship?"

"Yes, that's her. She saved all our lives," Kama says, bowing again. She glances at me, probably wondering why I look upset. It takes willpower not to tell her Kayo and Erity are missing, knowing she'll share my fear. But that would shame her in front of her rulers.

"We have taken excellent care of your young girls," Sven says smoothly, "as you have now heard from two of them. You may go," he says to Kama. "Four of my people are waiting outside to speak to you about two of your friends."

"Kama will tell them where you parted from Kayo and Erity. They will find them," Agatha murmurs to me.

"I trust you are also taking excellent care of our people, those who lived among you and have recently been... detained," Sven continues, speaking to the Salarians. "We will be happy to release your children to you, as I am sure you will be happy to release our people."

The apparent leader of the Ruling Triad—or at least the most vocal one—demands to know if the fifteen-year-olds are hostages.

"They are our guests," Sven says. "Why? Are our people your hostages?"

"They are murderers!"

"A few of them. Not all. I have given you the names of those involved in the explosions. Some of them you already have, and the others we will turn over to you. We do not condone violence. You are free to judge and punish them. However, those who are innocent of any wrongdoing must be released."

The three Salarians look outraged, until the Adept looks intently at them.

"Acceptable," their spokesperson says.

"What did she say to get them to be so agreeable?" I murmur in Edoan to Agatha, for whom I'm translating everything being said.

"She informed them that the Interplanetary Council is waiting to hear from her as to whether they should intercede here."

"Next there is the matter of the crystal mines," the Adept says.

I look up to hear what she has to say about the slaves in the mines.

She turns to Sven. "It has come to my attention that you have found a vein of crystals while digging out one of your settlements."

He shoots a nasty look at Agatha, clears his throat, and admits it's true.

"Unacceptable!" the vocal Salarian cries. "They aren't citizens! They can't own land."

"I believe interplanetary law granted them squatters' rights several generations ago," the Adept replies. "They have the right to create their own state and govern it themselves. That could be an unfortunate business, though. I believe their settlements cover more land than yours do, spread out as they are. The Interplanetary Council would have to come in to help decide who owns what territory. Far simpler just to grant them all citizenship and learn to live with them, don't you think?"

The Salarians look unconvinced in the extreme.

"Wait a minute," Sven says. "We would end up with most of the land?"

"Acceptable!" the vocal Salarian cries. "We will grant them citizenship, after we have punished those who murdered our people."

The Adept looks at Sven.

"Acceptable," he says. "On the condition that we have representation in the government and judicial system, and that we own the land we currently live on."

Back and forth they go, and no one—no one!—mentions the slaves.

"When will they talk about Lady Celeste?" I ask Agatha in Edoan when we're on a refreshment break.

"The Adept is in charge," she replies. "But what good can come of mentioning the atrocities that brought us here?"

"When will she bring up the slave issue, then?"

"She might not. The Salarians are discussing peace with the desert people, and have agreed to come here to do so. That's something we can be proud we helped accomplish. The Adept knows better than we do how far she can push them. Giving up their miners might be one step too far."

"It's important! The slaves matter as much as your desert people."

She looks at me. I'm ashamed. I know her better than that.

"Important enough to risk losing the peace we're trying to secure?" she asks mildly. "We have to trust the Adept."

"We're the ones who were in the vision," I remind her.

When we return to the negotiations, I look around the room. Salarians and desert people. No one is here to represent those who gambled themselves into servitude. *Do better than your best,* Agatha told me. So should the Adept. So should everyone. They should care about those who have no voice, no power, as much as those who do. But of course, they don't.

Whatever else I did here, I came for only one reason: to free my sister. I haven't given that my best.

I nod my head to Agatha, as though following her instruction, and begin speaking Salarian: "There's also the matter of the indentured servants to discuss."

They all turn and stare at me. If any one here speaks Edoan I'm going to be caught. I'll be out of the university so fast, and likely in prison. Interpreting for my own agenda is an interplanetary criminal offense, let alone inventing words and pretending I'm interpreting for someone. Well, I've committed it, no use stopping short of making it mean something. I bow to the Ruling Triad, glance quickly at Agatha as if these are her words, and continue.

"Many of your miners have died in the conflict between you and the desert people, and countless others die in the mines every year. That's not servitude, that's slavery."

The Adept is looking intently at me. I avoid looking at her.

"Nothing excuses slavery, not their bad choices or any justification you use." I turn to the Adept, not quite meeting her eyes, "Or anything the O.U.B. does to legitimize it. None of us are free until they are free. If they can be bought, we can all be bought—it's only a matter of price."

"Enough." The Adept speaks calmly, but her voice conveys an overpowering command. Even without the force of her gaze I freeze, unable to say another word.

She looks at Agatha. Agatha returns her gaze steadily, backing me up even though she doesn't speak enough Salarian to know what I said. She probably has a good idea, though.

No luck. The Adept can't be fooled. She speaks Edoan. She only has to mentally replay what she heard Agatha and me saying while she was focused on the others, to know I wasn't asked to interpret these words. I've ruined myself, and for nothing; they aren't even considering what I said.

"It has become apparent that you are not able to keep your indentured servants safe," Agatha says, nodding at me to interpret her Edoan words. I glance at the Adept. She's staring at Agatha. This wasn't on her agenda.

"We did not set off those explosions!" the vocal Salarian objects when I've finished.

"They died unprotected in the midst of a conflict you helped create," Agatha says. "Moreover, many die before their term is up, working with crystals that are poisonous to them."

"They give their oaths willingly. You oversee that."

I hate translating the words of this woman, but after my one act of rebellion, I'm meekly professional again. Particularly since the Adept is watching me now, and listening closely.

"We oversee their oaths and your statement of their debt. It's up to you to ensure they forfeit only the years they owe you, not their lives. You have failed to do so, in a great many cases. They are extraplanetary citizens, which makes their deaths a sustai—"

"We are prepared to take this to the Interplanetary Council," the Adept says, cutting Agatha off abruptly, while sounding like she's weighing in with us.

The Salarians all stare, horrified, at the Adept. A sustained disregard for the lives of extraplanetary citizens on the part of the ruling government of a planet is an act of interplanetary war.

I translate what she said to Agatha. We know this Adept. She is thoroughly ticked behind her expressionless face. We'll hear about it afterwards. Not a hint of that shows on any of our faces now, though.

"Unless?" the Salarian spokeswoman croaks, taking our calm appearance for real solidarity. As, of course, she is meant to. The O.U.B. never disagree. They are all working together under God's guidance toward a benevolent human universe. No one is supposed to know that the right hand often has no idea what the left hand is doing.

"You will free all indentured servants on Salaria before any others come to harm in your care," the Adept says. "And in future, work in your mines will no longer be part of any off-world gambling." It's all I can do not to grin as I translate that for Agatha. Oghogho will be coming home with me!

The Salarians blanch, dumb with shock.

"Impossible," one of them says, weakly.

"You will ruin us," the vocal member of the Ruling Triad protests.

"It would take a great deal more than having to pay your miners to ruin you," the Adept says coolly.

"The heat on this planet, having to work underground, the trace elements of scorpion and snake poison where the crystals are mined…" Agatha lists all the drawbacks to working in the Salarian mines. "You would have to pay well to get willing miners here." I glance at Sven and his advisors and this time I do grin as I interpret her words.

&

Negotiations continue as the leaders of the Salarians and the desert people work out a tolerable agreement. I interpret for Agatha, and occasionally she makes a suggestion, but our—or rather her—main input is over. The fact that she's here, part of this, will help Sven convince his people to agree to it. The Adept and her threat of far greater interference will help the Salarians convince their people. Fortunately I won't be around for that part.

At the back of my mind, through the days of interpreting, is my fear for Kayo and Erity.

"I should have gone myself," I tell Kama, as we sit in the evenings at the edge of the settlement staring out at the desert, in the direction the four men went searching for them.

"We'd only have slowed them down," she says.

"They'll find them."

She never answers when I say that. She could at least hold up her side, reassure me back. If it was Kama out there, Erity and Kayo would be so reassuring it would make me sick. I'd be doing what Kama's doing: not tempting fate.

"You really want to be in a triad with Erity?" I ask Kama while we watch for them. Erity doesn't take anything seriously; Kama takes everything seriously. "And Kayo?" I can't even begin to list the ways they're opposite. "What about your friends? What about Akako?"

"They're still my friends. But they'd be better to form new triads. Akako and I don't always... bring out the best in each other."

She stops abruptly. I'm thinking she wants to drop it, when she adds, "I think I could learn something from Erity and Kayo. And they could learn from me. It would be a good triad for all of us."

"It would be an interesting one." I almost wish I could make that triad a quad. I gaze out at the desert, willing myself to see them coming.

"What will you do? After this is all over, I mean?" Kama asks.

"Go home." And finish my interpreter's degree, if I can manage to avoid any more interruptions. "Finish my schooling," I say.

"Without a triad?"

I shrug. *I could start my own,* I'm thinking, but I'm not ready to share that thought.

Sometime during the third night after we learned they were missing, I hear footsteps aboveground. I jump out of bed, race down the hall and climb up through the hatch. Four weary figures are walking slowly through the village. They didn't find them. I turn aside and take a shaky breath. Then I notice they're carrying two still, white shapes.

Are they alive? The words stick in my throat.

"Are they alive?" Kama calls. Three hatches down I see her climbing aboveground.

"Barely," one of the men says as they carry Kayo and Erity toward the med dugout.

"Heat, dehydration, exhaustion—another day and we'd have been too late. But they're young and strong. I think we got to them in time," one of the others says more optimistically.

I race barefoot across the sand toward them, and hear Kama running, too. I fall into step beside two of the men and take Kayo's hand. "I'm here, Kayo. You're safe now, you'll be okay." Behind me, I hear Kama saying similar things to Erity.

Kayo opens her eyes. She tries to say something. I lean down, my ear near her mouth.

"You made it." Her voice is so raw it's painful to hear it.

"I made it," I agree. "Thanks to you and Norio and Kama and Erity and Nyah and all the fifteens…" I smile down at her.

She mumbles something, barely moving her cracked lips. I lean down closer.

"Good backup," she mumbles again, in her raspy voice.

"Yeah," I say. "I guess I needed it after all."

She smiles and closes her eyes.

I walk beside her, holding her hand, all the way to the med dugout.

☙

The initial talks wrap up in another day. We receive information through the aircar comp that all the fifteens with Nyah have been transferred home safely. I remember them trudging across the desert to find me, with no idea how they could help or what they were getting into. Just showing up to make sure I got home with them. I never thought I'd be part of something like that, that I'd have friends who would risk their lives for me.

Chapter Twenty-Four

The Salarian Ruling Triad takes Kama, Erity, and Kayo home with them. They intend to stop off at the Kicho-Ryo-Tomiko estate anyway. Grandmother Ryo is very influential. If they convince her of the new agreement, the other estates will fall in line. They'll certainly need the Adept with them when they talk to the dragon.

Agatha and I watch their aircar leave.

"Will I see you again?" Kayo asked me when I went to say good-bye to her last night.

"No," I had to tell her. "I can't come back, but I'll never forget you." Then I thought of how she'd feel if she knew there is no Idaro, that I lied to her and all the fifteens, and everyone, the whole time. "Kayo, if you hear anything bad about me…"

"I won't believe it," she said, a little fiercely.

"I was going to say, I want you to know you're the best friend I've ever had, you and Norio."

"I won't ever believe anything bad about you," she said, starting to cry.

Which embarrasses me even now, remembering it. "Hey," I said. "Maybe believe some things. Like, I lied to you about the desert chicken."

She hiccups. "I know that." She smiles a little. "They told me when I ate it here."

"And you puked it up, right?"

"Of course I did! It's *snake!*"

I grin, remembering that, and wave at Kayo, her face mashed against the aircar window, mouthing *goodbye* as it rises into the sky.

"Ready to go back to Tokosha?" Agatha asks when the aircar has left.

I look out over the burning sand. "You told them to send another aircar, right? Because I am not walking out through that desert."

Chapter
Twenty-Five

I'm waiting outside the Kicho-Ryo-Tomiko Number Two mine when the slaves are released. Some of them, anyway. Even the Adept could not convince my grandmother to release all her slaves. Dragon to dragon, they reached a compromise: Ryo agreed to free any who were ill or weak and therefore unlikely to finish out their terms of service without permanent damage, such as death. The rest have to work off their term. She'll have to hire desert people eventually, because there won't be any more indentured servants; the government passed a law against gambling debts being paid off in service.

Agatha warned me not to come today. "Your sister's young and strong, she won't be released. Even if she is among them, she won't recognize you, and you can't tell her who you are. It'll just upset you and confuse her."

I came anyway. If she's not here, at least I'll know right away that she's okay—so far. And, if possible, I'm prepared to find her.

The aircar stopped outside the gate of the wall around the mine and its surrounding buildings, alongside a dozen other aircars all waiting to take the released slaves to the port. Spaceships are waiting there for them; they've each been issued a ticket home, the only payment they'll get for their service.

It was surprisingly easy to convince the guards at the gate that I'm from the Kicho-Ryo-Tomiko estate so they'd let me in. I guess they've seen my picture in the news-holos, interpreting at the Summit of the Peace Accord, as it's being called. I imagine Norio laughing at that, such a distinguished name for a meeting in a desert dugout.

The first thing I see, a few yards away, is Matriarch Ryo's son,

Ichiro, standing beside two male Salarians. I assume one of them is a mine supervisor; the other is wearing the insignia of a customs official. They appear to be double-checking something on their hand comps, probably a list of the slaves being freed today. There's a long line of sorry-looking foreigners standing on the other side of them, waiting. Ichiro looks up and notices me. He looks surprised, and then, very briefly, sad. Before I can interpret that expression it's gone; he's looking down and tapping something on his hand comp again.

I go over to stand with a group of people waiting to receive the slaves: mostly government officials here to confirm their ability to travel and tell them how they'll get home, and a few relatives who heard of their release in time to get here. "I'm with the mining family," I tell the first anxious relative who tries to make conversation, and after that I don't need to worry about what to say to them.

This has all been planned, so I'm wondering what the hold-up is when at last Ichiro and the two men with him begin allowing the slaves past. One by one the weary men and women state their name, look into the hand comps of the mine supervisor and the customs official, and press their thumbs into a device attached to the customs' comps, before limping or staggering or coughing their way over to us. I hear the first ones to arrive responding to the officials' questions, *no they weren't working in this condition, they were granted sick days, they've been treated fairly, considering…* I only half listen, still trying to see if Oghogho is in the line.

I see a dark head, tall, behind six or eight other people. There's something about her face, but then she turns away and the person ahead of her shifts sideways, obstructing my view. It's not like there won't be anyone else from Seraffa who gambled and lost, but I rise on my tip toes, straining to see the person. Her head—I think it's a woman—moves forward as another slave is sent on. She seems to be moving easily, not limping, but all I can see now is the top of her head. Two more people prove their identity and shuffle over to us before the line has shifted enough for me to see her whole head, and then she turns.

It is Oghogho! I think it is, but her eyes are hidden under some kind of cups or flaps. Her hand rests on the shoulder of the person ahead of her, like he's steering her forward. What's happened to her? I bounce on my feet, resisting the urge to run forward. I can't make a scene here. I'm Idaro, there's no connection between me and this woman except a shared birthplace.

The line of people creeps forward, one by one, as slowly as the sun crosses the sky. Yes, her eyes *are* covered. She walks without limping, unhurt except…

Except that she's blind. I wait in agony as the slaves file forward. When it's her turn she can't look into the comps; they accept her thumb print and let her pass. The man ahead has waited to walk with her across the sand toward us.

"You've been hurt," I say, as calmly as my shaking voice will allow. I don't use her name, or touch her, nothing to show familiarity. "Will you… be all right?" *Stupid, stupid! Of course she's not all right!* "I'll help you to the aircar." I speak our home language, Edoan. Oghogho's a trader and knows several languages, but I don't know if Salarian is one of them.

It never occurred to me that, without being able to rely on her eyes, Oghogho would be relying on her ears.

"Akhié? Is that you? How did you get here?" She grabs my arm.

I look around quickly. Oghogho's voice is too loud. But there are at least a dozen wounded slaves around us now, asking questions and receiving information and instructions from the government officials in several different languages, and two of the waiting relatives are greeting their loved ones exuberantly. No one is paying any attention to us.

"My name is Idaro," I tell my sister, keeping my voice low. "I'm from Seraffa, too. We can go back together."

She takes this in without comment.

"How did you get hurt?"

"There was an explosion. I was hit in the face by some shrapnel." She pauses, then adds, "The medic says my eye nerves aren't damaged. Surgery could repair my sight. The cups are there so I won't strain them while they heal enough for the surgery." There's a don't-worry tone to her voice that lets me know she doesn't believe my cover for a minute.

I don't know what to say next.

"How did you know I'm from Seraffa?" she asks in Malemese.

My mouth falls open. She can't see that, but I guess my silence is just as telling because she smiles. "They'll just think we're speaking a local dialect if anyone overhears us in all this noise."

She's right. No one's paying attention to us as more and more freed slaves make their way over, adding their voices to the general din. No one speaks Malemese, anyway, except for a small group of people on one small, distant planet most people haven't even heard of. And my father, and us.

"When did you learn?" I ask in Malemese.

"When Father was dying."

"You never let on!"

"We weren't supposed to talk to him in Malemese. I only wanted to understand him when he spoke it."

"You acted so—" *superior,* but I stop myself from saying it. What are we doing, arguing here like when we were kids? But the injustice of her learning Malemese too, after our mother was so angry at me for learning it, goads me. "You could have admitted you learned it too," I tell her.

"I couldn't. I always had to be the good girl, the obedient daughter."

"What does that make me? The bad one?"

"I didn't mean… but yes, you were, weren't you? You never did

257

what you were told. You spoke Malemese to Father, you ran away from home after he died. I'm not criticizing, I—"

"Of course you're criticizing me!"

"—I always admired your independence."

"You never liked me."

"You never liked me. So what are you doing here, pretending to be someone else?"

"I came to get you."

"To get me? Like, rescue me?" She laughs.

I flush, feeling as useless as Kayo when she showed up to rescue me. I'm glad I didn't laugh at her.

"Didn't I tell you to stay on Seraffa?" Oghogho demands "When you objected to them taking me away, I told you to stay out of it! You could have got killed, coming here!"

"I never do what I'm told," I remind her.

She sighs. "Here we are, quarrelling again."

"Let's just go home. Come with me." I start to lead her through the growing crowd of people, toward the gate.

Half way there, we're intercepted by two guards. One of them glances toward Ichiro, who nods.

"Come with us," the guard says.

"Why?" I switch to Salarian. "We're just leaving." I take another step toward the gate.

He grabs my arm. "Come quietly, please. Both of you."

"Where are you taking us?" Oghogho demands, in Salarian.

"You have no right!" I look at the government officials, raising my voice a little. "You have to free the wounded slaves!"

The officials pretend not to notice, focusing on the people they're helping.

"We have the right to question you—and her. Inside the gates of this mining compound, we are the law." He's holding my arm tightly enough to hurt. The second guard has Oghogho's arm, but he holds her more gently than my guard's grasp on me. I stop objecting so he'll continue to hold her gently.

They take us to one of the buildings, a straightforward rectangle with rooms along each side of a central hallway down the middle. We are locked in a room with a table, four straight chairs, and a small, darkened window. This building must house the business offices for the mine, and the other, larger one I saw, the residences. I help Oghogho to a chair.

"Do you know why they've brought us here?" she asks in Malemese.

"No."

"Does it have to do with you pretending to be someone else?"

"I don't think so."

"Tell me about that anyway."

"It's a long story. Just call me Idaro. You don't know me. We happen to be from the same planet, so I spoke to you, nothing more than that. I'm sure they'll let you go."

"And you?"

"I don't know. I really don't know why we're here."

"Okay, we'll figure it out. Tell me about this Idaro."

How do older sisters do it? Blind and hurt and knowing nothing about the situation, she just takes charge of my problem, and somehow I find myself letting her. It's even a relief. In the safety of an unknown language, I tell her Idaro is the granddaughter of Matriarch Ryo, who owns this mine, and about the estrangement between Philana and Ryo, and that Idaro supposedly came to meet her family, the ruse I used to get here to look for her, Oghogho…

"Why are Philana and Ryo estranged?" she asks.

Hitting perfectly on the single important thing in my whole story. As soon as she says it, I know why I'm here. I let out my breath as though I've been punched.

The door opens.

Grandmother Ryo stands framed by it, glaring at me. "Take her away," she says, motioning toward Oghogho.

Ichiro enters and takes Oghogho's arm. "Don't be alarmed," he tells her. "I'm taking you to another room. You won't be harmed." He doesn't look at me once.

"Let her go! She's just one of the freed slaves. I spoke to her because we're both from Seraffa."

"Be quiet!" Grandmother Ryo snaps. "You have no say here. This is not a negotiation you can manipulate to your ends!" She glares at me while the others leave.

"Do you remember what I told you when you first arrived?" she says when we're alone.

I will not tolerate a single word against my way of life, I remember. The Summit meetings have been constantly in the news, as well as the words and holos of everyone at them.

"I was interpreting." I look straight at her, refusing to show the terror I feel, but when I look in her eyes all I see is fire. She is the law here. How far does that go? Slaves have died, and no one has questioned that. She can kill me, I believe it, and right now she wants to. Agatha warned me not to come.

I want to cringe away from her, to fall on my knees and beg for mercy. I'm not too proud to do it, either, but this is a dragon facing me, and that's not the way to survive a dragon's wrath. I meet her eyes and do not look away.

I will not have another traitor crawl out of my nest, so do not think to shame me, and survive, she warned me.

Why are Philana and Ryo estranged, my sister asked. I thought it was a difference of opinion, but people never fight because they disagree; they fight because of *how* they disagree.

"I will not bring shame on you," I tell my grandmother, the same words I said then. Something changes in her face. She's still furious, a proud and pitiless woman, but staring into her eyes I feel again, as I did then, that strange connection between us. I know what it is to hold onto an anger, to fasten it to your pride so it won't slip away over time.

"I will return when I've decided what to do with you," she says, leaving. The door locks behind her.

I didn't expect Oghogho to be in the line of slaves being freed. I expected her to be working in the mine, or resting in a locked dorm. So I brought what I needed.

Opening an outside lock from inside the room is tricky. The locking mechanism is actually between the two sides of the door, however, and since this building was never intended as a jail, it's possible to spring the lock from inside the room if you know how and you have the right tools. Thanks to Messer Sodum I do, and I have. I wait till I'm certain my grandmother has left, and open the door as quietly as possible. No one in the corridor.

I creep down the hall, silently trying each door. The first one begins to open at my touch. I close it and continue; the one I want will be locked. I hate the construction of this building. If any-one enters from either end, they'll be able to see down the entire hallway. I'm panting with fear, like a rabbit without so much as a shadow to hide in as I make my way from door to door, check-ing each one for noises inside before trying to open it. It's not just my life that depends on my not getting caught, but possibly Oghogho's, too.

Finally I reach a door that doesn't open to my touch. No sounds from inside, at least none that I can hear. I take a breath and unlock it as quietly as I can. Then I'm afraid to open it. Has someone heard me and is waiting calmly inside for me to show myself? That would be so like my grandmother. I grit my teeth and open the door.

No one's inside. I let out my breath in relief. Directly in front of me is a desk with a comp on it, turned on. My grandmother's signature style of security: lock the door, not the comp. I put the voice override in my mouth and say: "Interplanetary." When the messaging system comes up, I state the link Philana made me memorize, and take the voice override out, hiding it under my shirt again.

After an agonizingly long delay—which is probably only about ten minutes—Philana's face appears. I smile in relief at reaching her and open my mouth to greet her—

"How did you get in here?"

I freeze. Philana's image on the screen freezes in the middle of saying *hello*.

I'm trying desperately to come up with something that would explain my getting through two locked doors, when my grandmother steps around the desk to stand beside me, looks at the screen, and she freezes too.

The three of us stand shocked into silence, staring at each other.

Everything depends on Philana, now, and I haven't had any time to prepare her. Everything I intended to tell her—about her mother's pride and the way she looked when she asked me if Philana was alive; about my own mother dying before I had a chance to forgive her and be forgiven; about the hollow, aching pain your anger turns into when it's too late, there's nothing you can ever do to make it up—I can't tell her any of that while her mother is standing here. I look from one stiff face to the other and I know I've lost this gamble and I will pay for it, and probably Oghogho as well just because I spoke to her.

Grandmother Ryo is the first to regain command of herself. "What is this?" She looks from the screen to me, and back at the screen. I can feel her anger rising by the second.

"So my daughter has found you," Philana says. I feel a flicker of hope. Philana knows her mother, she knows what's at stake here.

"Did you send her?" My grandmother's voice is dangerously quiet.

Please, I think. Please hear what's underneath the anger. *Yes*, I think, very hard, as Philana hesitates. *Say yes.* I look at the screen, trying to put the thought into my eyes. She's a Select, she can read the emotions people write on their faces. *Say yes! Don't, whatever you do, don't reject her again in front of me!*

"No," Philana says. "It was her idea."

I look at the dragon. I'm ready to beg now, to fall on her mercy; she might at least spare my sister's life.

"She's smarter than I am," Philana says. "If I knew my heart as well as she knows hers, I would have come to see you long before now."

Chapter
Twenty-Six

I've always disliked spaceships, but it's a relief to board this one. No more burning heat and blinding sun; in three weeks I'll be home. I intend to stand in the shower for five hours, wasting water. Maybe all day.

I swipe open the door to my cabin and stop dead. Murdock the medic and his jolly assistant are waiting for me.

"What are you doing here?"

"No time for pleasantries. We have to get started right away," Murdock says. "You won't be leaving this room again until we land. Don't worry," he holds up his hand before I can object. "You won't want to."

I take a step back.

"Oh dear." Agatha arrives in the hallway behind me. She steers me into the cabin and closes the door. "I hoped to get here before you. Sit down, Kia."

The name sounds strange. Kia? I sit down on my cot. How long has it been since anyone called me Kia? Am I still Kia? I glance at the mirror on the back of the door. Idaro stares back at me mockingly. What would it be like to have Kia look back at me when I look into a mirror?

"I'm listening."

"That's a start. Now, here's what's going to happen. Idaro is going to lock herself in her cabin for three days; then, in the night, she's going to steal a shuttle and launch into space. Ten minutes later, the shuttle will explode. Her DNA will be found on some of the retrieved pieces."

I imagine red streaks exploding into space along with pieces of shuttle, and feel myself beginning to hyperventilate. "You're going to space a body?"

"Of course not. What are you thinking? Oh, I see you're not thinking. Take a deep breath."

I take several. It doesn't help. "Just tell me."

"Philana has provided the DNA samples that will be found on the salvage. Traces only. Some strands of hair. No body involved."

"Why—" I croak, swallow, start again. "Why would Idaro do something like that?" I glance at the mirror. She looks sane.

"You know she was diagnosed with PTSD after the explosion on the lightspeed platform. It's perfect, really. We couldn't have planned it better."

"I... She recovered. She joined the desert game. She interpreted for you! She wouldn't do this now."

"That's what we'll all think. But what a brave girl, to do all those things when inside she was fighting off panic attacks and depression."

"No. I don't want everyone with PTSD to be slurred like that. Be made to look suicidal."

"Many of them are, Kia. You'll be—Idaro will be—helping them. We've known about PTSD since Old Earth was the only human world. We understand the brain's response to trauma, we can treat it now—and yet too many sufferers refuse to. They deny it, think it's a weakness, blame themselves instead of seeking help. Idaro is well-known on Salaria. People who survived the explosions, or came back from a desert walk changed forever, they need her to force them to acknowledge their pain, and get help."

"You're making this up."

"Well, yes, of course I am. Idaro doesn't exist. But if she's real to you, then let us make her death count for something."

"I already did," I mutter, thinking of my promise to Philana. No one is more surprised than I am that I kept it. Not to mention getting her and her mother talking again.

"Idaro has to die, Kia. They can never know you tricked them."

"Can we get started?" Murdock whines. "I only have three weeks."

"I won't be able to visit Oghogho?" We've only just begun to talk rationally after years of fighting and misunderstanding each other. I decided if Philana and the dragon can make peace, Oghogho and I can. But what will she think if I never once come to her cabin to see her?

"I've already explained the situation to her, that's why I was late getting here. She'll come see you tomorrow. Right now I believe she's processing it, in her cabin. I thought she, at least, should know of your contribution to freeing the slaves."

"I wish you hadn't," I say. My relationship with my sister is complicated enough without Agatha making me look better than I am.

"Don't worry. Everyone else believes Idaro did it, and she won't be around to give you any credit."

I glance in the mirror, thinking of the fifteens and Nyah and even my grandmother, the dragon. I can never let them know I'm still alive. I won't be, not to them. "They won't believe she'd do that," I murmur to Idaro's face in the mirror.

"They'll have to. We'll let them see the report," Agatha says.

Kayo will be devastated. She's already lost her brother.

If she believes it, that is. *I won't ever believe anything bad about you,* she told me. And she won't, no matter what evidence they provide. She won't let Erity and Kama believe it either, if they're in her triad. I smile. It doesn't matter if everyone else believes it.

"What about the ship's records? Of who came aboard and who disembarked?"

"It's an O.U.B. ship. They're our records."

"Does that mean...?"

Chapter Twenty-Six

Agatha nods. "The Adept is travelling with us."

Murdock was right: I don't want to leave my cabin.

In my mirror, I watch Idaro take a deep breath. "Give me a sheet," she says.

Murdock's assistant hands me the spare sheet for my cot.

"Goodbye, Idaro," I whisper, covering the mirror. I hold out my arm to the assistant, standing nearby with her IV needle.

I'm ready to be Kia again.

About the Author

 J. A. McLachlan lives with her husband in Waterloo, Ontario. She is the author of a short story collection, *Connections,* two non-fiction textbooks on professional ethics, and three science fiction novels: *Walls of Wind, The Occasional Diamond Thief,* and *The Salarian Desert Game.* Find out more about her and her books and sign up to receive free stories on her website, www.janeannmclachlan.com or connect with her on Facebook, Twitter, or Google+.

Other Science Fiction Books by J. A. McLachlan

Walls of Wind, an alien science fiction novel that explores gender relations, can be found on Amazon and Kobo.

The Occasional Diamond Thief, the first book in the series about Kia and Agatha, can be found in bookstores and on Amazon and Kobo.

Acknowledgements

First, as always, I am grateful to my family for their help, support, encouragement and love: Ian, Amanda and Jeff, Tamara and Steve, Caroline and Karl, Richard, Linda and Peter, Pete and Jan, and my beloved nieces, nephews, cousins, and grandchildren. You are the air I breathe.

I also owe thanks to everyone who helped me with their critiques and editing: Lori Christy, Barbara Strang, Linda Barron, and Ian Darling. Thanks also goes to my amazing launch team, who helped give this book a great start.

I am very grateful to my friend and publicist, Janice Shoults, to my talented cover designer, Marija Vilotijevic and my interior designer Catherine Murray, both from Expert Subjects, and to my publisher, Brian Hades, of EDGE Science Fiction & Fantasy Publishing.

Finally, I am deeply grateful to my readers and fans who have bought, enjoyed, talked about, written reviews on Amazon, and generally spread the word about my books. You are the reason I sit at my laptop laughing, weeping, swearing, cheering, and generally sweating blood. (Yes, this *is* something I am deeply grateful for!)

~Jane Ann McLachlan

To the Readers of this Book

I'm surprised I'm not mentioned in the acknowledgements, since there wouldn't even be a book if I hadn't come back from Salaria and told the author what happened there. I had a tough time convincing her they actually changed the way I looked, but then the cover artist showed her a picture of Idaro and me, and she had to believe it.

The first thing I'm going to do when I get back to the university is form my own triad. I know I'm a smart-mouth and a loner, and I don't expect to change all that much. But I was part of a group on Salaria, the fifteens, and even though I didn't like it at first, I got used to having friends (after I got over being surprised about it) and then I got to like it. I intend to try that again, sometime. Otherwise I'll always think back to this one world, this one time, when I was part of something. I don't want it to be a single memory.

The desert part of it, I'm okay as a one-off, though.

However, do NOT expect another story from me. No way! I am going to stay put on Seraffa and finish my Interpreter's degree. No more space travel and potentially fatal adventures for me. If you see anyone from the O.U.B. (blue and white robe, with a hood) you should tell me at once so I can hide. Then you should hide, too. And if anyone says the word "vision" to you—unless it's your optometrist—you should RUN!

Oh, and if you know anyone who'd like to be part of my triad, tell them to email me at: kia@execulink.com. I have learned you can never have too much back-up!

~ Kia

Our titles are available at major book stores
and local independent resellers who support
Science Fiction and Fantasy readers like you.

EDGE Science Fiction
and Fantasy Publishing

www.edgewebsite.com

Our titles are available at major book stores and local independent resellers who support Science Fiction and Fantasy readers like you.

Dreams of the Sea (Part 1 of Tyranaël) by Élisabeth Vonarburg (tp)
   - ISBN: 978-1-895836-96-7
   Dreams of the Sea (Part 1 of Tyranaël) by Élisabeth Vonarburg (hb)
      - ISBN: 978-1-895836-98-1
Druids by Barbara Galler-Smith and Josh Langston (tp) - ISBN: 978-1-894063-29-6

Eclipse by K. A. Bedford (tp) - ISBN: 978-1-894063-30-2
Elements by Suzanne Church (tp) - ISBN: 978-1-77053-042-3
Europa Journal by Jack Castle (tp) - ISBN: 978-1-77053-106-2
   Europa Journal by Jack Castle (POD) - ISBN: 978-1-77053-104-8
   Europa Journal by Jack Castle (ebk) - e-ISBN: 978-1-77053-091-1
Even The Stones by Marie Jakober (tp) - ISBN: 978-1-894063-18-0
Evolve: Vampire Stories of the New Undead edited by Nancy Kilpatrick (tp)
   - ISBN: 978-1-894063-33-3
Evolve Two: Vampire Stories of the Future Undead edited by Nancy Kilpatrick (tp)
   -ISBN: 978-1-894063-62-3
Expiration Date edited by Nancy Kilpatrick (tp) - ISBN: 978-1-77053-062-1

Fires of the Kindred by Robin Skelton (tp) - ISBN: 978-0-88878-271-7
Forbidden Cargo by Rebecca Rowe (tp) - ISBN: 978-1-894063-16-6

Game of Perfection, A (Part 2 of Tyranaël) by Élisabeth Vonarburg (tp) - ISBN:
   978-1-894063-32-6
Gaslight Arcanum: Uncanny Tales of Sherlock Holmes edited by Jeff Campbell &
   Charles Prepolec (tp) - ISBN: 978-1-8964063-60-9
Gaslight Grimoire: Fantastic Tales of Sherlock Holmes edited by Jeff Campbell &
   Charles Prepolec (tp) - ISBN: 978-1-8964063-17-3
Gaslight Grotesque: Nightmare Tales of Sherlock Holmes edited by Jeff Campbell
   & Charles Prepolec (tp) - ISBN: 978-1-8964063-31-9
Genius Asylum, The by Arlene F. Marks (ebk) - e-ISBN: 978-1-77053-111-6
Green Music by Ursula Pflug (tp) - ISBN: 978-1-895836-75-2
   Green Music by Ursula Pflug (hb) - ISBN: 978-1-895836-77-6

Healer, The (Children of the Panther Part One) by Amber Hayward (tp)
   - ISBN: 978-1-895836-89-9
   Healer, The (Children of the Panther Part One) by Amber Hayward (hb)
      - ISBN: 978-1-895836-91-2
Hell Can Wait by Theodore Judson (tp) - ISBN: 978-1-978-1-894063-23-4
Hounds of Ash and other tales of Fool Wolf, The by Greg Keyes (tp)
   - ISBN: 978-1-894063-09-8
Hydrogen Steel by K. A. Bedford (tp) - ISBN: 978-1-894063-20-3

i-ROBOT Poetry by Jason Christie (tp) - ISBN: 978-1-894063-24-1
Immortal Quest by Alexandra MacKenzie (tp) - ISBN: 978-1-894063-46-3

Jackal Bird by Michael Barley (pb) - ISBN: 978-1-895836-07-3
   Jackal Bird by Michael Barley (hb) - ISBN: 978-1-895836-11-0
JEMMA7729 by Phoebe Wray (tp) - ISBN: 978-1-894063-40-1

Keaen by Till Noever (tp) - ISBN: 978-1-894063-08-1
Keeper's Child by Leslie Davis (tp) - ISBN: 978-1-894063-01-2

Land/Space edited by Candas Jane Dorsey and Judy McCrosky (tp)
   - ISBN: 978-1-895836-90-5
   Land/Space edited by Candas Jane Dorsey and Judy McCrosky (hb)
      - ISBN: 978-1-895836-92-9